Bred of the Desert

Marcus Horton

BRED OF THE
DESERT

A HORSE AND A ROMANCE

BY

MARCUS HORTON

1915

TO

A. D. B. S. H.

WHO TAUGHT CONSIDERATION FOR THE DUMB
THIS WORK IS LOVINGLY INSCRIBED

CONTENTS

CHAPTER I
A COLT IS BORN

It was high noon in the desert, but there was no dazzling sunlight. Over the earth hung a twilight, a yellow-pink softness that flushed across the sky like the approach of a shadow, covering everything yet concealing nothing, creeping steadily onward, yet seemingly still, until, pressing low over the earth, it took on changing color, from pink to gray, from gray to black–gloom that precedes tropical showers. Then the wind came–a breeze rising as it were from the hot earth–forcing the Spanish dagger to dipping acknowledgment, sending dust-devils swirling across the slow curves of the desert– and then the storm burst in all its might. For this was a storm–a sand-storm of the Southwest.

Down the slopes to the west billowed giant clouds of sand. At the bottom these clouds tumbled and surged and mounted, and then, resuming their headlong course, swept across the flat land bordering the river, hurtled across the swollen Rio Grande itself, and so on up the gentle rise of ground to the town, where they swung through the streets in ruthless strides–banging signs, ripping up roofings, snapping off branches–and then lurched out over the mesa to the east. Here, as if in glee over their escape from city confines, they redoubled in fury and tore down to earth–and enveloped Felipe Montoya, a young and good-looking Mexican, and his team of scrawny horses plodding in a lumber rigging, all in a stinging swirl.

"Haya!" cried Felipe, as the first of the sand-laden winds struck him, "Chivos–chivos!" And he shot out his whip, gave the lash a twist over the off mare, and brought it down with a resounding thwack. "R-run!" he snarled, and again brought the whip down upon the emaciated mare. "You joost natural lazy! Thees storm–we–we gettin'–" His voice was carried away on the swirling winds.

But the horses seemed not to hear the man; nor, in the case of the off mare, to feel the bite of his lash. They continued to plod along the beaten trail, heads drooping, ears flopping, hoofs scuffling disconsolately. Felipe, accompanying each outburst with a mighty swing of his whip, swore and pleaded and objurgated and threatened in turn. But all to no avail. The horses held stolidly to their gait, plodding–even, after a time, dropping into slower movement. Whereat Felipe, abandoning all hope, flung down reins and whip, and leaped off the reach of the rigging. Prompt with the loosened lines the team came to a full stop; and Felipe, snatching up a blanket, covered his head and shoulders with it and squatted in the scant protection of a forward wheel.

The storm whipped and howled past. Felipe listened, noting each change in its velocity as told by the sound of raging gusts outside, himself raging. Once he lifted a corner of the blanket and peered out–only to suffer the sting of a thousand needles. Again, he hunched his shoulders guardedly and endeavored to roll a cigarette; but the tempestuous blasts discouraged this also, and with a curse he dashed the tobacco from him. After that he remained still, listening, until he heard an agreeable change outside. The screeching sank to a crooning; the crooning dropped to a low, musical sigh. Flinging off the blanket, he rose and swept the desert with eyes sand-filled and blinking.

The last of the yellow winds was eddying slowly past. All about him the air, thinning rapidly, pulsated in the sun's rays, which, beaming mildly down upon the desert, were spreading everywhere in glorious sheen. To the east, the mountains, stepping forth in the clearing atmosphere, lay revealed in a warmth of soft purple; while the slopes to the west, over which the storm had broken, shone in a wealth of dazzling yellow-white light–sunbeams scintillating off myriads of tiny sand-cubes. The desert was itself again–bright, resplendent-gripped in the clutch of solitude.

Felipe tossed his blanket back upon the reach of the rigging. Then he caught up reins and whip, ready to go on. As he did so he paused in dismay.

For one of the mares was down! It was the off mare, the slower and the older mare of the two. She was lying prone and she was breathing heavily. Covered as she was with a thin layer of fine sand, and tightly girdled with chaotic harness straps, she was a spectacle of abject misery.

But Felipe did not see this. All he saw, in the blinding rage which suddenly possessed him, was a horse down, unready for duty, and beside her a horse standing, ready for duty, but restrained by the other. Stringing out a volley of oaths, he stepped to the side of the mare and jerked at her head, but she refused stubbornly to get up on her feet.

Gripped in dismay deeper than at first, Felipe fell back in mechanical resignation.

Was the mare dying? he asked himself. He could ill afford to lose a mare. Horses cost seven and eight dollars, and he did not possess so much money. Indeed, all the money he had in the world was three dollars, received for this last load of wood in town. So, what to do! Cursing the mare had not helped matters; nor could he accuse the storm, for there had been other storms, many of them, and each had she successfully weathered–been ready, with its passing, to go on! But not so this one! She–Huh? Could it be possible? Ah!

He looked at the mare with new interest. And the longer he gazed the more his anger subsided, became finally downright compassion. For he was reviewing a something he had contemplated at odd times for weeks with many misgivings and tenacious unbeliefs. Never had he understood it! Never would he understand that thing! So why lose time in an effort to understand it now?

Dropping to his knees, he fell to work with feverish haste unbuckling straps and bands. With the harness loose, he dragged it off and tossed it to one side. Then, still moving feverishly, he led the mate to the mare off the trail, turned to the wagon with bracing shoulder, backed it clear of the prostrate animal, and swung it out of the way of future passing vehicles. It was sweltering work. When it was done, with the sun, risen to its fierce zenith, beating down upon him mercilessly, he strode off the trail, blowing and perspiring, and flung himself down in the baking sand, where, though irritated by particles of sand which had sifted down close inside his shirt, he nevertheless gave himself over to sober reflections.

He was stalled till the next morning–he knew that. And he was without food-supplies to carry him over. And he was ten miles on the one hand, and five up-canyon miles on the other, from all source of supplies. But against these unpleasant facts there stood many pleasant facts–he was on the return leg of his journey, his wagon was empty, and he had in his possession three dollars. Then, too, there was another pleasant fact. The trip as a trip had been unusual; never before had he, or any one else, made it under two days–one for loading and driving into town, and a second for getting rid of the wood and making the return. Yet he himself had been out now only the one day, and he was on his way home. He had whipped and crowded his horses since midnight to just this end. Yet was he not stalled now till morning? And would not this delay set him back the one day he had gained over his fellow-townsmen? And would not these same fellow-townsmen rejoice in this opportunity to overtake him–worse, to leave him behind? They would!

"Oh, well," he concluded, philosophically, stretching out upon his back and drawing his worn and ragged sombrero over his eyes, "soon is comin' a *potrillo*." With this he deliberately courted slumber.

Out of the stillness rattled a wagon. Like Felipe's, it was a lumber rigging, and the driver, a fat Mexican with beady eyes, pulled up his horses and gazed at the disorder. It was but a perfunctory gaze, however, and revealed to him nothing of the true situation. All he saw was that Felipe was drunk and asleep, and that before dropping beside the trail he had had time, and perhaps just enough wit, to unhitch one horse. The other, true to instinct and the law of her underfed and overworked kind, had lain down. With this conclusion, and out of sheer exuberance of alcoholic spirits, he decided to awaken Felipe. And this he did–in true Mexican fashion. With a curse of but five words–words of great scope and finest selection, however–he mercilessly raked Felipe's ancestors for five generations back; he objurgated Felipe's holdings–chickens, adobe house, money, burro, horses, pigs. He closed, snarling not obscurely at Felipe the man and at any progeny of his which might appear in the future. Then he dropped his reins and sprang off the reach of his rigging.

Felipe was duly awakened. He gained his feet slowly.

"You know me, eh?" he retorted, advancing toward the other. "All right–*gracios!*" And by way of coals of fire he proffered the fellow-townsman papers and tobacco.

The new-comer revealed surprise, not alone at Felipe's sobriety, though this was startling in view of the disorder in the trail, but also at the proffer of cigarette material. And he was about to speak when Felipe interrupted him.

"You haf t'ink I'm drunk, eh, Franke?" he said. "Sure! Why not?" And he waved his hand in the direction of the trail. Then, after the other had rolled a cigarette and returned the sack and papers, he laid a firm hand upon the man's shoulder. "You coom look," he invited. "You tell me what you t'ink thees!"

They walked to the mare, and Franke gazed a long moment in silence. Felipe stood beside him, eying him sharply, hoping for an expression of approval–even of congratulation. In this he was doomed to disappointment, for the other continued silent, and in silence finally turned back, his whole attitude that of one who saw nothing in the spectacle worthy of comment. Felipe followed him, nettled, and sat down and himself rolled a cigarette. As he sat smoking it the other seated himself beside him, and presently touched him on the arm and began to speak. Felipe listened, with now and again a nod of approval, and, when the *compadre* was finished, accepted the brilliant proposition.

"A bet, eh?" he exclaimed. "All right!" And he produced his sheepskin pouch and dumped out his three dollars. "All right! I bet you feety cents, Franke, thot eet don' be!"

Frank looked his disdain at the amount offered. Also, his eyes blazed and his round face reddened. He shoved his hand into his overalls, brought forth a silver dollar, and tossed it down in the sand.

"A bet!" he yelled. "Mek eet a bet! A dolar!" Then he narrowed his eyes in the direction of the mare. "Mek eet a good bet! You have chonce to win, too, Felipe–you know!"

Felipe did not respond immediately. Money was his all-absorbing difficulty. Never plentiful with him, it was less than ever plentiful now, and was wholly represented in the three dollars before him. A sum little enough in fact, it dwindled rapidly as he recalled one by one his numerous debts. For he owed much money. He owed for food in the settlement store; he owed for clothing he had bought in town; and he owed innumerable gambling debts–big sums, sums mounting to heights he dared not contemplate. And all he had to his name was the three dollars lying so peacefully before him, with the speculative Franke hovering over them like a fat buzzard over a dead coyote. What to do! He could not decide. He had ways for this money, other than paying on his debts or investing in a gambling proposition. There was to be a *baile* soon, and he must buy for Margherita (providing her father, a caustic *hombre*, bitter against all wood-haulers, permitted him the girl's society) peanuts in the dance-hall and candy outside the dance-hall. The candy must be bought in the general store, where, because of his many debts, he must pay cash now–always cash! So what to do! All these things meant money. And money, as he well understood, was a thing hard to get. Yet here was a chance, as Franke had generously indicated, for him to win some money. But, against this chance for him to win some money was the chance also, as conveyed inversely by Franke, of his losing some money–money he could ill afford to lose.

"You afraid?" suddenly cut in Franke, nastily, upon these reflections. "I don' see you do soomt'ing!"

Which decided Felipe for all time. "Afraid?" he echoed, disdainfully. "Sure! But not for myself! You don' have mooch money to lose! But I mek eet a bet–a good bet! I bet you two dolars thot eet–thot eet don' be!"

It was now the other who hesitated. But he did not hesitate for long. Evidently the spirit of the gambler was more deeply rooted in him than it was in Felipe, for, after gazing out in the trail a moment, then eying Felipe another moment, both speculatively, he extracted from his pockets two more silver dollars and tossed them down with the others. Then he fixed Felipe with a malignant stare.

"I bet you t'ree dolars thot eet cooms what I haf say!"

Felipe laughed. "All right," he agreed, readily. "Why not?" He heaped the money under a stone, sank over upon his back with an affected yawn, drew his hat over his eyes, and lay still. "We go to sleep now, Franke," he proposed. "Eet's long time–I haf t'ink."

Soon both were snoring.

Out in the trail hung the quiet of a sick-room. The long afternoon waned. Once a wagon appeared from the direction of town, but the driver, evidently grasping the true situation, turned out and around the mare in respectful silence. Another time a single horseman, riding from the mountains, cantered upon the scene; but this man, also with a look of understanding, turned out and around the mare in careful regard for her condition. Then came darkness. Shadows crept in from nowhere, stealing over the desert more and more darkly, while, with their coming, birds of the air, seeking safe place for night rest, flitted about in nervous uncertainty. And suddenly in the gathering dusk rose the long-drawn howl of a coyote, lifting into the stillness a lugubrious note of appeal. Then, close upon the echo of this, rose another appeal in the trail close by, the shrill nicker of the mate to the mare.

It awoke Felipe. He sat up quickly, rubbed his eyes dazedly, and peered out with increasing understanding. Then he sprang to his feet.

"Coom!" he called, kicking the other. "We go now—see who is winnin' thot bet!" And he started hurriedly forward.

But the other checked him. "Wait!" he snapped, rising. "You wait! You in too mooch hurry! You coom back—I have soomt'ing!"

Felipe turned back, wondering. The other nervously produced material for a cigarette. Then he cleared his throat with needless protraction.

"Felipe," he began, evidently laboring under excitement, "I mek eet a *bet* now! I bet you," he went on, his voice trembling with fervor—"I bet you my wagon, thee horses—thee whole shutting-match—against thot wagon and horses yours, and thee harness—thee whole damned shutting-match—thot I haf win!" He proceeded to finish his cigarette.

Felipe stared at him hard. Surely his ears had deceived him! If they had not deceived him, if, for a fact, the *hombre* had expressed a willingness to bet all he had on the outcome of this thing, then Franke, fellow-townsman, *compadre*, brother-wood-hauler, was crazy! But he determined to find out.

"What you said, Franke?" he asked, peering into the glowing eyes of the other. "Say thot again, *hombre!*"

"I haf say," repeated the other, with lingering emphasis upon each word–"I haf say I bet you everyt'ing–wagon, harness, *caballos*–everyt'ing!–against thot wagon, harness, *caballos* yours–everyt'ing–thee whole shutting-match–thot I haf win thee bet!"

Again Felipe lowered his eyes. But now to consider suspicions. He had heard rightly; Franke really wanted to bet all he had. But he could not but wonder whether Franke, by any possible chance, knew in advance the outcome of the affair in the trail. He had heard of such things, though never had he believed them possible. Yet he found himself troubled with insistent reminder that Franke had suggested this whole thing. Then suddenly he was gripped in another unwelcome thought. Could it be possible that this scheming *hombre*, awaking at a time when he himself was soundest asleep, had gone out into the trail on tiptoe for advance information? It was possible. Why not? But that was not the point exactly. The point was, had he done it? Had this buzzard circled out into the trail while he himself was asleep? He did not know, and he could not decide! For the third time in ten hours, though puzzled and groping, trembling between gain and loss, he plunged on the gambler's chance.

"All right!" he agreed, tensely. "I take thot bet! I bet you thees wagon, thees *caballos*, thees harness–everyt'ing–against everyt'ing yours–wagon, horses, harness–everyt'ing! Wait!" he thundered, for the other now was striding toward the mare. "Wait! You in too mooch hurry yourself now!" Then, as the other returned: "Is eet a bet? Is eet a bet?"

The fellow-townsman nodded. Whereat Felipe nodded approval of the nod, and stepped out into the trail, followed by the other.

It was night, and quite a dark night. Stretching away to east and west, the dimly outlined trail was lost abruptly in engulfing darkness; while, overhead, a starless sky, low and somber and frowning, pressed close. But, dark though the night was, it did not wholly conceal the outlines of the mare. She was standing as they approached, mildly encouraging a tiny something beside her, a wisp of life, her baby, who was struggling to insure continued existence.

And it was this second outline, not the other and larger outline, that held the breathless attention of the men. Nervously Felipe struck a match. As it flared up he stepped close, followed by the other, and there was a moment of tense silence. Then the match went out and Felipe straightened up.

"Franke," he burst out, "I haf win thee bet! Eet is not a mare; eet is a li'l' horse!" He struck his *compadre* a resounding blow on the back. "I am mooch sorry, Franke," he declared–"not!" He turned back to the faint outline of the colt. "Thees *potrillo*," he observed, "he's bringin' me mooch good luck! He's–" He suddenly interrupted himself, aware that the other was striding away. "Where you go now, Franke?" he asked, and then, quick to sense approaching trouble: "Never mind thee big bet, Franke! You can pay me ten dolars soom time! All right?"

There was painful silence.

"All right!" came the reply, finally, through the darkness.

Then Felipe heard a lumber rigging go rattling off in the direction of the canyon, and, suddenly remembering the money underneath the stone, hurried off the trail in a spasm of alarm. He knelt in the sand and struck a match.

The money had disappeared.

CHAPTER II
FELIPE CELEBRATES

It was well along in the morning when Felipe pulled up next day before his little adobe house in the mountain settlement. The journey from the mesa below had been, perforce, slow. The mare was still pitiably weak, and her condition had necessitated many stops, each of long duration. Also, on the way up the canyon the colt had displayed frequent signs of exhaustion, though only with the pauses did he attempt rest.

But it was all over now. They were safely before the house, with the colt lying a little apart from his mother–regarding her with curious intentness–and with Felipe bustling about the team and now and again bursting out in song of questionable melody and rhythm. Felipe was preparing the horses for the corral at the rear of the house, and soon he flung aside the harness and seized each of the horses by the bridle.

"Well, you li'l' devil!" he exclaimed, addressing the reclining colt. "You coom along now! You live in thees place back here! You coom wit' me now!" And he started around a corner of the adobe.

The colt hastily rose to his feet. But not at the command of the man. No such command was necessary, for whither went his mother there went he. Close to her side, he moved with her into the inclosure, crowding frantically over the bars, skinning his knees in the effort, coming to a wide-eyed stand just inside the entrance, and there surveying with nervous apprehension the corral's occupants–a burro, two pigs, a flock of chickens. But he held close to his mother's side.

Felipe did not linger in the corral. Throwing off their bridles, he tossed the usual scant supply of alfalfa to the horses, and filled their tub from a near-by well. Then, after putting up the bars, he set out with determined stride across the settlement. His direction was the general store, and his quest was the loan of a horse, since his team now was broken, and would be broken for a number of days to come.

The store was owned and conducted by one Pedro Garcia. Pedro Garcia was the mountain Shylock. He loaned money at enormous rates of interest, and he rented out horses at prohibitive rates per day. Also, being what he was, Pedro had gained his pounds of flesh–was alarmingly fat, with short legs of giant circumference. Usually these legs were clothed in tight-fitting overalls, and his small feet incased in boots of high-grade leather wonderfully roweled. Yet many years had passed since Pedro had been seen in a saddle. Evidently he held to the rowels in fond memory of his days of slender youth and coltish gambolings. Pedro was seated in his customary place upon an empty keg on the porch, and Felipe, ignoring his grunted greeting, plunged at once into the purpose of his call.

He had come to borrow a horse, Felipe explained. One of his own was unfit for work, yet the cutting and drawing must go on. While the mare was recuperating, he carefully pointed out, he himself could continue to earn money to meet some of his pressing debts. Any kind of horse would do, he declared, so long as it had four legs and was able to carry on the work. The horse need not have a mouth, even, he added, jocosely, for reasons nobody need explain. After which he sat down on the porch and awaited the august decision.

Pedro remained silent a long time, the while he moistened his lips with fitful tongue, and gazed across the tiny settlement reflectively. At length he drew a deep breath, mixed of disgust and regret, and proceeded to make slow reply.

It was true, he began, that he had horses to rent. And it was further true, he went on, deliberately, that he kept them for just this purpose. But–and his pause was fraught with deep significance–it was no less true that Felipe Montoya bore a bad reputation as a driver of horses–was known, indeed, to kill horses through overwork and underfeed–and that, therefore, to lend him a horse was like kissing the horse good-by and hitching up another to the stone-boat. Nevertheless, he hastened to add, if Felipe was in urgent need of a horse, and was prepared to pay the customary small rate per day, and to *pay in advance–cash–*

Here Pedro paused and popped accusing eyes at Felipe, in one strong dramatic moment before continuing. But he did not continue.

Felipe was the check. For Felipe had leaped to his feet, and now stood brandishing an ugly fist underneath the proprietor's nose. Further–and infinitely worse–Felipe was saying something.

"Pedro Garcia," he began, shrilly, "I must got a horse! And I have coom for a horse! And I have thee money to pay for a horse! And if I kill thot horse," he went on, still brandishing his fist–"if thot horse he's dropping dead in thee harness–I pay you for thot horse! I haf drive horses–"

"*Si, si, si!*" began Pedro, interrupting.

"I haf drive horses on thees trail ten years!" persisted Felipe, yelling, "and in all thot time, Pedro Garcia, I'm killin' only seven horses, and all seven of thees horses is dyin', Pedro Garcia, when I haf buy them, and I haf buy all seven horses from you, Pedro Garcia, thief and robber!" He paused to take a breath. "And not once, Pedro Garcia," he went on, "do I keeck about thot-a horse is a horse! But I haf coom to you before! And I haf coom to you now! I must got a horse quick! And I bringin' thot horse back joost thee same as I'm gettin' thot horse–in good condition–better–because everybody is knowin.' I feed a horse better than you feed a horse–and I'm *cleanin'* the horse once in a while, too!" Which was a lie, both as to the feeding and the cleaning, as he well knew, and as, indeed, he well knew Pedro knew, who, nevertheless, nodded grave assent.

"*Si,*" admitted Pedro. "*Pero ustede–*"

"A horse!" thundered Felipe, interrupting, his neck cords dangerously distended. "You give me a horse–you hear? I want a horse–a horse! I don' coom here for thee talk!"

Pedro rose hastily from the keg. Also, he grunted quick consent. Then he stepped inside the store, followed by Felipe, who made several needed purchases, and, since he had his enemy cowed, and was troubled with thirst created by the protracted harangue, to say nothing of the strong inclination within him to celebrate the coming of the colt, he made a purchase that was not needed–a bottle of *vino*, cool and dry from Pedro's cellar. With these tucked securely under his arm, he then calmly informed Pedro of the true state of his finances, and left the store, returning across the settlement, which lay wrapped in pulsating noonday quiet. In the shade of his adobe he sat

upon the ground, with his back comfortably against the wall.
Directly the quiet was broken by two distinct sounds–the pop of a
cork out of the neck of a bottle, and the gurgle of liquid into the
mouth of a man.

Thus Felipe set out upon a protracted debauch. In this debauch he
did nothing worth while. He used neither the borrowed horse nor
his own sound one. Each day saw him redder of eye and more
swollen of lip; each day saw him increasingly heedless of his debts;
each day saw him more neglectful of his duties toward his animals.
The one bottle became two bottles, the two bottles became three,
each secured only after threatened assault upon the body of Pedro,
each adding its store to the already deep conviviality and reckless
freedom from all cares now Felipe's. He forgot everything–forgot the
stolen money, forgot the colt, forgot the needs of the mare–all in
exhilarated pursuit of phantoms.

Yet the colt did not suffer. Becoming ever more confident of himself
as the days passed, he soon revealed pronounced curiosity and an
aptitude for play. He would stare at strutting roosters, gaze after
straddling hens, blink quizzically at the burro, frown upon the
grunting pigs, all as if cataloguing these specimens, listing them in
his thoughts, some day to make good use of the knowledge. But
most of all he showed interest in and playfulness toward his mother
and her doings. He would follow her about untiringly, pausing
whenever she paused, starting off again whenever she started off–
seemingly bent upon acquiring the how and why of her every
movement.

But it was his playfulness finally that brought him first needless
suffering. The mare was standing with her nose in the feed-box. She
had stood thus many times during the past week; but usually,
before, the box had been empty, whereas now it contained a
generous quantity of alfalfa. But this the colt did not know. He only
knew that he was interested in this thing, and so went there to
attempt, as many times before, to reach his nose into the mysterious
box. Finding that he could not, he began, as never before, to frisk
about the mare, tossing up his little heels and throwing down his
head with all the reckless abandon of a seasoned "outlaw." He could
do these things because he was a rare colt, stronger than ever colt

before was at his age, and for a time the mare suffered his antics with a look of pleased toleration. But as he kept it up, and as she was getting her first real sustenance since the day of his coming, she at length became fretful and sounded a low warning. But this the colt did not heed. Instead he wheeled suddenly and plunged directly toward her, bunting her sharply. Nor did the single bunt satisfy him. Again and again he attacked her, plunging in and darting away each time with remarkable celerity, until, her patience evidently exhausted, she whisked her head around and nipped him sharply. Screaming with pain and fright, he plunged from her, sought the opposite side of the inclosure, and turned upon her a pair of very hurt and troubled eyes.

Yet all the world over mothers are mothers. After a time–a long time, as if to let her punishment sink in–the mare made her way slowly to the colt, and there fell to licking him, seeming to tell him of her lasting forgiveness. Under this lavish caressing the colt, as if to reveal his own forgiveness for the dreadful hurt, bestowed similar attention upon her–in this attention, though he did not know it, softening flesh that had experienced no such consideration in years. Thus they stood, side by side, mother and son, long into the day, laying the foundation of a love that never dies–that strengthens, in fact, with the years, though all else fail–love between mother and her offspring.

Other things, things of minor consequence, added their mite to his early development. One morning, while the mare was asleep, the colt, alert and standing, was startled by the sudden movement of a large rooster. The rooster had left the ground with loud flapping of wings, and now stood perched upon the corral fence, like a grim and mighty conqueror, ruffling his neck feathers and twisting his head in pre-eminent satisfaction. But the colt did not understand this. Transfixed, he turned frightened eyes upon the cause of the unearthly commotion. Then suddenly, with another loud flapping of wings, the rooster uttered a defiant crow, a challenge that echoed far through the canyon. Whereat the colt, eyes wide with terror, whirled to his mother, whimpering babyishly. But with the mare standing beside him and caressing him reassuringly, all his nervousness left him, and he again turned his eyes upon the rooster and watched him till the cock, unable to stir combat among his neighbors, left the fence with another loud flapping of wings, and returned to earth, physically and spiritually, there to set up his customary feigned quest for worms for the ladies. But the point was this–with this last flapping of wings the colt remained in a state of perfect calm.

Thus he learned, and thus he continued to learn, in nervous fear one moment, in perfect calm the next. And though his hours of life were few indeed, he nevertheless revealed an intelligence far above the average of his kind. He learned to avoid the mare's whisking tail, to shun or remove molesting flies, to keep away from the mare when she was at the feed-box. All of which told of his uncommon strain, as did the rapidity with which he gained strength, which last told of his tremendous vitality, and which some day would serve him well against trouble.

Yet in it all lurked the great mystery, and Felipe, blustering to occasional natives outside the fence during his week of debauch, while pointing out with pride the colt's very evident blooded lineage, yet could tell nothing of that descent. All he could point out was that the mare was chestnut-brown, and when not in harness was kept close within the confines of the corral, while here was a colt of a dark-fawn color which would develop with maturity into coal-black. And there was not a single black horse in the mountains for miles and miles around. Nor was the colt a "throw-back," because–

"Oh, well," he would conclude, casting bleared eyes in the direction of the house, wearily, "I got soom *vino* inside. You coom along now. We go gettin' a drink." Which would close the monologue.

One morning early, Felipe, asleep on a bed that never was made up, heard suspicious sounds in the corral outside. He sprang up and, clad only in a fiery-red undershirt, hurried to a window. Cautiously letting down the bars, with a rope already tied around the colt's neck, was the mountain Shylock, Pedro Garcia, intent upon leading off the innocent new-comer. Pedro no doubt had perceived an opportunity either to force Felipe to meet some of his debts, or else hold the colt as a very acceptable chattel. Also, he evidently had calculated upon early dawn as the time best suited to do this thing, in view of Felipe's long debauch upon unpaid-for wine. At any rate, there he was, craftily letting down the bars. Raging with indignation and a natural venom which he felt toward the storekeeper, Felipe flung up the window.

"*Buenos dias, señor!*" he greeted, cheerfully, with effort controlling his anger. "Thee early worm he's takin' thee *potrillo*! How cooms thot, *señor*?" he asked, enjoying the other's sudden discomfiture. "You takin' thot li'l' horse for thee walk–thee exercise?" And then, without waiting for a reply, had there been one forthcoming, which there was not, he slammed down the window, leaped to the door, flung it open–all levity now gone from him. "Pedro Garcia!" he raged. "You thief and robber! I'm killin' you thees time sure!" And, regardless of his scant attire, and stringing out a volley of oaths, he sprang out of the doorway after his intended victim.

But Pedro Garcia, though fat, was surprisingly quick on his feet. He dropped the rope and burst into a run, heading frantically past the house toward the trail. And, though Felipe leaped after him, still clad only in fiery-red undershirt, the storekeeper gained the trail and set out at top speed across the settlement. Felipe pursued. Hair aflaunt, shirt-tail whipping in the breeze, bare feet paddling in the dust of the trail, naked legs crossing each other like giant scissors in frenzied effort, he hurtled forward exactly one leap behind his intended victim. He strained to close up the gap, but he could not overtake the equally speedy Pedro, whose short legs fairly buzzed in the terror of their owner. Thus they ran, mounting the slight rise before the general store, then descending into the heart of the settlement, with Pedro whipping along frantically, and Felipe still one whole leap behind, until a derisive shout, a feminine exclamation of shrieking glee, awoke Felipe to the spectacle he was making of himself before the eyes of the community. He stopped; growled disappointed rage; darted back along the trail. Once in the privacy of his house, he hurriedly donned his clothes and gave himself over to deliberations. The result of these deliberations was that he concluded to return to work.

After a scant breakfast of chili and coffee he moved out to the corral. He leaned his arms upon the fence and surveyed the colt with fresh interest.

"Thot li'l' *caballo*," he began, "he's bringin' me mooch good luck. Thot *potrillo* he's wort' seven–he's wort'–*si*–eight dolars–thot *potrillo*.

I t'ink I haf sell heem, too–queek–in town! But first I must go cuttin' thee wood!" With this he let down the bars and entered the inclosure. Then his thoughts took an abrupt turn. "I keel thot Pedro Garcia soomtime–bet you' life! He's stealin' fleas off a dog–thot *hombre!*"

Felipe drove the borrowed horse out of the inclosure, and then singled out the mate to the mare. As he harnessed up this horse, the colt, standing close by, revealed marked interest. Also, as Felipe led the horse out of the corral the colt followed till shut off by the bars, which Felipe hurriedly put up. But they did not discourage him. He remained very close to them, peering out between the while Felipe hitched the team to his empty lumber rigging. Then came the crack of a whip, loud creaking of greaseless wheels, the voice of Felipe in lusty demand, all as the outfit set out up the trail toward the timber-slopes. But not till the earth was still again, the cloud of dust in the trail completely subsided, did the colt turn away from the bars and seek his mother, and then with a look in his soft-blinking eyes that told of concentrated pondering on these mysteries of life.

CHAPTER III
A SURPRISE

Next morning, having returned from the timber-slopes, Felipe, fresh and radiant, appeared outside the corral in holiday attire. Part of this attire was a pair of brand-new overalls. Indeed, the overalls were so new that they crackled; and Felipe appeared quite conscious of their newness, for he let down the bars with great care, and with even greater care stepped into the inclosure. Then it was seen, since he was a Mexican who ran true to form, there was a flaw in all this splendor. For he had drawn on the new overalls over the older pair–worse, had drawn them on over *two* older pairs, as revealed at the bottoms, where peered plaintively two shades of blue–lighter blue of the older pair, very light blue of the oldest pair–the effect of exposure to desert suns. So Felipe had on three pairs of overalls. Yet this was not all of distinction. Around his brown throat was a bright red neckerchief, while between the unbuttoned edges of his vest was an expanse of bright green–the coloring of a tight-fitting sweater.

There was reason for all this. Felipe was going to town, and he was taking the mare along with him, and the mare naturally would take her colt; and because he had come to know the value of the colt, Felipe wished to appear as prosperous in the eyes of the Americans in town as he believed the owner of so fine a colt ought to appear.

Therefore, still careful of his overalls, he set about leisurely to prepare the team for the journey. He crossed to the shed, hauled out the harness, tossed it out into the inclosure. Promptly both horses stepped into position. Also, the older mare, whether through relief or regret, sounded a shrill nicker. This brought the colt to her side, where he fell to licking her affectionately, showing his great love for her bony frame. And when Felipe led the horses out of the corral he followed close beside her, and when outside held close to her throughout the hitching, and to the point even when Felipe clambered to the top of the high load and caught up the reins and the whip. Then he stepped back, wriggling his fuzzy little tail and blinking his big eyes curiously.

"Well, *potrillo*," began Felipe, grinning down upon the tiny specimen of life, "we goin' now to town! But first you must be ready! You ready? All right! We go now!" And he cracked the whip over the team.

They started forward, slowly at first, the wagon giving off many creaks and groans, then fast and faster, until, well in the descent of the hard canyon trail, the horses were jogging along quite briskly.

The colt showed the keenest interest and delight. For a time he trotted beside the mare, ears cocked forward expectantly, eyes sweeping the canyon alertly, hoofs lifting to ludicrous heights. Then, as the first novelty wore off, and he became more certain of himself in these swift-changing surroundings, he revealed a playfulness that tickled Felipe. He would lag behind a little, race madly forward, sometimes run far ahead of the team in his great joy. But he seemed best to like to lag. He would come to a sudden stop and, motionless as a dog pointing a bird, gaze out across the canyon a long time, like one trying to find himself in a strange and wonderful world. Or, standing thus, he would reveal curious interest in the rocks and stumps around him, and he would stare at them fixedly, blinking slowly, a look of genuine wonderment in his big, soft eyes. Then he would strain himself mightily to overtake the wagon.

Once in a period of absorbed attention he lost sight of the outfit completely. This was due not so much to his distance in the rear as to the fact that the wagon, having struck a bend in the trail, had turned from view. But he did not know that. Sounding a baby outcry of fear, he scurried ahead at breakneck speed, frantic heels tossing up tiny spurts of dust, head stretched forward–and thus soon caught up. After that he remained close beside his mother until the wagon, rocking down the mouth of the canyon, swung out upon the broad mesa. Here the outfit could be seen for miles, and now he took to lagging behind again, and to frisking far ahead, always returning at frequent intervals for the motherly assurance that all was well.

As part of the Great Scheme, all this was good for him. In his brief panic when out of sight of his mother he was taught how very necessary she was to his existence. In his running back and forth, with now and again breathless speeding, he developed the muscles of his body, to the end that later he might well take up an independent fight for life. In the curious interest he displayed in all subjects about him he lent unknowing assistance to a spiritual development as necessary as physical development. All this prepared him to meet men and measures as he was destined to meet them–with gentleness, with battle,–with affection–like for like–as he found it. It was all good for him, this movement, this change of environment, this quick awakening of interest. It shaped him in both body and spirit to the Great Purpose.

This interest seemed unbounded. Whenever a jack-rabbit shot across the trail, or a covey of birds broke from the sand-hills, he would come to a quick pause and blink curiously, seeming to understand and approve, and to be grateful, as if all these things were done for him. Also, with each halt Felipe made with *compadres* along the trail, friends who entered with him in loud badinage over the ownership of the colt–an ownership all vigorously denied him–the colt himself would cock his ears and fix his eyes, seemingly aware of his importance and pleased to be the object of the cutting remarks. And thus the miles from mountain to the outskirts of town were covered, miles pleasurable to him, every inch revealing something of fresh interest, every mile finding him more accustomed to the journey.

They reached a point on the outskirts where streets appeared, sharply defined thoroughfares, interlacing one with the other. And as they advanced vehicles began to turn in upon the trail, a nondescript collection ranging from an Indian farm-wagon off the Navajo reservation to the north to a stanhope belonging to some more affluent American in the suburbs. With them came also many strange sounds–Mexican oaths, mild Indian commands, light man-to-man greetings of the day. Also there was much cracking of whips and nickering of horses along the line. And the result of all this was that the colt revealed steadily increasing nervousness, a condition enhanced by the fact that his mother, held rigidly to her duties by Felipe, could bestow upon her offspring but very little attention. But he held close to her, and thus moved into the heart of town, when suddenly one by one the vehicles ahead came to a dead stop. Felipe, perched high, saw that the foremost wagons had reached the railroad crossing, and that there was a long freight-train passing through.

Team after team came into the congestion and stopped. Cart and wagon and phaeton closed in around the colt. There was much maneuvering for space. The colt's nervousness increased, and became positive fear. He darted wild eyes about him. He was completely hedged in. On his right loomed a large horse; behind him stood a drowsing team; on his left was a dirt-cart; while immediately in front, such was his position now, stood his mother. But, though gripped in fear, he remained perfectly still until the locomotive, puffing and wheezing along at the rear of the train, having reached the crossing, sounded a piercing shriek. This was more than he could stand. Without a sound he dodged and whirled. He plunged to the rear and rammed into the drowsing team; darted to the right and into the teeth of the single horse; whirled madly to the left, only to carom off the hub of a wheel. But with all this defeat he did not stop. He set up a wild series of whirling plunges, and, completely crazed now, darted under the single horse, under a Mexican wagon, under a team of horses, and forth into a little clearing. Here he came to a stop, trembling in every part, gazing about in wildest terror.

Following its shrill blast, the engine puffed across the crossing, the gates slowly lifted, and the foremost vehicles began to move. Soon the whole line was churning up clouds of dust and rattling across the railroad tracks. Felipe was of this company, cracking his whip and yelling lustily, enjoying the congestion and this unexpected opportunity to be seen by so many American eyes at once in his gorgeous raiment. In the town proper, and carefully avoiding the more rapidly moving vehicles, he turned off the avenue into a narrow side street, and pulled up at a water-trough. As he dropped the reins and prepared to descend, a friend of his–and he had many– hailed him from the sidewalk. Hastily clambering down, he seized the man's arm in forceful greeting, and indicated with a jerk of his head a near-by saloon.

"We go gettin' soomt'ing," he invited. "I have munch good luck to tell you."

Inside the establishment Felipe became loquacious and boasting. He now was a man of comfortable wealth, he gravely informed his friend–a wizened individual with piercing eyes. Besides winning a bet of fifteen dollars in money, he explained, he also held a note against Franke Gamboa for fifty dollars more on his property. But that was not all. Aside from the note and the cash in hand, he was the owner of a colt now of great value–*si*–worth at least ten dollars–which, added to the other, made him, as anybody could see, worthy of recognition. With this he placed his empty glass down on the bar and swung over into English.

"You haf hear about thot?" he asked, drawing the back of his hand across his mouth. Then, as the other shook his head negatively, "Well, I haf new one–*potrillo*–nice li'l' horse–*si!*" He cleared his throat and frowned at the listening bartender. "He's comin' couple days before, oop on thee mesa." He picked up the glass, noted that it was empty, placed it down again. "I'm sellin' thot *potrillo* quick," he went on–"bet you' life! I feed heem couple weeks more mebbe–feed heem beer and soom cheese!" He laughed raucously at the alleged witticism. "Thot's thee preencipal t'ing," he declared, soberly. "You must feed a horse." He said this not as one recommending that a horse be well fed, but as one advising that a horse be given something to eat occasionally. "*Si!* Thot's thee preencipal t'ing! Then he's makin' a fast goer–bet you' life! I haf give heem–" He suddenly interrupted himself and laid firm hold upon the man's arm. "You coom wit' me!" he invited, and began to drag the other toward the swing-doors. "You coom look at thot *potrillo!*"

They went outside. On the curb, Felipe gazed about him, first with a look of pride, then with an expression of blank dismay. He stepped down off the curb, roused the drowsing mare with a vigorous clap, again looked about him worriedly. After a long moment he left the team, walking out into the middle of the street, and strained his eyes in both directions. Then he returned and, heedless of his new overalls, got down upon his knees, sweeping bleared eyes under the wagon. And finally, with a last despairing gaze in every direction, he sat down upon the curb and buried his face in his arms.

For the colt was gone!

CHAPTER IV
A NEW HOME

With the beginning of the forward movement across the railroad the colt, ears cocked and eyes alert, moved across also. Close about him stepped other horses, and over and around him surged a low murmuring, occasionally broken by the crack of a whip. Yet these sounds did not seem to disturb him. He trotted along, crossing the tracks, and when on the opposite side set out straight down the avenue. The avenue was broad, and in this widening area the congestion rapidly thinned, and soon the colt was quite alone in the open. But he continued forward, seeming not to miss his mother, until there suddenly loomed up beside him a very fat and very matronly appearing horse. Then he hesitated, turning apprehensive eyes upon her. But not for long. Evidently accepting this horse as his mother, he fell in close beside her and trotted along again in perfect composure.

Behind this horse was a phaeton, and in the phaeton sat two persons. They were widely different in age. One was an elderly man, broad of shoulders and with a ruddy face faintly threaded with purple; the other was a young girl, not more than seventeen, his daughter, with a face sweet and alert, and a mass of chestnut hair–all imparting a certain esthetic beauty. Like the man, the girl was ruddy of complexion, though hers was the bloom of youth, while his was toll taken from suns and winds of the desert. The girl was the first to discover the colt.

"Daddy!" she exclaimed, placing a restraining hand upon the other. "Whose beautiful colt is that?"

The Judge pulled down his horse and leaned far out over the side. "Why, I don't know, dear!" he replied, after a moment, then turned his eyes to the rear. "He must belong with some team in that crush."

The girl regarded the colt with increasing rapture. "Isn't he a perfect dear!" she went on. "Look at him, daddy!" she suddenly urged, delightedly. "He's dying to know why we stopped!" Which, indeed, the colt looked to be, since he had come to a stop with the mare and now was regarding them curiously. "I'd love to pet him!"

The Judge frowned. "We're late for luncheon," he declared, and again gazed to the rear. "We'd better take him along with us out to the ranch. To-morrow I'll advertise him in the papers." And he shook up the mare. "We'd better go along, Helen."

"Just one minute, daddy!" persisted the girl, gathering up her white skirts and, as the Judge pulled down, leaping lightly out of the phaeton. "I've simply *got* to pet him!" She cautiously approached the colt.

He permitted her this approach. Nor did he shy at her outstretched hand. Under her gentle caresses he stood very still, and when she stooped before him, as she did presently, bringing her eyes upon a level with his own, he gazed into them very frankly and earnestly, as if gauging this person, as he had seemed to tabulate all other things, some day to make good use of his knowledge. After a time the girl spoke.

"I wish I could keep you always," she said, poutingly. "You look so nice and babyish!" But she knew that she could not keep him, and after a time she stood up again and sighed, and fell to stroking him thoughtfully. "I'll have you to-day, anyway," she declared, finally, with promise of enjoyment in her voice, as one who meant to make the most of it. Then she got back into the phaeton.

The Judge started up the horse again. They continued through the town, and when on its northwestern outskirts turned to the right along a trail that paralleled the river. The trail ran north and south, and on either side of it, sometimes shielding a secluded ranch, always forming an agreeable oasis in the flat brown of the country, rose an occasional clump of cottonwoods. The ranch-houses were infrequent, however; all of them were plentifully supplied with water by giant windmills which clacked and creaked above the trees in the high-noon breeze. To the left, across the river, back from the long, slow rise of sand from the water's edge, rose five blunt heights like craters long extinct; while above these, arching across the heavens in spotless sheen, curved the turquoise dome of a southwestern midday sky, flooding the dust and dunes below in throbbing heat-rays. It was God's own section of earth, and not the least beautiful of its vistas, looming now steadily ahead on their right, was the place belonging to Judge Richards. House and outhouses white, and just now aglint in the white light of the sun, the whole ranch presented the appearance of diamonds nestling in a bed of emerald-green velvet. Turning off at this ranch, the Judge tossed the reins to a waiting Mexican.

Helen was out of the phaeton like a flash. Carefully guiding the colt around the house and across a *patio*, she turned him loose into a spacious corral. Then she fell to watching him, and she continued to watch him until a voice from the house, that of an aged Mexican woman who presided over the kitchen, warned her that dinner was waiting. Reluctantly hugging the colt–hugging him almost savagely in her sudden affection for him–she then turned to leave, but not without a word of explanation.

"I must leave you now, honey!" she said, much as a child would take leave of her doll. "But I sha'n't be away from you long, and when I come back I'll see what I can do about feeding you!"

The colt stood for a time, peering between the corral boards after her. Then he set out upon a round of investigation. He moved slowly along the inside of the fence, seeming to approve its whitewashed cleanliness, until, turning in a corner, he stood before the stable door. Here he paused a moment, gazing into the semi-gloom, then sprang up the one step. Inside, he stood another moment, sweeping eyes down past the stalls, and finally set out and made his way to the far end. In the stall next the last stood a brown saddle-horse, and in the last stall the matronly horse he had followed out from town. But he showed no interest in these, bestowing upon each merely a passing glance. Then, discovering that the flies bothered him here more than in the corral, he walked back to the door and out into the sunlight again. In the corral he took up his motionless stand in the corner nearest the house.

He did not stand thus for long. He soon revealed grave uneasiness. It was due to a familiar gnawing inside. He knew the relief for this, and promptly set out in search of his mother. He hurried back along the fence, gained the door of the stable, and stepped into the stable, this time upon urgent business. He trotted down past the stalls to the family horse, and without hesitation stepped in alongside of her. Directly there was a shrill nicker, a lightning flash of heels, and the colt lay sprawling on the stable floor.

Never was there a colt more astonished than this one. Dazed, trembling, he regained his feet and looked at the mare, looked hard. Then casting solicitous eyes in the direction of the saddle-horse, he stepped in alongside. But here he met with even more painful objections. The horse reached around and bit him sharply in the neck. It hurt, hurt awfully, but he persisted, only to receive another sharp bite, this time more savage. Sounding a baby whimper of despair, he ran back to the door and out into the motherless corral.

He made for the corner nearest the house. But he did not stand still. He cocked his ears, pawed the ground, turned again and again, swallowed frequently. And presently he set out once more in search of his mother; though this time he wisely kept out of the stable. He held close to the fence, following it around and around, pausing now and again with eyes strained between the boards. But he could not find his mother. Finally, resorting to the one effort left to him that might bring result, he flung up his little head and sounded a piteous call–not once, but many times.

"Aunty," declared the girl, rushing into the genial presence of the Mexican cook, "what shall I do about that colt? He must be hungry!"

The old woman nodded and smiled knowingly. Then she stepped into the pantry. She filled a long-necked bottle with milk and sugar and a dash of lime-water, and, placing the bottle in the girl's hands, shoved her gently out the door and into the *patio*.

Racing across to the corral, Helen reached the colt with much-needed aid. He closed upon the bottle with an eagerness that seemed to tell he had known no other method of feeding. Also, he clung to it till the last drop was gone, which caused Helen to wonder when last the colt had fed. Then, as if by way of reward for this kindly attention, he tossed his head suddenly, striking the bottle out of her hands. This was play; and Helen, girlishly delighted, sprang toward him. He leaped away, however, and, coming to a stand at a safe distance, wriggled his ears at her mischievously. She sprang toward him again; but again he darted away. Whereupon she raced after him, pursuing him around the inclosure, the colt frisking before her, kicking up his heels and nickering shrilly, until, through breathlessness, she was forced to stop. Then the colt stopped, and after a time, having regarded her steadfastly, invitingly, he seemed to understand, for he quietly approached her. As he came close she stooped before him.

"Honey dear," she began, eyes on a level with his own, "they have telephoned the city officials, and your case will be advertised to-morrow in the papers. But I do wish that I could keep you." She peered into his slow-blinking eyes thoughtfully. "Brownie–my saddle-horse–is all stable-ridden, and I need a good saddler. And some day you would be grown, and I could–could take lots of comfort with you." She was silent. "Anyway," she concluded, rising and stroking him absently, "we'll see. Though I hope–and I know it isn't a bit right–that nothing comes of the advertisement; or, if something does come of it, that your rightful owner will prove willing to sell you after a time." With this she picked up the bottle and left him.

And nothing did come of the advertisement. Felipe did not read the papers, and his knowledge of city affairs was such that he did not set up intelligent quest for the colt.

So the colt remained in the Richards' corral. Regularly two and three times a day the girl came to feed him, and regularly as his reward each time he bunted the bottle out of her hand afterward. Also, between meals she spent much time in his society, and on these occasions relieved the tedium of his diet with loaf sugar, and, after a while, quartered apples. For these sweets he soon developed a passion, and he would watch her comings with a feverish anxiety that always brought a smile to her ready lips. And thus began, and thus went on, their friendship, a friendship that with the passing months ripened into strongest attachment, but which presently was to be interrupted for a long time.

Hint of this came to him gradually. From spending long periods with him every day his mistress, after each feeding now, took to hurrying away from him. Sometimes, so great was her haste to get back to the house, she actually ran out of the corral. It worried him, and he would follow her to the gate, and there stand with nose between the boards and eyes turned after her, whimpering softly. And finally, with his bottle displaced by more solid food, and the visits of his mistress becoming less frequent, he awoke to certain mysterious arrivals and departures in a buggy of a sharp-eyed woman all in black, and he came to feel, by reason of his super–animal instinct, that something of a very grave nature was about to happen to him. Then one morning late in August he experienced that which made his fears positive convictions, though precisely what it was he did not immediately know.

His mistress stepped into the corral with her usual briskness, and, walking deliberately past him, turned up an empty box in a far corner and sat down upon it, and called to him. From the instant of her entrance he had held himself back, but when she called him he rushed eagerly to her side. She placed her arms around his neck, drew his head down into her lap, and proceeded to unfold a story–later, tearful.

"It's all settled," she began, with a restful sigh. "We have discussed it for weeks, and I've had a dreadful time of it, and aunty–my Mexican aunty, you know–and my other aunty, my regular aunty–I have no mother–and everybody–got so excited I didn't really know them for my own, and daddy flared up a little, and–and–" She paused and sighed again. "But finally they let me have my own way about it–though daddy called it 'infant tommyrot'–and so here it is!" She tilted up his head and looked into his eyes. "You, sir," she then went on–"you, sir, from this day and date–I reckon that is how daddy would say it–you, sir, from this day and date shall be known as Pat. Your name, sir, is Pat–P-a-t–Pat! I don't know whether you like it or not, of course! But I do know that I like it, and under the circumstances I reckon that's all that is necessary." Then came the tears. "But that isn't all, Pat dear," she went on, tenderly. "I have something else to tell you, though it hurts dreadfully for me to do it. But–but I'm going away to school. I'm going East, to be gone a long time. I want to go, though," she added, gazing soberly into his eyes; "yet I am afraid to leave you alone with Miguel. Miguel doesn't like to have you around, and I know it, and I am afraid he will be cruel to you. But–but I've got to go now. The dressmaker has been coming for over a month; and–and I'm not even coming home for vacation. I am to visit relatives, or something, in New York–or somewhere–and the whole thing is arranged. But I–I don't seem to want–to–to go away now!" Which was where the tears fell. "If things–things could only be–be put off! But I–I know they can't!" She was silent, silent a long time, gazing off toward the distant mountains through tear-bedimmed eyes. "But when I do come back," she concluded, finally, brightening, "you will have grown to a great size, Pat dear, and then we can go up on the mesa and ride and ride. Can't we?" And she hugged him convulsively. "It will be glorious. Won't it?"

He didn't exactly say. His interest was elsewhere, and, resisting her hugging, he began to nuzzle her hands for sweets. Whereupon she burst into laughter and forcibly hugged him again.

"I forgot," she declared, regretfully. "You shall have them, though–right away!" Then she arose and left him–left him a very much mystified colt. But when she returned with what he sought he looked his delight, and closed over the sweets with an eagerness that forced her into sober reflection. "Pat," she said, after a time, "I don't think you care one single bit for me! All you care about, I'll bet, is what I bring you to eat!" Then she began to stroke him. "Just the same," she concluded, after a while, tenderly, "you're the dearest colt that ever lived!" She dallied with him a moment longer, then abruptly left him, running back to the house.

The days which followed, however, were full of delight for him. Now that the mysterious activity in the house was over with, his mistress began to visit him again with more than frequent regularity. And with each visit she would remain with him a long time, caressing him, talking to him, as had been her wont in the earlier days of their friendship. But as against those earlier days he had changed. Possibly this was due to her absence. Instead of frisking about the inclosure now, as he had used to frisk–whirling madly from her in play–he would remain very still during her visits, standing motionless under her caresses and love-talk. Also, when she took herself off each time, instead of hurrying frantically after her to the gate, he would walk slowly, even sedately, into his corner, the one nearest the house, and there watch her soberly till she disappeared indoors. Then–further evidence of the change that had come upon him–he would lie down in the warm sunlight and there fight flies, although before he had been given to worrying the family horse or irritating the brown saddler–all with nervous playfulness.

And he was dozing in his corner that morning when his mistress came fluttering to him to say good-by. He slowly rose to his feet and blinked curiously at her.

"Pat dear," she exclaimed, breathlessly, "I'm going now!" She flung her arms around his neck, held him tightly to her a moment, then stepped back. "You–you must be good while–while I'm gone!" And dashing away a persistent tear, she then hurriedly left him, speeding across the *patio* and stepping into the waiting phaeton.

He watched the vehicle roll out into the trail. And though he did not understand, though the seriousness of it all was denied him, he nevertheless remained close to the fence a long time; long after the phaeton had passed from view, long after the sound of the mare's paddling feet had died away, he stood there, ears cocked, eyes wide, tail motionless, in an attitude of receptivity, spiritual absorption, as one flicked with unwelcome premonitions.

CHAPTER V
LONELINESS

Pat's mistress was gone. He realized it from his continued disappointed watching for her at the fence; he realized it from the utter absence out of life of the sweets he had learned to love so well; and he realized it most of all from the change which rapidly came over the Mexican hostler. Though he did not know it, Miguel had been instructed, and in no mistakable language, to take good care of him, and, among other things, to keep him healthily supplied with sweets. But Miguel was not interested in colts, much less in anything that meant additional labor for him, and so Pat was made to suffer. Yet in this, as in all the other things, lay a wonderful good. He was made to know that he was not wholly a pampered thing–was made to feel the other side of life, the side of bitterness and disappointment, the side at times of actual want. And this continued denial of wants, of needs, occasionally, hardened him, as his earlier experiences had hardened him, toughened him for the struggles to come, brought to him that which is good for all youth–realization that life is not a mere span of days with sweets and comforts for the asking, but a time of struggle, a battle for supremacy, and it is only through the battle that one grows fit and ever more fit for the good of the All.

Not the least of his trials was great loneliness. One day was so very like another. Regularly each morning, after seeking out his favorite corner in the corral, he would see the sun step from the mountain-tops, ascend through a cool morning, pour down scorching midday rays, descend through a tense afternoon, and drop from view in the chill of evening. Always he would watch this thing, sometimes standing, other times reclining, but ever conscious of the dread monotony of it all. Nothing happened, nobody came to caress him, no one paid him the least attention. A forlorn colt, a lonely colt, doubly so for lack of a mother, he spent long days in moody contemplation of an existence that irked.

One day, however, came something of interest into the monotony of his life. Evidently tiring of attending each horse in turn in the stalls, Miguel built a general box for feed in one corner of the inclosure, and then, by dint of loud swearing and the free use of a pitchfork, instructed the colt to feed from it with the others. Not that Pat required instruction as to the feeding itself–he was too much alive to need driving in that respect. But he did show nervous timidity at feeding with the other horses, and so Miguel cheerfully went to the urging with fork and tongue. But only the one time. Soon the colt took to burying his nose in the box along with the others, and would wriggle his tail with a vigor that seemed to tell of his gratitude at being accepted as part of the great establishment and its devices. And then another thing. With this change in his method of feeding, he soon came to reveal steadily increasing courage and independence. Oftentimes he would be the first to reach the box, and, what was more to the point, would hold his position against the other horses–hold it against rough shouldering from the family horse, savage nipping from the saddler, even vigorous cursing and flaying from the swarthy hostler.

With the approach of winter he revealed his courage and temerity further. Of his own volition one night he abruptly changed his sleeping-quarters. Since the memorable occasion when the mare had kicked him out of her stall he had sought out a stall by himself with the coming of night, and there spent the hours in fear-broken sleep. But this night, and every night thereafter, saw him boldly approaching the mare and crowding in beside her in her stall, where, in the contact with her warm body and in her silent presence, he found much that was soothing and comfortable. Which, too, marked the beginning of a new friendship, one that steadily ripened with the passing winter and, by the time spring again descended into the valley, was an attachment close almost as that between mother and offspring. When in his playful moments, rare indeed now for one of his age, he would inadvertently plunge into her, or stumble over a water-pail, she would nicker grave disapproval, or else chide him more generously by licking his neck and withers a long time in genuine affection.

Thus the colt changed in both spirit and physique. And the more he changed, and the larger he grew, the greater source of trouble he became to the Mexican. Before, he had feared the man. Now he felt only a kind of hatred, and this lent courage to make of himself a frequent source of annoyance.

With the return of warm weather he resumed his old place in his favorite corner. He did this through both habit and a desire to warm himself in the sun's rays. And it was all innocent enough–this thing. Yet, innocent though it was, more than once, in passing, the Mexican struck him with whatever happened to be in his hands. At such times, whimpering with pain, he would dart to an opposite corner, there to stand in trembling fear, until, his courage returning, and his hatred for the man upholding him, he would return and defiantly resume his day-dreaming in the corner. This happened for perhaps a dozen times before he openly rebelled. And when he did rebel–when the Mexican struck him sharply across the nose–he whipped around his head like lightning and, still only half awake, sank his teeth savagely into the man's shoulder. Followed a string of oaths and sudden appearance of a club, which might have proved serious but for the Judge's timely call for the horse and phaeton. Whereupon the Mexican slunk off into the stable. But as he went Pat saw the gleam in his black eyes, and knew that some day punishment most dire and cruel would descend upon him.

He passed through his second summer, that period of trial and sickness for many infants, in perfect health. In perfect health also he passed through the autumn and on into his second winter. Growing ever stronger with the passing seasons, he came to reveal still further his wonderful vitality, and to reveal it in many ways. Often he would take the initiative against the Mexican, kicking at him without due cause, refusing always to get out of his way, once nipping him sharply as he hurried past under pressing orders from the house. Also, having grown to a size equal to the brown saddler, he began to reveal his antipathy for this animal. Not only would he shoulder him away from the feed-box, but he would kick and snap at him, and once he tipped over the water-pail for no other reason, seemingly, than to deprive the saddler of water. The result of all this was that, with the passing seasons, both the Mexican and the saddler showed increasing respect for him, and the former went to every precaution to avoid a serious encounter.

But it was bound to come in spite of all his efforts to avoid it. Fighting spring flies in the stable one morning, Pat was aroused by a familiar sound in the corral. It was the sound which usually accompanied feeding, and, whirling, he plunged eagerly toward the door. As he did so the Mexican, about to enter the stable, appeared on the threshold. Pat saw him too late. He crashed headlong into the Mexican and sent him reeling out into the inclosure. From that moment it was to the death.

The Mexican painfully gained his feet and, swearing a mighty vengeance, caught up a heavy shovel. Pat saw what was coming and, dashing out into the corral, sought protection behind the feed-box. But the infuriated man hunted him out, dealing upon his quivering back blow after blow, until, stung beyond all caution, Pat sprang for the object of his suffering. But the man leaped aside, delivering as he did so another vicious blow, this time across Pat's nose—most tender of places. Dazed, trembling, raging with the spirit of battle, he surveyed the man a moment, and then, with an unnatural outcry, half nicker, half roar, he hurtled himself upon his enemy, striking him down. But he did not stop here. When the man attempted to rise he struck him down again, and a third time. Then, seeing the man lying motionless, he uttered another outcry, different from the other, a whimpering, baby outcry, and, whirling away from the scene, hurried across the corral and into the stable, where he sought out the family horse and, still whimpering babyishly, stood very close beside her, seeking her sympathy and encouragement.

This closed the feud for all time. Miguel was not seriously hurt. But he had learned something, even as Pat had learned something, and thereafter there existed tacit understanding between them.

The seasons passed, and the third year came, and with it the beginning of the end of Pat's loneliness. One morning late in June he was aroused by the voice of the Mexican, who, with brushes and currycomb in hand, had come to clean him. Pat was in need of just this cleaning. Though wallowing but little, leaving that form of exercise to the older horses, he nevertheless was gritty with sand from swirling spring winds. So he stood very still under the hostler's vigorous attention. But Miguel's ambition did not stop here. He turned to the other horses and curried and brushed them also, working till the perspiration streamed from him. But this was not the end. He set to work in the stable, and scraped and cleaned to the last corner, and rubbed and scoured to the smallest harness buckle. It was all very unusual, and Pat, standing attentive throughout it all, revealed marked interest and something of surprise. Soon he was to know the reason.

Along toward noon, as he was feeding at the box, he saw a very dignified young woman leave the house, cross the *patio* in his direction, and come to a stop immediately outside the fence. Though the feed-box always held his interest above all other things, and though it was strongly attracting him now, he nevertheless could not resist the attention with which this young woman regarded him. He returned her gaze steadily, wondering who she was and what she meant to do. He soon found out, for presently she set out along the fence and came to a stop directly in front of him. She did more. She held out a hand and sounded a single word softly.

"Pat!" she called.

And now something took place inside the colt. With the word, far back in his brain, in the remotest of cells, there came an effort for freedom. It was a grim struggle, no doubt, for the thing must fight its way against almost all other thoughts and scenes and persons in his memory. But at length this vague memory gained momentum and dominance. And now he understood. The young woman outside the fence was his little mistress of early days! Lifting his head, he gave off a shrill and protracted nicker of greeting.

Helen dropped her hand. "Bless you!" she cried, and sped along the fence, opened the gate, and ran inside. "You do know me, don't you?" she burst out, and, hurrying to his side, hugged him convulsively. "And I'm so glad, Pat!" she went on. "It–it has been a long three years!" She stepped back and looked him over admiringly. "And you have grown so! Dear, oh, dear! Three years!" Again she stepped close and hugged him. "I am so proud of you, Pat!"

All this love-talk, this caressing and hugging, was as the lifting of a veil to Pat. Within him all that had lain dormant for three years– affection, desires, life itself–now pressed eagerly to the surface. And though his mistress did not look the same to him–though he found himself gazing down now instead of up to engage her eyes–yet, as if she had been gone but a day, he suddenly nuzzled her hand for loaf sugar and quartered apples. Then as suddenly he regretted this. For she had left him–was running across the corral. Frantically he rushed after her and, with a shrill cry of protest, saw her enter the house. But soon she appeared again, and when close, and he saw the familiar sweets in her hand, he nickered again, this time in sheer delight. And if he had doubted his good fortune before, now, with his mouth dripping luscious juices, he knew positively that he had come into his own again.

Sometime during the feast Helen noticed a scar across his nose. "Why, Pat!" she exclaimed. "How ever did you get that?"

But Pat did not say. Indeed, it is doubtful whether, in this happiest of moments, he would have descended to such commonplaces. But it was no commonplace to Helen, and she promptly sought out the Mexican. Yet Miguel declared that he knew nothing of the scar. He had been very watchful of the colt, he lied, cheerfully, and the scar was as much a mystery to him as it was to her. Whereupon Helen decided that Pat had brought it about through some prank, and, after returning to him and indulging in further caresses and love-talk, reluctantly took leave of him, returning to the house, there to begin unpacking her numerous trunks.

Thus their friendship was renewed. Pat was older by three years, as the girl was older by three years. But each was much older than that in point of development. Where before had been baby affection in him and girl affection in her, now was a thing of greater worth and more lasting quality–affection of a grown horse and a grown woman. In the days which followed this was brought out in many ways. The colt did not once frisk and play about the inclosure, a trait she remembered best; yet she did not wish it. She preferred him as he was, finding in his mature conduct something that enhanced his beauty; and rare beauty it was, as she frequently noted in running proud eyes over his lines, and in noting it came more and more to feel not alone great pride for him, but a sure love as well–not the love woman gives to man, of course, but the love she can give, and does give, without stint, to all dumb animals.

CHAPTER VI
THE FIRST GREAT LESSON

Helen spent much time in the society of the horse. Aside from attending to his wants, such as food and water, she more than once took comb and brush in hand and gave him a thorough cleaning. This invariably brought a grin to the ugly features of Miguel, and when the Judge was present, which was not often, a smile of delight mixed with derision to his ruddy features. But never would Helen permit them to discourage her. She would brush and curry Pat till his coat shone like new-mined coal, and then, after surveying the satiny sheen critically, she would comb out his long tail, sometimes braid his glossy mane, and, after that, scour his hoofs till they were as clean and fresh as the rest of him. In her pride for him she liked to do these things, and often regretted that he did not require her attention more than he did.

One day, with characteristic suddenness, she decided to have him broken to saddle. Therefore, next morning, three horse-breakers–one professional and two assistants–armed with ropes and saddles, appeared in the corral. Pat was sunning himself in his corner, and at their entrance only cocked his ears and blinked his eyes lazily. Outside the inclosure Helen, together with a scattering of spectators, attracted by the word of this treat in town, stood quietly expectant. One of the assistants, a raw-boned individual with hairy wrists, drove Pat out of his corner, while the professional, a large man of quiet demeanor, turned to Miguel, who was standing in the stable door, and put a question to him. Miguel, out of his own experience, warned them against the horse. Whereupon the large man neatly roped Pat, settling the noose skilfully around the horse's neck.

Instantly Pat was a quivering bundle of nerves. Bracing his legs, he drew back on the rope. But the man held to it grimly. The man did more. He suddenly raced across the inclosure, gave the rope a deft twist, and followed the twist with a vigorous jerk. Pat plunged heavily to the ground.

He lay dazed, breathing laboriously, till the rope slackened. Then he started to rise. But he only gained his fore legs. The second assistant, a slender youth, resisted his efforts, forcing Pat's head back by sitting upon it. Pat twisted and writhed to throw him off. But the man stayed with him, and finally had him prone to earth again. Whereupon Pat experienced the chagrin of his first defeat. Yet he could see. Upon the retina of each eye danced a picture. It was that of his mistress, surrounded by open-mouthed spectators, outside the fence, gazing down upon him with seeming approval. This once, but only this once, he felt dislike for her.

One of the men approached with a halter. Pat had seen these things in the stable, and he instinctively knew what they were for. But he would not accept this one. Embittered by his fall, chafing under the weight upon his head, he struggled so successfully that he finally dislodged the man. Then he sprang to his feet again, and, trembling in every part, glared savagely at his tormentors.

"Better give him a twist," quietly suggested the professional.

Pat heard the remark. But he did not understand, and so remained quiet. Presently he felt a light hand creeping up along his neck, pausing, patting him, creeping along farther, pausing and patting him again. It was not unpleasant, and under the soothing influence he came to believe that his tormentors had experienced a change of attitude. But he was mistaken. Suddenly his ear was gripped as in a vise. Also, it was twisted sharply, once, twice, and then held in a relentless grip. He stood still as death. Up and down his spine, from his ear to his tail, coursed shrieking pain, hacking him like the agony of a thousand twisting knives. Under the terror of it he stopped breathing–stopped till he must breathe or swoon. Then he did take air, in short, faint gasps, but each gasp at terrible cost. And standing thus, fearing to move, he accepted the halter. He could do naught else.

The raw-boned assistant turned to Helen apologetically. "Lively hoss, Miss Richards," he declared. "Reckon we're in for a little exercise." And he grinned.

Anxiously Helen mounted the fence, standing upon a lower board. "You won't hurt him, I hope–that is, needlessly! I don't want that, you know!" And she gazed at Pat with pitiful eyes.

The other laughed. "No; 'tain't that," he hastened to reassure her. "He's lively–that's all."

The professional looked Pat over speculatively, and again made a suggestion. "Better blindfold him, Larry," he said.

Pat heard this as he had heard the other. And because he was coming to know this man's voice, and to interpret it correctly, despite the agony it cost him he went on his guard, spreading and bracing his legs as against shock. He did not receive shock, however. Merely a piece of soft flannel was tucked gently under his halter and drawn carefully over his eyes. Against the soft pressure of it he closed his eyes. As he did so the hand released his ear. Conscious of sweet relief from the dread pain now, he opened his eyes again, only to discover that he could not see!

Here was new distress! He did not understand it. He knew that his eyes were open; knew that it was the time of sunshine; knew with grim certainty that he was awake. Yet he could not see! He flung up his head; tossed it across and back; flung it down again. Yet the unnatural darkness! He took to pawing the ground. He began to recall his surroundings before this strange darkness had descended upon him–the girl outside the fence, the spectators upon the fence, the tormentors inside the fence, the glorious sunlight, the distant shimmering mountains, the stable and outhouses and cottage. But all were gone from him now. Everything was black with the blackness of night! Again he tossed his head–and again and again. But still the darkness! He was afraid.

Here came a change. Across his vision leaped sudden flashing lights, myriads of them, dancing strangely before him. Gripped in new fear, he watched them closely, saw them hurry, pause, hurry again, all in dazzling array. They kept it up. Breathlessly he saw them dart to and fro, speed near, whirl and twist, until out of sheer distress he closed his eyes for relief. But he got no relief. He saw the lights as before, saw them dancing and pirouetting before his eyes, and suddenly whisk away, as though satiated with their fiendishness. But they left him limp and faint and with a throbbing pain in his head. Again he stamped the earth and shook his head. But the darkness clung. He could not throw off the thing before his eyes. Yet he persisted. He tossed his head until dizziness seized him. Then he stopped all effort and relaxed. His head began to droop; he let it droop, low and lower, until he smelled the earth. This aroused him. His spirit of fight rose again. He jerked up his head, sounded a defiant outcry, stiffened his legs for action. This for a moment only, for he did not act–somehow felt it was not yet time. But he gave way to a grim restlessness. He took to rocking like a chained elephant–from right hind to left fore, from left hind to right fore legs–changing, always changing.

"Well, old son," came a voice on his chaotic thoughts, "we've just found a bridle that'll suit. But it took us a mean long time to do it, didn't it?"

Pat stopped swaying. He stopped suddenly, as one checked by a mighty force. And so he was. For he knew now that the time had come. Here was his tormentor! Here was one of them within reach! The time had come to strike, to strike this man, to crush him to earth, to kill the cause of his suffering–

"Here, hoss," went on the voice, soothingly, the while Pat smelled a something of the stable underneath his nose. "Go to it! It's right harmless–now, ain't it?" Which it seemed to be from the smell.

But Pat struck–reared with the speed of lightning and struck.

The blow was unexpected. It sent the man spinning, whirling across the inclosure. He dropped into a corner like a log.

There was a tense moment. Spectators sat dazed; horsemen stood rigid; the girl screamed. Then the large man ran to the prostrate form. He bent over, gazed briefly, straightened up with a reassuring smile. Presently the assistant arose and, rubbing his shoulder ruefully, caught up the fallen bridle. Soon the work of breaking was resumed as though nothing had happened.

Pat was standing motionless. But he was keenly alert. He heard the man draw near, felt the hand creeping along his neck, but he had learned his lesson well. He reared and struck again–this time only empty air. Yet, as he returned to earth, almost before he touched ground, the hand was around his ear, another was around his other ear, he was feeling the dread twist again, twofold. Every twitch of muscle, every least gasp for air, sent excruciating pain throughout the ends of him. Fearing to move, yet clamoring for breath, he slowly opened his mouth.

Which was what they wanted, evidently. He felt a cold something suddenly thrust between his teeth. It was hard as well as cold. He tasted it, rolled it over his tongue, and found it not painful. Then came something else. His head was being hurriedly fitted with a leathery contrivance. But neither was this painful, save only as it touched his twisted ears, and he therefore experienced no increasing alarm. Then, with this adjusted, he was introduced to something else–a something held close under his nose. He smelled this carefully; noted that it reeked with odors of the stable; smelled it again. Next he knew it was being placed gently upon his back. It was soft, and quite hairy, and though it irritated him a little, he accepted it without loss of composure. But when it was followed, as it was directly, by a heavier something, a something fitting his back snug and hard, he instantly determined to rebel, despite his twisted ears. But he could not withstand the increased pain, and he permitted the thing to be made secure with straps around his body. And now came a heavier something, a free and loose weight, something with spring and give to it, and which had flung up from the ground. And suddenly, flaying his pained senses, understanding flashed upon him. This was a man. There was a tormentor upon his back, gripping the thing in his mouth, holding him solidly to the ground. He–

"Go!"

It was a word of command. With the word Pat felt his ears released. As he thrilled with relief the cloth was jerked off his eyes. For a time the fierce daylight blinded him. Then the pupils of his eyes contracted and all objects stood out clearly again–the men in the corral, the spectators on the fence, his mistress outside the fence. Also he saw the sunlit stable, and Miguel in the doorway, and the house in the trees. All had come back to him, and he stood gazing about him blinkingly, trying to understand, conscious of straps binding his body and restraining his breathing.

Then suddenly he understood–remembered–remembered that he had been abused, had been tortured as never before. And he awoke to the fact that he was still being tortured. There was this thing in his mouth. There was this contraption on his head. There was that thing on his back, and the weight upon the thing. Also, there was that binding of his belly, and the irritation due to the prickly something pressing his back and sides. All these facts stung him, and under the whip of them he awoke to a mighty urging within. It was his fighting spirit rekindling–the thing that was his birthright, the thing come down to him from his ancestors, the thing that told him to rebel against the unnatural. And heeding this, voice, heeding it because he knew no other, he decided to give decisive battle.

In a frenzy of effort he suddenly reared. He pirouetted on hind legs; pawed the air with fore legs; lost his balance. Failing to recover himself, he went over backward. He struck the earth resoundingly, but he realized that the weight was gone, and he felt a faint glow of victory!

"Wow!" yelled a spectator, excitedly.

Pat heard this and hastily regained his feet. And because he was uncertain of his next move he remained motionless. This was a mistake, as he soon discovered. For he saw two men leap, grasp both his ears; felt the dread twist again. So he remained still, and he felt the man mount again. Then came rumbling in upon his tortured soul again the insistent voice telling him to rebel further, and to keep on rebelling until through sheer brute strength he had mastered these unnatural things. With the grip on his ears released he once more gave heed to this clamoring within.

He leaped straight up into the air. Returning to earth with nerve-shattering shock, he whirled suddenly, pitched and bucked, tossed and twisted, all in mad effort. But the weight clung fast. He whirled again, and again leaped, leaped clear of the ground, returning to it this time on stiffened legs. But he could not shake off the weight. He flung across the corral, twisting, writhing, bucking; flung back again–heart thumping, lungs shrieking for air, muscles wrenching and straining; and again across, responding, and continuing to respond, to the ringing voice within, like the king of kings that he was. But he could not dislodge the weight.

"Great!" yelled an excited spectator.

"See that hoss sunfishin'!" burst out another.

"An' corkscrewin'!" added a third.

"Better 'n a outlaw!" amplified a fourth.

42

And now the first again: "Stay with him, Alex! I got two dollars–Oh, hell!"–this disgustedly. "Come out o' that corner!" Then suddenly he turned, face red as fire, and apologized to Helen. "I beg your pardon, Miss Richards," he offered, meekly. But he turned back to the spectacle and promptly forgot all else in his returning excitement. "Shoot it to him, Alex!" he yelled. "Shoot it; shoot it! He's a helldinger, that hoss!" Frenziedly he then yawped, cowboy fashion: "Whe-e-e-o-o-o-yip-yip! Whe-e-e-o-o-o-yip-yip!"

Yet Helen–poor Helen!–had not heard. Holding her breath in tense fear, eyes upon her pride fighting his fight of pride, half hopeful that he would win, yet fearful of that very thing, she watched the strife of man skill against brute strength, keyed up almost to snapping-point.

But her horse did not win. Neither did he lose. She saw him take up, one after another, every trick known to those familiar with horses, and she marveled greatly at his unexpected knowledge of things vicious. Along one side of the inclosure, across the side adjacent to it, back along the side opposite to the second, then forward along the first again–thus round the corral–he writhed and twisted in mighty effort, bucking and pitching and whirling and flinging, the while the sun rose higher in the morning sky. Spectators clambered down from the fence, stood awhile to relieve cramped muscles, clambered on the fence again; but the horse fought on; coat necked with white slaver, glistening with streaming sweat in the sunlight, eyes wild, mouth grim, ears back, he fought on and on till it seemed that he must stop through sheer exhaustion. But still he fought, valiantly, holding to the battle until, with a raging, side-pitching twist, one never before seen, he lost his footing, plunged to the ground, tore up twenty feet of earth, crashed headlong into the fence, ripped out three boards clean as though struck by lightning–lay motionless in a crumpled heap.

The man was thrown. He arose hastily. As he wiped away his perspiration and grime he saw blood on his handkerchief. He was bruised and bleeding, and wrenched inwardly, yet when Pat, returning to consciousness, hastily gained his feet, the man leaped for the horse, sounding a muffled curse. But he did not mount. And for good reason. For Pat was reeling like a drunken man–head drooping, fore parts swaying, eyes slowly closing. At the sight one of the spectators made a plea in Pat's behalf.

"Whyn't you take him outside?" he demanded. "Into the open. This ain't no place to bust a horse like him! That horse needs air! Get him out into about three-quarters of these United States! Git ginerous! Git ginerous! I hate a stingy man!"

Whereupon Helen at last found voice. "Wait!" she cried, evenly, and, turning, sped along the fence to the gate. Inside the corral she hurried to the horse and flung her arms around his neck. "Pat dear," she began, tenderly, "I am so sorry! But it's 'most over with now, if you'll only accept it! Can't you see, Pat? It is so very necessary to both of us! For then I myself can ride you! Please, Pat–please, for my sake!" Whereupon Pat, as if all else were forgotten–all the torture, all the struggle and shock–nickered softly and nuzzled her hands for sugar and apples. Suppressing a smile, and accepting this as a good omen, she stroked him a few times more and then stepped back. "Later, dear!" she promised and left him, suddenly mindful of spectators. But, though she felt the blood rush into her cheeks, she did not leave the inclosure. The horse-breaker stepped resolutely to Pat and, laying firm hands upon the bridle, waited a moment, eying Pat narrowly, then flung up into the saddle. Pat's sides heaved, his knees trembled, but he did not resist. Eyes trained upon his mistress, as if he would hold her to her promise, he set out peacefully, and of his own volition, across the inclosure. Further, even though he could not see his mistress now, he turned in response to the rein and started back across the inclosure. And he kept this up, holding to perfect calm, breaking into a trot when urged to it, falling back into a walk in response to the bridle, round and round and round until, with a grunt of satisfaction, the man dismounted close beside the girl and handed her the reins.

"Rides easy as a single-footer, Miss Richards," he declared. "Where can I wash up?"

Which ended Pat's first great lesson at the hands of man. But though this lesson had its values, since he was destined to serve mankind, yet he had learned another thing that held more value to him as an animal than all the teachings within the grasp of men–he had learned the inevitable workings of cause and effect. His nose was scraped and his knees were scraped, and all these places burned intensely. And, intelligent horse that he was, he knew why he suffered these burns–knew that he had brought them about through his own sheer wilfulness. True, he was still girt with bands and straps, and in a way they were uncomfortable. But they did not pain him as the wounds pained him. Not that he reasoned all this out. He was but a dumb animal, and pure reasoning was blissfully apart from him. But he did know the difference between what had been desired of him and what he himself had brought on through sheer wilfulness. Thus he awakened, having learned this lesson with his headlong plunge into the fence, and having added to the lesson of the futility of rebellion the very clear desires of his mistress. Other and less intelligent horses would have continued to respond to the ancestral voice within till death. But Pat was more than such a horse.

With the men gone, he revealed his intelligence further. Helen commissioned Miguel to fit him with her saddle and bridle, then hurried herself off to the house. Returning, clad in riding-habit and with hands full of sugar and quartered apples, she fed these delectables to him till his mouth dripped delightful juices. Then, while yet he munched the sweets, she mounted fearlessly. Sitting perfectly still for a time to accustom him to her weight, she then gave him the rein and word. Without hesitation he responded, stepping out across the inclosure, acknowledging her guiding rein in the corner, returning to the starting-place and, with the word, coming to a stop. It was all very beautiful, rightly understood, and, thrilled with her success, Helen sat still again, sat for a long time, gazing soberly down upon him. Then she bent forward.

"Pat," she began, her voice breaking a little with emotion suddenly overwhelming her, "this begins our real friendship and understanding. Let us try to make it equal"–she straightened up, narrow eyes off toward the mountains–"equal to the best that lies within us both."

CHAPTER VII
A STRANGER

As the weeks passed, each day bringing its period of companionship, this friendship and understanding between them became perfect in its simplicity. Pat learned to know her wishes almost without the reins, and he showed that he loved to carry her. Also, with these daily canters on the mesa he developed in bodily strength, and it was not long before he was in the pink of condition. Yet it was a perfection that was only natural for him. The quality of his blood was shown in his nostrils, which were wide and continuously atremble; in his eyes, which were bright and keenly alert; and in his ears, which were fine and vibrant. Stepping through town each morning under Helen's restraining hand, he would pick up his hoofs with a cleanliness and place them down with a grace that always commanded the attention of admiring eyes. But he seemed unconscious of his quality.

Dressed in her usual dark riding-habit, Helen entered the corral one morning for her daily canter across the mesa. Already Pat was bridled and saddled. But as she stepped alongside to mount, Miguel appeared in the stable door with a brief tale of trouble and a warning. It seemed that he had experienced difficulty in preparing the horse, and between puffs at a cigarette he strongly advised Helen to be careful.

"He's a-very fresh thees mornin'," he concluded, with an ominous shake of his head.

Helen looked Pat over. He appeared in anything but a cantankerous mood. He was standing quietly, eyes blinking sleepily, ears wriggling lazily, in an attitude of superior indifference toward all the world. So, untroubled by the hostler's tale, she slipped her foot into the stirrup. Instantly the horse nickered queerly and stepped away.

"Steady, Pat!" she gently admonished, and again attempted to mount. But, as before, he stepped away, this time more abruptly. He began to circle around her, prancing nervously, pausing to paw the ground, prancing again nervously. She held firm grip on his bridle, however, and sharply rebuked him. "Pat," she exclaimed, "this is a new trait!" And then, before he could resist again, she caught hold of the saddle-horn, leaped up, hardly touching the stirrup, and gathered the reins quickly to meet further rebellion.

But with her in the saddle Pat was quite another horse. He snapped his ears at attention, wheeled to the gate, and cantered briskly out of the corral.

It was a beautiful morning. The air nipped with a tang of frost, and she rode swiftly through town and up the hill to the mesa in keen exhilaration. Once on the mesa, Pat dashed off ecstatically in the direction of the mountains. The pace was thrilling. The rush of the crisp wind, together with the joy of swift motion, sent tingling blood into Helen's cheeks, while the horse, racing along at top speed, flung out his hoofs with a vigor that told of the riot of blood within him. Thus they continued, until in the shadow of the mountains–just now draped in their most delicate coloring, the pink that accompanies sunbeams streaming through fading haze–she pulled Pat down and gave herself over to the beauty of the scene. The horse, also appreciative, came to a ready stop and turned his eyes out over the desert in slow-blinking earnestness.

"Pat!" suddenly cried Helen. She pulled his head gently around in the direction of the mountain trail. "Look off there!"

Above the distant trail hung a thin cloud of dust, and under the cloud of dust, and rolling heavily toward town, creaked a lumber rigging, piled high with wood and drawn by a pair of plodding horses–plodding despite the bite and snarl of a whip swung with merciless regularity. The whip was in the hands of a brawny Mexican, who, seated confidently on the high load, appeared utterly indifferent to the trembling endeavors of his scrawny team. He was inhaling the smoke of a cigarette, and with every puff mechanically flaying the horses. The spectacle aroused deep sympathy in the girl.

"Only consider, Pat!" she exclaimed, after a while. "Those poor, miserable horses–half-starved, cruelly beaten, yet of God's own making!" She was silent. "Suppose you had been born to that service, Pat–born to that oppression! You are one of the fortunate!" And she bent forward and stroked him. "One of the fortunate!" she repeated, thoughtfully.

Indeed Pat was just that. But not in the way Helen meant. For such was the whim of Fate, and such is the limit of human understanding, she did not know, and never would know, save by the grace of that Fate, that Pat had been born in just that service, born to just that oppression; that only by the kindness of Fate he had been released from that service, that oppression, that he had been guided out of that environment and cast into a more kindly, bigger, and truer environment–her own!

But Pat only blinked stolid indifference at the spectacle. He appeared to care nothing for the misery of other horses, nor to appreciate her tenderness when directed elsewhere than toward himself. After a time, as if to reveal this, he set out of his own volition toward a particularly inviting bit of flower, dainty yellow in the brown of the desert. Plucking this morsel, he fell to munching it in contentment, and continued to munch it till the last vestige disappeared. Then, again of his own volition, he broke into a canter. Helen smiled and pulled him down.

"You're a strange horse, Pat," she declared, and fell to stroking him again. "And not the least strange thing about you is your history. Sometimes I wonder whether you are actually blooded. Certainly you look it, and at times assuredly you act it; yet if you are so valuable, why didn't somebody claim you that time? It is all very mysterious." And she relapsed into silence, gazing at him thoughtfully.

Aroused by sudden faint gusts of wind, she glanced around and overhead. She saw unmistakable signs of an approaching storm, and swung Pat about toward home. As the horse broke into a canter the gusts became more fitful and sharper, while the sun, growing dim and hazy, cast ever-increasing shadow before her. Presently, as far as the eye could reach, she saw the landscape spring into active life. Dust-devils whirled about in quick eddies, stray sheets of paper leaped up, tumbleweed began steady forward movement, rabbit-like, scurrying before the winds, the advance occupied by largest growths, the rear brought up with smallest clumps, the order determined by the area each presented to the winds. It was all very impressive, but, knowing the uncertain character of the elements, and uncertain whether this foretold violent sand-storm or milder wind-storm, she was gripped with apprehension. She urged Pat to his utmost.

And Pat responded, though he really needed but little urging. With each sudden gust he became increasingly afraid. Holding himself more and more alert to every least movement about him, he was steadily becoming keyed up to a dangerous pitch. Rollicking tumbleweed did not worry him any more than did the swirling dust-devils. These were things of the desert, each the complexion of the desert. But not so with scraps of paper. Their whiteness offered a startling contrast to the others, and, whisking about frantically, they increased his fears. Then suddenly a paper struck him, whipped madly across his eyes. It was unexpected, and for an instant blinded him. Gripping the bit in his teeth, he bolted.

His sudden plunge almost unseated Helen. But, recovering, she braced herself grimly in the stirrups and pulled mightily on the reins. But she could not hold him. He increased his speed, if anything, and hurtled across the desert–head level, ears flat, legs far-reaching. She braced herself again, flinging back head and shoulders, thrusting her feet far forward, and continued to pull. But it counted for nothing. Yet she did not weaken, and under her vigorous striving, coupled with the jolting of the horse, her tam-o'-shanter flew off, and her hair loosened and fell, streaming out whippingly behind. And then suddenly, struck with terror herself, she cried out in terror.

"Pat!" she burst out. "Pat! Pat!"

But the horse seemed not to hear. Thundering madly forward, he appeared blind as well as fear-stricken, and Helen, suddenly seeing a barb-wire fence ahead, felt herself go faint, for she had never taken a fence, and she knew that Pat never had. She must get control of herself again. And this she did. Stiffening in the stirrups, she gripped a single rein in both hands and pulled with all her strength. But she could not swerve the horse. On he plunged for the obstruction, evidently not seeing it. She screamed again.

"Pat! Pat! Pat!"

But, as before, the horse did not heed. He dashed to the fence. He hesitated, but only for an instant. Throwing up his head, he rose and took the fence cleanly. Once on the other side, he resumed his frantic racing–pounding along in the mountain trail, his course clearly defined, hurtling madly straight toward town. With the fence safely cleared, and the way ahead free of vehicles, Helen regained much of her composure. Settling calmly to the rhythmic movement, she permitted the horse free rein. Once she reached back to gather up her hair, but the motion of the horse forbade this. So she fell to watching his splendid energy, finding herself quite calm and collected again, vaguely wondering how it would end. For the horse seemed tireless.

Wise in his knowledge of first principles, and remembering the terrible slap across his eyes, Pat continued to rush forward. As he ran he kept eyes alert about him, fearing another blow. He knew that the thing was white, and he watched for a white something. Instead of a white something, however, there presently loomed up beside him a brown something, browner even than the desert, a something racing along beside him, moving with a speed equal to his own–even greater than his own! But he did not pause to analyze this. Instead, he forced himself to greater efforts, pounding the hardened trail with an energy that hurt his ankles, stretching neck and legs to their utmost limit of fiber–on and on in increased frenzy. But he could not best this object beside him. Yet that did not discourage him. He continued grimly forward, stung to desperation now by a double purpose, which was to outrun this thing on his right as well as get away from the other possible pursuing object. Yet the brown thing gained upon him–drew steadily nearer, steadily closer–he saw a hand shoot out. He felt a strong pull on his bridle, a tearing twist on the bit in his mouth, and found himself thrown out of his stride. But not even with this would he accept defeat. He reared in a nervous effort to shake off the hand. Finding this futile, he dropped back again, and at last came to a trembling, panting, nerve-racked pause.

The thing was a horseman. He hurriedly dismounted, still retaining hold on Pat's bridle, and smiled up at Helen.

"I–I tried to overtake you–to overtake you before you reached the fence," he began to explain, pausing between words for breath. "This horse of yours can–can claim–claim anything on record–for speed." And he looked Pat over admiringly.

Helen did not speak at once. In the moment needed to regain her self-possession she could only regard him with mute gratitude. She saw that he was young and well-built, though lean of features, but with frank, healthy eyes. He was not at all bad-looking. Also she observed that he was neatly garbed in puttees and knickerbockers, and she quickly appraised him as the usual type of Easterner come into the valley to spend the winter. Then she suddenly remembered her hair. Woman-like, she hastily gathered it up into a knot at the back of her head before she answered this young man smiling up at her.

"Pat never ran like that before," she explained, a bit nervously. "I was beginning to wonder what would happen at the railroad crossing. You checked him just in time. I–I really owe–"

"Sure he won't charge again?" interrupted the young man, evidently wishing to avoid any expression of gratitude on her part.

"I–I am quite certain," she replied, and then, after thanking him, slowly gathered up the reins. But she did not ride on, for the reason that the other, now absorbed in a cool survey of Pat's outlines, retained his hold on the bridle. Yet neither the survey nor the grip on the bridle displeased her.

"A splendid horse," he declared, after a moment. "A beautiful animal!" Then, evidently suddenly mindful that he was detaining her, he stepped back.

Helen again prepared to ride on.

"Pat is a beautiful horse," she agreed, still a little nervous. "And like all beauty," she added, "he develops strange moods at times." Then, her sense of deep gratitude moving her, she asked, "Were you going toward town?"

For reply he swung into the saddle. He wheeled close, and they set out. He appeared a little ill at ease, and Helen took the initiative.

"From the East, I take it?" she inquired. "There are not a few Easterners down here. Some have taken up permanent residence."

"Yes," he replied, "I'm from the East–New York."

She liked his voice.

"We are here for the winter–mother and myself. Mother isn't strong, and your delightful climate ought to improve her. I myself came along"–he turned twinkling eyes toward her–"as guide and comforter and–I fear–all-round nuisance." He was silent. "I like this country," he added, after a moment.

Helen liked him for liking her country, for she had true Western pride for her birthplace. So she said the natural thing, though without display of pride. "Everybody likes it down here."

He looked at her hesitatingly. "You're not from the outside, then?"

"No," she rejoined. "I am a native."

He showed restless curiosity now. "Tell me," he began, engagingly, "about this country. What, for instance, must one do, must one be, to–to be–well, to be accepted as a native!" He said this much as one feeling his way among a people new to him, as if, conscious of the informal nature of their meeting, he would ease that informality, yet did not know precisely how.

Yet Helen found herself quite comfortable in his society now, and, permitting herself great freedom, she spoke almost with levity.

"You have asked me a difficult question," she said. "Offhand I should say you must ride every morning, sleep some part of the early afternoon, and–oh, well, ride the next morning again, I reckon." And she smiled across at him. "Are you thinking of staying with us?"

He nodded soberly. Then he went on. "What else must one do?" he asked. "Is that all?" His eyes were still twinkling.

Helen herself was sober now. "No," she replied, "not quite. One must think a little, work a little, do a little good. We are very close together down here–very close to one another–and very, very far from the rest of the world. So we try to make each day register something of value, not alone for ourselves, but for our neighbors as well." She was silent. "We are a distinct race of people," she concluded, after a moment.

He turned his head. "I like all that," he declared, simply. "Though I'm afraid I won't do–much as I dislike to admit it. You see, I've never learned to live much in the interest of others." He regarded her with steady eyes.

Helen liked him for that, too. Evidently he had had too much breeding, and, from his remark, knew it. So she took it upon herself at least to offer him encouragement.

"You will learn," she rejoined, smiling. "Everybody does."

With this, Helen discreetly changed the subject. She entered upon less intimate matters, and soon, sweeping off into a rhapsody over the country–its attraction for Easterners, its grip on Westerners–she was chatting with a freedom typical of the country. For by now she was interested, and for some inexplicable reason she found herself drawn to the smiling stranger.

Also, Pat was interested. But not in the things which appealed to his mistress. Pat was pondering the sullen nature of the horse beside him, and as they rode slowly toward town he stole frequent sidelong glances at his unfriendly companion. But all he could arrive at was that, while appearing peaceable enough, this horse was the most self-satisfied animal chance had ever thrown his way. After a time he ceased all friendly advances, such as pressing close beside him and now and again playfully nipping at him, and took up his own affairs, finding deep cause for satisfaction in the return of his breath after the long race, and in the passing of pain from his strained legs, to say nothing of the complete absence of flying papers around him.

They crossed the railroad track and entered the town. Here the young man took a polite leave of Helen, and Pat, seeing the unfriendly horse canter away at a brisk gait, himself set out briskly, feeling somehow called upon to emulate the step of the other. And thus he continued through town to the river trail, which he followed at an even brisker stride, and thence to the ranch and the corral. Here his mistress took leave of him–abruptly, it seemed–and made her way straight into the house. Directly the Mexican came and removed his saddle and bridle. With these things off, he shook himself vigorously, and then took up his customary stand in the corner, and confidently awaited the reappearance of his mistress with sugar and apples–a reward she never had denied him.

But he waited this time in vain.

CHAPTER VIII
FELIPE MAKES A DISCOVERY

Pat waited in vain two whole days. Not once did she come to him, not once did he lay eyes upon her. He became nervous and irritable, and in this emptiness, equal to that which he had suffered during the three years she was away, he spent every waking moment in the corral, standing in his favorite corner, eyes strained toward the house, occasionally interrupting the silence with a pleading nicker. But his vigil gained him nothing, his watching remained unrewarded, his outcries went unanswered. Finally, with the close of each day he would enter the stable, but only to brood through half the night–wondering, wondering. But never did he give up hope. Nor had he given up hope now, this morning of the third day, when, standing in his corner as usual, he heard a door close in the house.

As always, his heart leaped with expectation, and he gave off a protracted whinny. Also he pressed close to the fence. This time he was not disappointed. For coming slowly toward him, with her hands behind her back, was his mistress.

"Pat," she began, standing close before him, "I have neglected you purposely. And I did it because I have lost confidence in you." She regarded him a long moment coldly, then was forced to smile. "I suppose I feel toward you much as I used to feel toward a doll of mine that had fallen and cracked its head. I want to shake you, yet I can't help but feel sorry for you, too." And again she was silent.

Pat shifted his feet uneasily. He did not quite understand all this, though he knew, despite the smile of his mistress, that it was serious. Still, encouraged by the smile, he pressed close and asked for sweets, nuzzling her coat-sweater persistently. But she stepped away. Whereupon he reached his neck after her, and became almost savage in his coaxing. Finally he was relieved to see her burst into a peal of laughter.

"Here!" she said, and held out both hands. "I don't care if your head is broken!"

Glory be! Two red apples in one hand; a whole handful of loaf sugar in the other! If ever a horse smiled, he smiled then. Also, he promptly accepted some of the sugar, and, enjoying every delicious mouthful, reached for an apple. But she drew back. Evidently she was not yet finished with her reprimand.

"Blissfully unconscious of your behavior that morning, aren't you?" she continued. "Not a bit ashamed; not one speck regretful!"

Well–he wasn't. He was not a bit ashamed, not one speck regretful. Merely, he was sweet-hungry. And now that the sugar was gone, he wanted one of those apples mightily. Finally she gave him one, and then the other, feeding them to him rapidly, but not more rapidly than he wanted them. Then she spoke again.

"Pat dear," she said, her voice undergoing change, "I'm troubled. I am foolish, I know. But I can't help it. I advised that very nice young man to ride every morning. And he may do it. But if he does, sooner or later, perhaps the very first morning, we shall meet up there on the mesa. I want that, of course; but for reasons best known to Easterners, I don't want it–not yet." She gazed off toward the mountains. "I reckon, Pat dear," she concluded, after a moment, turning her eyes back to him, "we'd better ride in the afternoons for a time. Yet the afternoons are so uncomfortably hot. Oh, dear! What shall I do?"

But the horse did not answer her. All he did was stand very still, eyes blinking slowly, seemingly aware of the gravity of the situation, yet unable to help her. Indeed, that her serious demeanor had struck a note of sympathy within him he presently revealed by once more pressing very close to her–this in the face of the fact that she had no more sweets with her and he could see that she had no more. The movement forced her back, and evidently he perceived his mistake, for he quickly retraced one step. Then he fell to regarding her with curious intentness, his head twisting slowly in a vertical plane, much as a dog regards his master, until, evidently finding this plane of vision becoming awkward, he stopped. After which Helen playfully seized his ears and shook his head.

"You're a perfect dear!" she exclaimed. "And I love you! But I'm afraid we–we can't ride mornings any more–not for a while, at any rate." With this she left him.

He followed her to the gate, and with reluctance saw her enter the house. Then he rested his head upon the topmost board and, though he hardly expected it, waited for her return. Finally he abandoned his vigil, making his way slowly into the stable. He found both horses in their stalls, restlessly whisking their tails, offering nothing of friendliness or invitation. Also he awoke to the depressing atmosphere here, and after a time returned to the corral, where he took up a stand in his favorite corner and closed his eyes. Soon he was dreaming.

Sound as from a great distance awoke him. He opened his eyes. Outside the fence, and regarding him gloatingly, were two swarthy Mexicans in conversation. This was what had awakened him.

"Bet you' life!" one was saying, the taller man of the two. "Thot's my li'l' horse grown big lak a house—and a-fine! Franke, we gettin' thot *caballo* quick. We—"

A door had closed somewhere. The men heard it and crouched. But neither abandoned the ground. After some little time, hearing nothing further to alarm them, they set out along the fence to a rear door in the stable. It was not locked, and they lifted the latch and tiptoed inside. Up past the stalls they crept with cat-like stealth, gained the door leading into the corral, came to a pause, and gazed outside. The horse was still in his corner, his black coat glistening in the sunlight, and Felipe once more burst into comment, excited, but carefully subdued.

"A-fine! A-fine!" he breathed, rapturously. "He's lookin' joost lak a circus horse! You know, Franke," he added, turning to the other, "I haf see thee pictures on thee fences—" He interrupted himself, for the man had disappeared. "Franke!" he called, whispering. "You coom here. You all thee time—" He checked himself and smiled at the other's forethought. For Franke was emerging from a stall, carrying a halter. "Good!" he murmured. "I am forgettin' thot, *compadre*!" Then once more he turned admiring eyes upon the horse. "Never—*never*—haf I see a horse lak thot! Mooch good luck is comin' now, Franke! Why not?"

They stepped bravely forth into the corral. Yet their hour had been well timed. The house was still, quiet in its morning affairs, while the countryside around, wrapped in pulsating quiet, gave off not a sound. Cautiously approaching the horse, Franke slipped the halter into position, the while Felipe once more uttered his admiration. He was a little more direct and personal, however, this time.

"Well, you black devil!" he began, doubling his fist under Pat's nose. "You haf run away from me thot time, eh? But you don' run away again–bet you' life! I got you now and I keep you thees time! I haf work for you–you black devil–mooch work! You coom along now!"

They led the horse into the stable, down past the stalls, and out the back door. Then they set out toward the river trail, and, with many furtive glances toward the house, gained it without interruption. Felipe's lumber rigging and team of scrawny horses stood in the shade of a cottonwood, and Franke made the horse fast to the outhanging end of the reach. When he was secure both men seated themselves just back of the forward bolster, one behind the other, and Felipe sent his horses forward. Safely out of the danger zone, though Felipe entertained but little fear of the consequences of this act, believing that he could easily prove his ownership, he became more elated with his success and burst out into garrulous speech.

"You know, Franke," he began, with a backward glance at the horse ambling along peacefully in the dust, "thot *caballo* he's strong lak a ox. He's makin' a fine horse–a *fine* horse–in thees wagon! He's–" He suddenly interrupted himself. "Franke," he offered, generously, "for thees help I'm takin' off five dolars on thot debt now. You know? You haf never pay me thot bet–thee big bet–thee one on thee wagon and thee horses. And you haf steal seex dolars, too! But I'm forgettin' thot, now, too. All right?"

The other nodded grateful acceptance. Then, as if to show gratitude further, he very solicitously inquired into the matter, especially with reference to Felipe's discovery of the horse after all these years. They were clattering across the mesa now, having come to it by way of a long detour round the town, and before replying Felipe gave his team loose rein.

"Well," he began, as the horses fell back into a plodding walk, "I haf know about thot couple weeks before. I haf see thees *caballo* in town one mornin', and a girl she is ridin' heem, and everybody is lookin', and so I'm lookin'." He paused to roll a cigarette. "And then," he continued, drawing a deep inhale of smoke, "I haf know quick lak thot"–he snapped his fingers sharply–"quick lak thot"–he snapped his fingers again–"there's my *potrillo* grown big lak a house! And so–"

"But how you knowin' thot's thee horse?" interrupted the other. "How you knowin' thot for sure?" Evidently Franke was beginning to entertain grave doubts concerning this visit to the corral.

But Felipe only sneered. "How I know thot?" he asked, disdainfully. "I'm joost tellin' you! I know! Thot's enough! A horse is a horse! And I know thees horse! I know every horse! I got only to see a horse once–once only–and I'm never forgettin' thot horse! And I'm makin' no meestake now–bet you' life!" Nevertheless, flicked with doubt because of the gravity of the other, he turned his head and gazed back at the horse long and earnestly. Finally he turned around again. "I know thot horse!" he yelled. "And I'm tellin' you thees, Franke," he went on, suddenly belligerent toward the other. "If you don' t'ink I'm gettin' thee right *caballo*, I have you arrested for stealin' thot seex dolars thot time! Money is money, too. But a horse is a horse. I know thees horse. Thot's enough!" Yet he relapsed into a moody silence, puffing thoughtfully on his cigarette.

Behind the outfit, Pat continued along docilely. In a way he was enjoying this strange journey across the mesa. It was all very new to him, this manner of crossing, this being tied to the rear of a wagon, and he found himself pleasantly mystified. Nor was that all. Not once had he felt called upon to rebel. In perfect contentment he followed the rigging, eyes upon the outhanging reach, for he was intent upon maintaining safe distance between this thing and himself. Once, when they were mounting up to the mesa, he had met with a sharp blow from this projection–due to sudden change of gait in the horses–and he only required the one lesson to be ever after careful. As for the men forward, he knew nothing of them, and never, to his knowledge, had seen them before. But in no way was he concerning himself about them. Nor, indeed, was he worrying over any part of this proceeding. For in his dumb animal way he was coming to know, as all dumb servants of man come to know, that life, after all, is service, a kind of self-effacing series of tasks in the interests of others, and that this ambling along behind the vehicle was but one of the many kinds.

"And," suddenly broke out Felipe, who, having threshed the matter out to his satisfaction, now felt sure of his position once more, "I haf follow thees girl and thee horse. I haf see thee place where she's goin'–you know." And he winked foxily. "And then I haf coom to thees place, two, three times after thee horse. But always thee man is there. But thees mornin' I'm seein' thot *hombre* in town, and so I haf go gettin' you to coom help me. But you haf steal seex dolars. I'm forgettin' thot–not! And if you say soomt'ing to soombody soomtime, I'm havin' you arrested, Franke, for a t'ief and a robber– same as I ought to arrest thot Pedro Garcia oop in the canyon."

Franke maintained discreet silence. But not for long. Evidently he suddenly thought of a point in his own favor.

"You' havin' good luck thees time, Felipe," he declared, tranquilly, "especially," he hastened to add, "when I'm t'inkin' of thee halter. Without thee halter, you know, you don' gettin' thees *caballo*."

Felipe ignored this. "I haf need a horse," he went on, thoughtfully. "Thee mot'er of thees black fel'r–you know, thot's thee mot'er–she's gettin' old all time. She's soon dyin', thot *caballo*. Thees black horse he's makin' a fine one in thees wagon." Franke said nothing. Nor did Felipe speak again. And thus, in silence, they continued across the mesa and on up the canyon to the little adobe in the settlement. Arrived before the house, Franke quickly disappeared in the direction of his home, leaving Felipe to unhitch and unharness alone. But Felipe cared nothing for this. He was supremely happy–happy in the return of the long-lost colt, doubly happy in the possession of so fine a horse without outlay of money. Whistling blithely, he unhitched the team, led them back into the corral, returned to the wagon again. Here, still whistling, he untied the black and escorted him also into the inclosure. Then, after scratching his head a long moment in thought, he set out in the direction of the general store and a bottle of *vino*.

As the man disappeared, Pat, standing uncertainly in the middle of the corral, followed him with a look in his eyes that hinted of vague memories that would not down. And well he might be flicked with vague memories. For he was at last returned to the brief cradle of his babyhood.

Late that same afternoon, Helen, attired in riding-habit, left the house for her first afternoon canter. As she slowly crossed the *patio*, she noted the absence of Pat from his usual corner, but, assuming that he was inside the stable, called to him from the gate. But she received no answering whinny. Slightly worried, she entered the corral and stepped to the stable door, and again sounded his name. Again she received no answering whinny. She entered the stable, walked past the stalls, peered in at each with increasing alarm. Only the saddle-horse and the family horse met her troubled eyes. She stood for a moment dismayed, then once more she sounded the horse's name. But, as before, she received no answering whinny.

Puzzled, perplexed, troubled with misgivings, yet refusing to believe the worst, she fell to analyzing the thing. She knew that since coming to the ranch Pat at no time had been outside the corral save in her charge. Also she recalled that only a short hour or two before she had given him sweets and had talked with him. Nor could the horse have strayed out of the inclosure, because she remembered that the gate was latched when she had reached it. All these facts flashed across her as she stood with grave eyes sweeping the stable. Finally she stepped back to the door and gazed out into the sunlight of the corral; but, as before, the inclosure was empty and silent, and now, somehow, forbidding. She called again—called to the horse, called to the Mexican. But again came only the echo of her voice, sounding hollow and solemn and plaintive through the stable.

Suddenly her heart stopped beating. She remembered that the hostler had left for town on foot early in the morning. And now her fears broke bounds. The horse was gone! Some one had come in Miguel's absence. Her Pat had been stolen! He was gone for ever out of her life! Standing a moment, trembling with bitterness, she darted out of the stable, out of the corral, across the *patio*. She sped into the house and her father's study, caught up the receiver of the telephone.

And then, after a long time, the connection. And her father's voice. And her frantic inquiry. And the Judge's smiling reply. And her recital of the facts—pleading, pitiful, almost whimpering. And now the Judge's serious rejoinder. And then her imperious request that he come home. And the Judge's regretful reply–could not on account of pressing matters. And then her tearful, choking outburst into the transmitter! And now suddenly the wires crossing and a strange voice demanding that she get off. And with it her utter collapse. She whirled away from the telephone, flung herself down upon a couch, and gave way to a wild outburst of tears.

The thing *was* pitiful. The horse had occupied a very big place in her life. And because that place now was empty, and because she saw no promise of its ever being filled, she sobbed wretchedly a long time. Then, rising quietly, she ascended the stairs to her room. Here she sank into a chair, one that overlooked the corral, and began an analysis of the case, taking the affair up from the very first day of Pat's coming into her life. She did not go further than that. Woman that she was, endowed with strongest intuitions and insight, she knew she had sounded the mystery of his disappearance, had sounded it as clearly as though she had been present.

"Pat's rightful owners have found him and put in their claim!" She got up and began to pace the floor. "I know it," she declared with conviction. "I know it as well as I know I'm in this room. Pat–Pat has been–been taken and–and–" Tears choked back her words. Again she turned to her bed and gave way to a paroxysm of grief.

Her tears lasted until sleep mercifully descended. And thus she lay, outstretched and disheveled, until the sun, slanting across the room, settled its mellow rays upon her. And even though the touch was light and gentle and somehow sympathetic, it awoke her. She rose and hurried to a window. Out in the corral all was quiet. She dropped into a chair and turned her eyes to the east–out over the mesa to the distant mountains. The mountains were draped in their evening purple, which seemed to her like mourning for her lost happiness–a happiness that might have been hers always with the horse.

CHAPTER IX
THE SECOND GREAT LESSON

Next morning Pat, imprisoned in a tiny stable, tried to get out by thrusting his head against the door. But the door would not give. Alone in semi-darkness, therefore, he spent the day. Twice a Mexican youth came to feed and water him, but always the quantity was insufficient, and always the boy carefully locked the door after him. Because of this, together with the poor ventilation, Pat became irritable. He longed for the freedom of the big corral–its sunlight, the visits of his mistress–but these were steadfastly denied him. And so through another night and another day, until he became well-nigh distracted. He stamped the floor, fought flies, dozed, dreamed strange dreams, stamped the floor again. After three days of this, sounds outside told him of the return of man and horses. But not till the next morning, and then quite late, was he released from the odious confinement.

Felipe bustled in, all eager for business. He drove his recent acquisition out into the corral and set to work harnessing one of the team–the mate of the aged mare. When she was bridled and standing in the trail in front of his empty wagon, he hurriedly returned to the new horse, placed a bridle upon his head, led him forth, and swung him close beside the other horse. He winced just a little at the incongruity of the team, though he did not let it delay him. He picked up the half of the harness and tossed it over the mare's back. Then he caught up the other half, and, preparing to toss it upon the black, began to straighten out deep and unexpected tangles.

"Well, you black devil," he began, as he twisted and turned the much-bepatched harness, "you doin' soom work now! All you' life you havin' mooch good times! Eet is not for thee fun thot you live, you know?" he went on, academically, continuing to disentangle the harness. "Eet is for thee work thot you live! Work–thot's thee answer!" Then, having straightened the harness at last, with a grunt of satisfaction he tossed it lightly up.

Instantly there was wild commotion. With a kick and a plunge the horse flung off the harness.

Felipe stood dumfounded. It had never occurred to him that the horse was not broken to harness. Horses reared as this one evidently had been reared ought certainly to be educated to all kinds of service. Yet this horse evidently was not. He scratched his head in perplexity. To break a horse to harness was no child's play, as he well knew. To break a horse of this character to harness, as he well understood also, was a task that required exceptional patience and hardihood. What should he do? There was his constant press for money. The aged mare having almost dropped in the trail the evening before, was unfit for toil, and to break a horse to harness meant loss of time, and, as every one knows, loss of time meant loss of money. So what should he do? He was utterly at a loss.

Striding to the doorstep, he sat down and regarded the horse with malevolent disgust. After a time, jerking off his hat savagely, he burst out into a thundering tirade.

"You black devil! You haf give me more trouble than anyt'ing I haf ever own–chickens, burro, pigs, horses, money–money, even–money I haf owe thot robber Pedro! First you haf run away thot time! Then you haf mek me steal you out of thot place couple days before! And now"–he suddenly leaped to his feet–"now you haf mek me break you to thees wagon and harness!" He advanced to the startled horse and brandished his fist. "But I break you!" he snarled–"I break you like a horse never was broke before! And–and if I don' break you–if you don' do what I haf say–I break every bone inside!" With this he began feverishly to peel off his coat.

And this is the lot of the dumb. Merely for not knowing what a man believed he should know, Pat was to be humiliated, was to be punished far beyond justice and decency. And because he was a horse abnormally highstrung and sensitive, this punishment was to be doubly cruel. To him a blow was more painful than to the average horse, even as a word of kindness sank deeper and remained longer to soften his memory. On his maternal side he was the offspring of native stock, but he was blooded to the last least end of him, and while from his mother he had inherited his softer traits, like his affection for those who showed affection for him, it was from his sire, unknown though he was, that he inherited an almost human spirit of rebellion when driven by lash or harsh word, and also the strength to exercise it. In the face of these qualities, then, he was to be broken to harness and a wagon by a man!

Felipe lost little time in preparation. He set out through the settlement, his destination a distant and kindly neighbor. He moved at a stride so vigorous that the good townspeople, roused by the rare spectacle of a man in a hurry, interrupted their passive loafing beside well and in doorway, and turned wondering eyes after him. But if their eyes showed wonderment at his going, on his return they showed amazement and a kind of horror. For Felipe, acting for once in the capacity of work-horse, was straining along at the end of a huge wagon-tongue affixed to a crude and mastodonic axle which in turn supported two monolithic cart-wheels. It was a device by which he meant to break the horse to harness, and, perspiring freely, and swearing even more freely, he dragged it shrieking for grease through the settlement, really at work, but work which was not to be admired. Reaching the clearing in front of his house, he dropped the heavy tongue and whipped out a red handkerchief with a sigh of relief. Also, as he wiped away the perspiration on his forehead and neck and arms, he turned baleful eyes upon the innocent cause of his toil.

"You black devil!" he growled, after a moment. "I feex you now—bet you' life! And you can keeck—and keeck and keeck! You don' worry thees cart mooch! You black devil!"

Then he became active again. He strode back into the corral, sought out an old harness and a huge collar, and dragged them forward into the trail. Flinging them aside in the direction of the cart, he then turned to the mare, removed the work-harness from her, and led her into position before the warlike vehicle. Again perspiring freely, but losing no breath now in abusive talk, he quickly harnessed her up and then strode forward to the black. After eying him narrowly a moment, he seized his bridle and led him back alongside the mare, where he proceeded nervously to harness him.

"We see now," he began, as he picked up the massive collar. "You can stond still—thot's right! And maybe you can take thees t'ing—we see!"

The collar was much too large for workaday use, but it was not too large for this purpose. Its very size gave it freedom to pass over the head without the usual twisting and turning. Nor did the horse rebel when it was so placed–a fact which gave Felipe much relief, since he now believed that he would not have the trouble he had anticipated. Also, with the collar in position, he was but a moment in adjusting the hames, making fast the bottom strap, and hooking the tugs securely. With everything in readiness he then caught up the reins and the whip, and stepped away to begin the real work of breaking.

"*Haya!*" he cried, and touched up the off-horse. She started forward, as always with this command from her master. But she did not go far.

Pat was the cause of the delay. Understanding neither the contraption at his heels, nor the word of command from the man, he held himself motionless and pleasantly uninterested, gazing slowly about at the landscape. Nor did he offer to move when the man cut him viciously with the whip. The lash pitted his tender flesh and hurt mightily; but even though he now understood what was required of him, he only became stubborn–bracing his legs and flattening his ears, forcefully resisting the counter efforts of the mare beside him.

And this was his nature. Long before he had demonstrated that he would not be governed by a whip. That day in the Richardses' corral, when he was broken to saddle, cruelty alone would never have conquered him. Cruelty there had been, and much of it; but with the cruelty there had been other things–evidence of affection at the right moment, both in his mistress and in the men about him, and these, coupled with quick understanding, had made the breaking a success. And had there been evidence of kindness now, somewhere revealed early by this man, Pat might have drawn the cart as the straining mate at his side was attempting to draw it. But there was no evidence of kindness, and as a result he remained stubborn and wilful, standing braced and trembling, true in every particular to the spirit of his forebears.

Nor was Felipe less true to the spirit within himself. Infuriated, uncompromising, believing this to be merely the cussedness natural with the native horses, he abandoned all hope of instant success and gave way to brutality. Dropping the reins and reversing the whip in his hands, he began to beat the horse unmercifully, bringing the heavy butt down again and again, each mighty thwack echoing down the canyon. The result was inevitable. The horse began to kick–straight back at first, then, finding his hoofs striking the cart, he swung sideways to the tongue and kicked straight out. This last was sudden, and narrowly missed Felipe, who leaped to one side. Then, unable to reach the horse with the butt, he reversed the whip again and resumed his first torture, that of pitting the legs of the horse with the lash.

"Keeck!" he snarled, continuing to swing the whip. "Keeck! Keeck! I can keeck, too!" He swung his arm till it ached, when he stopped.

Whereupon the horse settled down. But his eyes were ablaze and he was trembling all over. Also, while undoubtedly suffering added distress from the taut and binding traces, he continued to stand at right angles to the mare–head high, nostrils quivering, mouth adrip with white slaver–until the spirit of rebellion appeared to grip him afresh. With a convulsive heave he moved again, making another quarter turn, which brought him clear of the tongue and facing the vehicle. Then he set up a nervous little prancing, whisking his tail savagely, now and again lifting his heels as if to strike. That was all. He gained no ground forward, nor did it appear as if he would ever move forward.

"You–you–" began Felipe, then subsided, evidently too wrathful for words. And he remained silent, gazing wearily toward the settlement, as though about to call assistance.

The stillness was heavy and portentous. Both horses were motionless. Felipe continued silent. Off toward the settlement all was still. Overhead, the early-morning sky pressed low, spotless and shimmering, brooding. Around and about, the flies seemed to stop buzzing. Everywhere lurked the quiet. The earth appeared bowed in humiliation, hushed in prayer as for the unfortunate one, while up and down the trail, basking in world-old light, lay dust of centuries, smug and contented in its quiescence. All nature was still, gripped in tense quiet.

The crack of a whip broke it. Felipe, suddenly bestirring himself, had sprung forward and dealt the horse a blow with the butt. Across the nose, it had sounded hollow and distant; and the horse, whipping up his head in surprised pain, now turned upon the man a look at once sorrowful and terrible, a look which spelled death and destruction. Nor did he only look. With a strange outcry, shrill and piercing, awaking the canyon in unnatural echoes, he whirled in his harness and reared, reared despite his harness, and struck out with venomous force. It was quick as a lightning flash, but, quick as it was, Felipe avoided it. And it was fortunate that he did. Terror-stricken and dropping the whip, he sped to the rear, to a point behind the cart, and there turned amazed eyes at the pirouetting horse.

What manner of horse was this, he asked himself. Could it be that this horse, black as night, was truly of the lower regions? Certainly he looked it, balancing there on his hind legs, with his reddened eyes and inflamed nostrils! And–But what was this? From the corral had come a shrill nicker, the voice of the aged mare. But that was not it! With the outcry, seemingly an answer to the black's maddened outcry, the black dropped to all-fours again, turning quick ears and eyes in the direction of the sound! What manner of horse was this, anyway? Never before had he seen such a horse! He felt himself go limp.

There is a call in nature that sounds for life against death. It is a call put forth in innumerable different tongues around the world, and it sounds somewhere every second of the day and darkness–through jungles, across swamps, down mountains, over plains, out of valleys. It is a cry of warning, a cry to disarm foes. It is an outcry of good as against evil–the squawk of a hen to her chicks, the bleat of a sheep to her lambs, the grunt of a sow to her sucklings, the bellow of a cow to her calf, the purr of a cat to her kittens, the whine of a dog to her puppies, the drum of a partridge to her young. A cry from the heart to the heart, an appeal of flesh to its own flesh, it is the world-old mother-call.

And the horse heard this call. He probably did not recognize in it a call of the mother-heart, any more than it was possible for the aged mare to recognize in his outcry the voice of her own flesh. What he did hear, no doubt, was the voice of a friend, one who understood and pitied, and would help if it could help. At any rate, he stood very still, seemingly grateful for the evidence of a champion, seemingly anxious that it sound again. But it did not sound again. Yet he made no further effort to give battle. He held to his attitude of intent listening, ears cocked forward and eyes straining and tail at rest, until Felipe, stung into action by an idea wrought out of all this, hastened out from behind the cart and away in the direction of the corral. At sight of him the horse became restless again, squaring himself once more to the mare, stamping his feet and champing his bit nervously. He seemed to lose all recollection of the outcry, all the peace it had engendered within him. Of such are the kingdom of the dumb.

Possessed by his idea, an idea so brilliant that he himself marveled, Felipe was not long in putting it to test. He hurriedly bridled the aged mare and led her out into the trail. He placed her alongside the black–for reasons which, had the *compadre* Franke been present, Felipe might have suggested with a crafty wink–then hastily began to unhitch the team-mate. And it was just here that he proved his foresight. In the work of unhitching the mate, he should have encountered, and had expected, trouble from the black. But he did not. The mare sounded another friendly nicker when arranged beside him, and the black, pricking up his ears sharply, turned to her and proceeded to establish his friendship by licking her. So Felipe did not meet with difficulty from that direction; nor did he have trouble in the direction of the team-mate herself. She seemed glad to be relieved from her unsuccessful task, and Felipe, glad to relieve her in the light of his brilliant idea, led her off to one side quickly, then returned and swung the old mare into her place. He hitched her up, picked up the reins and whip, and set about with his test.

"We see now," he began, his voice quiet and encouraging. "Maybe you work wit' thee old woman! We see!" And he gave a low command.

With the command Pat started forward, urged to it by the aged mare–pulling more than his share of the load. Perhaps it was due to her presence; perhaps to the note of kindness in Felipe's voice. At any rate, he moved, and he moved forward, and he moved with a steady pull. Yet he did not proceed far. Though he did not stop through rebellion. It was simply to renew his attentions to the old mare. He began to caress her as if he really recognized in this rack of an animal his own lost mother. But recognition, of course, was impossible. Long before, the only source of recognition, appeal made through digestive organs, had disappeared. Nevertheless, he lavished upon her unwonted affection until Felipe gently but firmly urged him forward again. Then again he proceeded, pulling all of the load this time, bringing about a slack in the traces of the mare and a consequent bumping of her hind legs against the cart which seemed to awaken some of her dying spirit.

Up and down the trail they moved, the mare sedately, the horse actively, prancing gaily, appearing to take gleeful pleasure in his task, until Felipe, kindled with elation and pride, decided to drive on into the settlement and there become the object of covetous eyes. Therefore he urged the team forward to a point in front of the general store, where in lordly composure sat Pedro, occupying his customary seat on an empty keg on the porch. At sight of him Felipe's joy leaped to the heavens, and he pulled up the team, ostensibly to adjust a forward buckle, but in reality to afford Pedro an uninterrupted view of the beautiful black. Moving forward to the head of the horses, he watched out of the tail of his eye Pedro's lazy survey of the team.

"Where you got thot horse?" inquired Pedro, after a long moment, as he slowly removed a cigarette from between his lips. "I mean," he added, "where you haf *steal* thot *caballo*?"

Felipe winced. But he did not immediately retort. He carried out his bluff, unbuckling and buckling one of the straps, then mildly straightened up and faced the man.

"Pedro," he began, tensely, "you haf know–José, Juan, Manuel, Francisco, Carlotta–all haf know–thot eet is only one t'ief in all thees place! And thot man–thot t'ief–is Pedro Garcia!"

Pedro grunted. "Where you haf steal thot horse?" he repeated, without show of anger. "You can give me thot horse," he continued, placidly. "You haf owe me mooch money. I take thot horse for payment–everyt'ing. You give thot *caballo* to me."

Felipe turned to the team. "I give you one keeck in thee belly!" he roared. Then he touched up the horses and started back toward the house. Gone was all elation, all pride, all gleeful consciousness of possession.

Gaining the clearing, he decided to try out the other horse with the black. He realized that the aged mare was unfit, even though in the last hour she had appeared greatly to improve, and he must accordingly match up a team. So he unhitched her and swung the mate into place. He met with disagreeable surprise, however. The black would not pull with this horse. Instead, he held himself quietly at rest, gazing about sleepily over the landscape, a trick of his, as Felipe had learned, when quietly rebelling. Felipe looked at him a moment, but did not try to force him with tongue or lash. For he was coming to understand this horse, and, concluding that sooner or later, under proper treatment, he would probably accept duty with any mate, determined to abandon work for the day. Whereupon he unhitched the horses and led them all back into the corral. Then he put up the bars and set out in the direction of the settlement.

Which ended Pat's second great lesson at the hand of man. He was sore and somewhat stiff from the struggle, but he did not fret long over his condition, for he soon awoke to the presence of that beside him in the corral which caused him to forget himself completely. It was the worn-out structure of skin and bones who had befriended him in his hour of trial. He gazed at her a moment, then approached and fell to caressing her, showing in this attention his power to forget self–aches, sores, troubles–in his affection and gratitude toward all things warranting affection and gratitude.

CHAPTER X
THE STRANGER AGAIN

Meantime, Helen was becoming desperate over her loss. Unwilling to accept the theory of her household, which was that Pat had been stolen by a band of organized thieves and ere this was well out of the neighborhood and probably the county, she had held firmly to her original idea, *viz.*, that the horse was in the possession of his rightful owners, and so could not be far out of the community. Therefore, the morning following his disappearance, having with sober reflection lightened within her the seriousness of it all, she had set out in confident search for him, mounted on her brown saddler. But though she had combed the town and the trails around the town, quietly interviewing all such teamsters and horsemen as might by any chance know something about it, yet in answer to her persistent inquiries all she had received was a blank shake of the head or an earnest expression of willingness to assist her. So, because she had continued her search for three days without success, inquiring and peering into every nook and corner of the community, she finally had come to regard her quest as hopeless, and to become more than ever an image of despair.

The evening of the fourth day there was a dance. It was one of the regular monthly affairs, and because Helen was a member of the committee she felt it her duty to attend. One of the young men, accompanied by his mother and sister, drove out for her, but she left the house with reluctance and a marked predisposition not to enjoy herself. But she forgot this when she presently beheld the young man from the East whom she had encountered on the mesa. He was standing close beside a rather frail little woman, undoubtedly his mother, who with the matrons of the town was seated near a fireplace watching the dancers. He was introduced. Later they sat out one of his numbers alone together in a corner behind some potted palms. In the course of their conversation Helen informed him of the disappearance of her horse, and asked him, as she asked everybody she met now, if he knew anything or had heard anything concerning the loss. The young man knew nothing of the great disappearance, however, though he did offer it as his belief that a horse of Pat's obvious value could not long remain in obscurity. This was encouraging, and Helen felt herself become hopeful again. But when he offered his services in the search, as he did presently, she felt not only hopeful again, but somehow quite certain now that it would all be cleared up. For there was that in this young gentleman which caused confidence. What she told him, however, was that she was grateful for his offer, and should be greatly pleased to have him with her.

And thus it was that, on the morning of the fifth day, Helen Richards and Stephen Wainwright–the young man's name–together with two of Helen's close friends, were riding slowly across the mesa, alert for any combination in harness which might reveal the lost Pat. Helen and Stephen were well in the lead, and Helen had broken the silence by addressing Stephen as a native, recalling their first meeting. Whereupon the young man, smiling quietly, had wanted to know why; but after she had explained that it was because he had enlisted himself in the search for a horse, adding that in doing so he had conformed with one of the unwritten laws of the country, he still confessed himself in the dark. This had been but a moment before, and she now settled herself to explain more fully.

"A horse is, or was, our most valued property," she began. "I reckon the past tense is better–though we'll never quite live down our interest in horses." She smiled across at him. "Long ago," she went on, "in the days of our Judge Lynch, you know, a stolen horse meant a hanged man–or two or three–as not infrequently happened. But all that is history now. Yet the feeling remains. And whenever one of our horses disappears–it is rare now–we all take it more or less as a personal loss. In your willingness to help find Pat, therefore, you declare yourself one of us–and are gladly admitted."

He rode along in silence. "Why was the feeling so intense in the old days?" he inquired, after a time.

"It was due to physical conditions," she replied–"the geography of the country. Water-holes were few and very far apart, and to get from one to another often entailed a journey impossible to a man without a horse. To steal his horse, therefore, was to deprive him of his sole means of getting to water–practically to deprive him of his life. If he didn't die of thirst, which frequently he did, at best it was a very grave offense. It isn't considered so now–not so much so, at any rate–unless in the desert wastes to the west of us. Yet the feeling still lurks within us, and a stolen horse is a matter that concerns the whole community."

He nodded thoughtfully, but remained silent. Suddenly Helen drew rein. Before her was a horned toad, peculiarly a part of the desert, blinking up at them wickedly. He drew rein and followed her eyes.

"A horned toad, isn't it?"

Helen shook her head. "Are you interested in such things?" she inquired.

"In a way–yes," he affirmed, doubtfully. "Though I can't see good reason for their existence." His eyes twinkled. "Can you?"

Helen was thoughtful a moment. "Well, no," she admitted, finally. "Yet there must be a good reason. Reptiles must live for some good purpose. All things do–don't you think?" Then, before he could make a rejoinder, she went on: "I sometimes feel that these creatures were originally placed here to encourage other and higher forms of life to come and locate in the desert–were placed here, in other words, to prove that life is possible in all this desolation."

He glanced at her. "Certainly it has worked out that way, at any rate," he ventured. "Good old Genesis!" He smiled.

"It seems to have," she agreed, thoughtfully. "Because you and I are here. But it goes a long way back–to Genesis–yes. Following the initial placing, other and higher organisms, finding in their migratory travels this evidence of life, accepted the encouragement to remain, and did remain, feeding upon the life found here in the shape of toads and lizards–to carry the theory forward a step–even as the toads and lizards–to carry it back again–fed upon the insects which they in their turn found here. Then along came other forms of life, higher in the cosmic setting, and these, finding encouragement in the presence of the earlier arrivals, fed upon them and remained. And so on up, to the forerunners of our present-day animals–coyotes and prairie-dogs. And after these, primitive man–to find encouragement in the coyotes and prairie-dogs–and to feed upon them and remain. Then after primitive man, the second type–the brown man; and after the brown man, the red man; and after the red man, the white man–all with an eye to sustenance, and finding it, and remaining."

Stephen's eyes swept around the desert absently. He knew–this young man–that he was in the presence of a personality. For he could not help but draw comparisons between the young woman beside him and the young women of his acquaintance in the East. While he had found Eastern girls vivacious, and attractive with a kind of surface charm, never had he known one to take so quiet and unassuming an outlook upon so broad a theme. It was the desert, he told himself. Here beside him was a type unknown to him, and one so different from any he had as yet met with, he felt himself ill at ease in her presence–a thing new to him, too–and which in itself gave him cause to marvel. Yes, it was the desert. It *must* be the desert! In this slender girl beside him he saw a person of insight and originality, a girl assuredly not more than twenty years of age, attractive, and thoroughly feminine. How ever did they do it?

He harked back in his thoughts to her theory. And he dwelt not so much upon the theory itself as upon her manner of advancing it. Running back over these things, recalling the music of her voice, together with her spoken musings, he came to understand why, with that first encounter, he had found himself almost instantly curious concerning desert folk. Not that he had known why at the time, or had given that phase of it consideration. He did remember that he had been strongly impressed by the way she had managed her bolting horse. But aside from that, there had been something in her personality, an indefinable calm and sureness, a grip upon herself, that he had felt the very first moment. Undoubtedly all this had flicked him into a novel curiosity. He pulled himself together with an effort.

"I like your theory," he answered, smiling. "And it must be true, because I am told horned toads are fast disappearing. Evidently they have served their purpose. But tell me," he concluded, "what is becoming of them? Where are they going?"

She laughed. "I can't tell you that. Perhaps they just vanish into the fourth–or maybe the fifth–dimension!"

And this was the other side of her, a side he had come to learn while with her at the dance, and which made her lovable as well as admirable. But she was speaking again, and again was serious.

"I have yet another theory," she said–"one as to why these creatures are here, you know." She smiled across at him. "It is all my very own, too! It is that in their presence among us–among mankind–they unwittingly develop us through thought. Thinking exercises the brain, we are told, and exercising the brain makes for world-advancement–we are told." Then, suddenly, "I hope you don't think me silly–Mr. Native?"

But he remained sober. "Tell me," he asked, after a time, "what it is about this country–I mean other than friendships, of course–that gets under a fellow's soul and lifts it–to the end that he wants to remain here? I know there is something, though I can't for the life of me place it. What is it, anyway?"

She turned upon him sharply. "Do you really feel that way?" she asked, evidently pleased.

"I feel that way. But why do I feel that way? What is it? You know what I mean. There is something–there must be!"

"I know what you mean–yes," she replied, thoughtfully. "Yet I doubt if I myself, even after all these years, can define it. What you 'feel' must be our atmosphere–its rarity, its power to exhilarate. Though that really doesn't explain it. I reckon it's the same thing–only much more healthful, more soulful–that one feels in large cities after nightfall. I mean, the glare of your incandescent lights. I honestly believe that that glare, more than any other single thing, holds throngs of people to an existence not only unnatural, but laden with a something that crushes as well." She was silent.

Again Stephen felt the strange pull on his interest, but he said nothing. After a time she went on.

"City-dwellers," she explained, "don't begin their day till the approach of dark. It's true of both levels of society, too–lower as well as upper. And I believe the reason for this lies, as I have said, in the atmosphere–their man-made atmosphere–just as the secret of your feeling the way you do lies in our atmosphere–God-made. Were this atmosphere suddenly to disappear, both out of your cities and out of my deserts, both your world and my own would lose all of their charm."

Stephen bestirred himself. "What psychology do you find in that?" he asked, dwelling upon the fact that she knew his East so well.

"Merely the effect of softening things–for the soul as well as the eye–through the eye, indeed, to the soul. Our atmosphere here does that–softens the houses, and the trees, and the cattle, and the mountains, and the distant reaches. It softens our nights, too. Perhaps you have noticed it? How everything appears shrouded in a kind of hazy, mellow, translucent something that somehow reacts upon you? I have. And I believe that is the secret of one's wanting to remain in the country, once he has exposed himself to it. It is a kind of spell–a hypnosis. When out of it one wants to get back into it.

"I know I felt it when I was East, attending school," she went on, quietly. "Living always in this atmosphere, I somehow had forgotten its charm–as one will forget all subtle beauty unless frequently and forcibly reminded of it. But in the East I missed it, and found myself restless and anxious to get back into it. Indeed, I felt that I must get back or die! So one day, when your Eastern spirit of sudden change was upon me, I packed and came home. It was a year short of my degree, too. But I could not remain away another day–simply had to get back–and back I came. My degree–my sheepskin"–she was smiling–"couldn't hold me!"

"Then you've spent some time in the East?" he asked, tentatively.

"Yes," she replied, "that much–three years. And I didn't like it."

"Why?" he asked, a little surprised.

She regarded him curiously. He saw a look of mild annoyance in her eyes, one that seemed to tell of her inability to understand so needless a question.

"I just didn't," she rejoined, after a moment. "I discovered that you Easterners value things which are diametrically opposite to the things we value, and that you value not at all those things which we value most of all."

76

He had to laugh. "What are they?" he wanted to know.

For an instant she showed shyness. "Oh, I can't say," she declared, finally. "Some day I may tell you."

Stephen realized that it must be serious. He was hesitating whether to press her further, when he saw her tighten her reins, put spurs to her horse, and go flashing off in the direction of the mountain trail. As she dashed off he heard her call out:

"Pat!" she cried. "Pat! It's Pat!" Then she glanced to the rear. "Adele! Sam! It's Pat! Come, quick!"

Stephen spurred on with the others. He galloped after this hard-riding girl–so intensely alive–a girl past his understanding. Over dunes and across flats he charged, followed closely by the others, urging his horse to his utmost. But, try as he might, he could not overtake her or even lessen the distance between them, so furious was her race for her lost horse. Finally he burst out upon the trail and drew rein beside her, standing with the others in the path of an oncoming wood-wagon, anxiously awaiting its slow approach.

It was a curious outfit. One of the team, an aged and decrepit horse, was laboring along with head drooping and hoofs scuffling the trail, while beside it, with head erect and nostrils aquiver and hoofs lifting eagerly, stepped the glorious Pat! Both horses were draped in a disreputable harness, crudely patched with makeshift string and wire, and both were covered with a fine coating of dust. Atop all this, high and mighty upon an enormous load of wood, sat a Mexican, complacently smoking a cigarette and contentedly swinging his heels, evidently elated with this prospect of parading his horse before a group of Americans. But as he drew close a look of uneasiness crept over him, and he pulled up his team and shrugged his shoulders, as a preliminary, no doubt, to disappearance behind the Mexican shield of "No sabe!"

Helen swung close to him. There was a choice between a contest and diplomatic concession. She decided to offer to purchase the horse at once, believing this to be the easiest way out of the trouble.

"*Señor*," she began in Spanish, "*deseo comprar aquel caballo negro. Puedo pagar cualquire cantidad razonable por el. Se perdio y nosotros lo cuidamos, y he aprendido a quererlo mucho. Si usted quiere venderlo me haria un gran favor. Siento mucho que me lo hayan quitado."*

The Mexican looked relieved. He slowly removed his hat with true Castilian courtesy.

"Señorita," he replied, *"lo venderia con gusto pero pienso que me paga lo que quiero por el."*

Which delighted Helen. *"Pagare lo que sea."*

The Mexican hesitated a moment. *"¿Pagara cuarenta pesos?"* he asked, finally. *"Yo tambien quiero al caballo mucho,"* he added. *"Pero por cuarenta pesos pienso–pienso que lo olvido."* And he grinned.

Helen turned to the others. For Stephen's benefit she explained what had been said, and the men promptly offered to make up the required forty dollars. Helen turned to the Mexican, accepted his price, and requested him to release Pat from the harness. Whereat the Mexican smiled broadly; shrugged his shoulders suddenly; forgot his rôle of "No sabe."

"How," he burst out–"how I'm gettin' thees wagon to town? I'm pullin' eet myself?"

The others laughed. Then Helen, deciding upon another arrangement, instructed him to drive forward. She could see her father in town, she explained to the others, and there also, after the exchange of money, the Mexican could purchase another horse. Which closed the matter. The Mexican started the team forward, while the others fell in alongside, ranging themselves on either side. Thus they journeyed into town–a strange cavalcade–Pat prancing, the mare drooping, the Mexican visibly pleased, the others gratified by their unexpected success. In town they turned into a side street, and there Helen left them, going off in the direction of her father's office. When she returned, the Judge was with her. He read the Mexican a brief but stern lecture on the law pertaining to the recovery of lost property, and closed the deal. Whereupon the wood-hauler unharnessed Pat, bestowed him smilingly upon Helen, and took himself off, evidently in quest of another horse, for he headed straight as a plumb-line for the city pound.

Pat was home again. He knew it from many things–the white fence, the clean stable, the Mexican hostler with broom in hand. And though he was at home where he wanted to be, yet he found himself filled with vague uneasiness. After a time he sought to relieve it. He made his way into the stable, but he found no relief there. He returned to the corral, and began slowly to circle inside the fence, but neither did this relieve him. Finally he took up his old stand in the sunlit corner, where he fell to listening with ears and eyes attentive to least sounds. But even this did not relieve him.

Nor would anything ever relieve him. Never would he find absolute solace from his inner disquiet. For what he sought and could not find, what he listened for and could not hear, was another of those sounds which had relieved the tedium of his brief stay in the mountains, the friendly nicker of the aged mare, gone to toil out her life in the racking treadmill between town and mountain.

CHAPTER XI
LOVE REJECTED

Pat had just been clipped. And never was there a horse nearer perfection! Shorn of all hair, his splendid physique, now in fullest maturity, stood out clean-cut and fascinating.

In weight he might have tipped the scales at ten hundred pounds. In color his skin, which now showed clearly, was a shade darker than that of the elephant, but it showed the richness of velvet. His body through the trunk was round and symmetrical; his haunches were wide without projection of the hip-bones; and his limbs, the stifle and lower thigh, were long and strong and fully developed. Added to these, he was high in the withers, the line of back and neck curving perfectly; his shoulders were deep and oblique; and his long, thick fore arm, knotty with bulging sinews, told of powerful muscles. And finally, his knees across the pan were wide, the cannon-bone below thin and short, the pasterns long and sloping, and the hoofs round and dark and neatly set on. While over all–over the small, bony head, beautiful neck and shoulders–over the entire body, clear down to the hoofs–ran a network of veins like those on the back of a leaf, only more irregular–veins which stood out as though the skin were but thin parchment through which the blood might burst. A rare horse, rare in any country, doubly rare in this land of the small Spanish product, was the rating given to Pat by men trained to judge value at sight. And so widespread did this appraisal become, along trail, beside camp-fire, in bunk-house, that it was known throughout the length and breadth of the Territory, and beyond the Territory, that Judge Richards was the owner of a horse the like of which never had been seen south of the Pecos.

For several days after the clipping, Helen did not choose to ride. So Pat was permitted the doubtful pleasure of loafing about in the inclosure. Then one morning, when the winter day was unusually warm, he awoke to a great clatter of hoofs outside the corral. Directly he saw a party of young people, men and girls under the chaperonage of a comely matron, dismounting in high spirits. As the party swung down he saw his mistress appear from the house, attired in her riding-habit, and, understanding the object of all this, since these parties had become frequent in the past two months, he pressed close to the fence, anxious to be off. The Mexican bridled and saddled him; his mistress and the others mounted; soon all clattered out upon the river-trail.

The day was beautiful, and Helen, riding, as usual, beside Stephen, both in the rear, enjoyed the morning keenly. Overhead, out of a shimmering azure sky, the sun beamed mildly down, penetrating the chill of the morning, yet leaving enough tang to bring a bloom to their cheeks. On their left the river, high with melted snows from the north, moved in slow eddies near the shore, quicker eddies away from the shore, steady and swift flow in the middle—a changing, fascinating panorama. There fell a long silence before she turned to the young man beside her.

"Well, Mr. Native," she began, smiling, "I hope you don't mean to bury yourself this morning! For more than a month you have had very little to say to me. I don't like it, because I can't understand it, and so I won't have it!" Then she became serious. "Whatever is the matter, Stephen?"

Pat, walking slowly beside the unfriendly horse, was attentive. He heard his mistress's voice, and somehow knew she was troubled. Then directly he had positive proof of this, for she suddenly began to stroke his neck and shoulders. Always she did this when thoughtful, but though he strained his ears for further sounds of her voice, he did not hear her. What he did hear presently was the voice of the young man, and having learned long before to discriminate between different shades of the human voice, he knew from its low and tense quality that the topic was a vital one. He listened sharply, heedful of any least change of intonation that might be interpreted as a climax. But instead he was relieved presently to hear the voice of his mistress again, breaking in upon the low, constrained tones of the young man.

Pat held his ears steadily back. He noted that her voice was well under control, and she appeared to be answering the young man. Also, it was quite evident that she was not accepting his argument, whatever it was. Yet her voice took on many delicate changes. Sometimes he heard a note of pleading; again, mild exasperation; and once a falling inflection which hinted at sadness. So it continued, his mistress talking as he had never heard her talk before, until the group ahead drew rein and wheeled, indicating their intention of returning. Then once more the voice of his mistress changed suddenly and became light, even gay, leaving Pat, as he himself was turned around, a very much mystified horse.

Yet this gaiety did not last. When they were well on their way back toward the ranch, with the sun higher and brighter in the heavens, and the trail correspondingly whiter and more dazzling to the eye, he found himself listening to grave tones again–the voice of the young man. He talked steadily now, his flow of words always tense, though occasionally interrupted by the other with a quiet rejoinder. Then suddenly he ceased altogether, and Pat, acutely conscious of the silence which descended upon them, was relieved when it was broken by sounds of laughter ahead. Still the pair above him did not speak. Each appeared to be adrift on a sea of thought the like of which he had never known. And it continued, this ominous silence, and became heavier, until he saw the ranch loom up ahead. Then he felt his mistress urge him into a canter that she might join the others for the parting. But when the party broke up, as it did with much good feeling, and he found himself turned loose to one side, with his mistress and the young man walking into the shade of a cottonwood, he found himself forced, since he now was out of range of their voices, to forego any further listening, keenly against his desires. So he gave it all up as a bad job.

"Stephen," began Helen, seating herself upon a hummock of earth, "I am sorry–sorry beyond words–that it has turned out this way! I must admit that I like you–like you very much! But–but I am afraid it is not the sort of liking you ask."

He was seated beside her, reclining upon one elbow, absently thrusting the tip of his riding-whip into a tuft of grass. And now again, as before that morning, he told her of his very great love for her, his deep voice vibrant with emotion, grimly acknowledging himself as unworthy of her, yet asking with rare simplicity that she take him anyway, take him in spite of his unworthiness, declaring it as his belief she would find him in time worthy–that he would try to make himself worthy–*would* make himself worthy–would overcome those faults which evidently–though she had not as yet told him what they were–made him impossible in her eyes. Then suddenly he asked her to tell him precisely what these faults were. He knew that he had many and could only blame himself for them. But which of them did she find chiefly objectionable? He was pitiable in his pleading.

But Helen shook her head. "I–I can't tell you, Stephen," she declared, her voice breaking. "It–it is too much to ask of–of any girl."

He rose, turning toward the distant mountains, bright and smiling in their noonday splendor. As his eyes dwelt upon them in brooding silence, Helen gained her feet. And, aware of her great part in this wretchedness, she took his hand very gently in her own. Subtly conscious of the touch, realizing the tumult in his soul, she found herself suddenly alive to a feeling within her deeper than mere pity and sympathy. It was the anguish preceding tears. Quickly withdrawing her hand, she turned and fled to the house. Inside, she slowly approached a window. He was leading Pat into the corral; and, watching him unsaddle and unbridle her horse, her treasure, she awoke to something else within her, a strange swelling of her heart, different from anything she had ever known. It was like ownership; it was a something as of maternal pride, a something new to her which she could not fathom. She turned away. When she looked out again, her eyes dry and burning, he was riding slowly along the trail toward town.

It was the beginning of the end. Winter passed, with horses abandoned for the delights, swift-following, of dinner and dance and house party. These affairs made deep inroads upon Helen's time, and so Pat was left pretty much to his own reflections.

Yet he managed to fill the days to his satisfaction. Standing in the stable, he loved to watch the snow-capped mountains, and the tiny white clouds scudding around them, and the mellow radiance of golden sunlight streaming over them. Also, gazing out of the little square window, he spent long periods in viewing the hard brown of the nearer mesaland–the dips and dunes and thread-like arroyos, with an occasional horseman crawling between. Or else, when he found himself yearning for his mistress, he would turn eyes upon the house, and with lazy speculation regard its sun-flecked windows, tightly shut doors, and smoking chimneys, in the hope that she might step forth. Then came more mild weather when he would spend long hours outside the stable, in his corner in the corral, there to renew his silent vigil over nature and the house from this vantage. Thus he filled his days, and found them not so long as formerly in his babyhood, when each hour was fraught with so many little things that demanded his closest interest and attention.

Nights found him early at rest. But not all nights. Nights there were when the house would be lighted from cellar to garret, when spectral forms would move in and out of doors, and when shadows would flicker across drawn shades. Such nights were always his nights, for he would hear sounds of merriment, and voices lifted in song, and above the voices, tinkling toward him on the crisp air, the music of a piano. Such nights were his nights, for he knew that his mistress was happy, and he would force open the stable door, step out under the cold stars, and take up his stand in his corner, there to rest his head upon the topmost board and turn steady eyes upon the scene of merriment until the last guest had departed.

Always on these nights, with wintry chills coursing down his legs or rollicking along his spine, he found himself wanting to be a part of this gaiety, wanting to enter the house, where he instinctively knew it was warm and comfortable, where he might nuzzle the whole gathering for sugar and apples. But this he could not do. He could only turn longing eyes upon the cottage and stand there until, all too soon, sounds of doors opening and closing, together with voices in cheery farewell, told him that the party was at an end. Then he would see mysterious forms flitting across to the trail, and lights in the house whisking out one by one, until the cottage gradually became engulfed in darkness. Then, but not till then, would he turn away from his corner, walk back slowly into the stable, and, because of the open door, which he could open but never close, suffer intensely from the cold throughout the long night.

One such occasion, when the round moon hung poised in the blue-black dome of heaven, and he was standing as usual in his corner, with eyes upon the brilliantly lighted house, he became suddenly aware of two people descending the rear porch and making slowly toward him. At first he did not recognize his own mistress and the young man who had been her almost constant companion since that memorable fright on the mesa eight months before. But as they drew closer, and he came to know the slender form in white, he sounded a soft whinny of greeting and pressed eagerly close to the fence. The pair came near, very near; but neither of them paid the least attention to him–a fact which troubled him deeply. And directly his mistress spoke, but, as she was addressing herself to the young man, this troubled him even more. But he could listen, and listen he did.

"Stephen," she was saying, "you *must* accept my answer as final. For you must know, Stephen," she went on, quietly, "that I have not changed toward you. My answer to-night, and my answer to-morrow night, and my answer for ever, in so far as I can see, will be what it was last autumn. I am more than sorry that this is so. But it is so, nevertheless." She was firm, though Pat, knowing her well, knew that it required all the force of her trembling soul to give firmness to her words.

Stephen felt something of this as he stood beside her in grim meekness. With his hungry eyes upon her, he felt the despair of one sunk to utter depths, of a man mentally and physically broken. For he loved this girl. And it was this love, God-given, that made him persist. In the spell of this love he realized that he was but a weak agent, uttering demands given him to utter, and unable, through a force as mighty as Nature herself, to do otherwise. Yet though he was utterly torn apart, he was able, despite this mighty demand within him, to understand her viewpoint. He had understood it from the first. But the craving within would not let him accept it.

"I suppose," he rejoined, "that the one decent course for me would be to drop all this. But somehow I can't. I love you that way, Helen! Don't you understand? I cannot let go! I seem to be forced repeatedly to make–make a boor of myself!" There was a moment's silence. "Yet I have resisted it," he went on. "I have fought it–fought it with all the power I have! But I–I somehow–cannot let go!"

Helen said nothing. She herself was coming to realize fully the depths of this man's passion. She knew–knew as few women have known–that here was a man who wanted her; but she knew also, and she was sorry to know it, that she could not conscientiously give herself to him. She regretted it not alone for his sake, but for her own as well. She liked him, liked him better than any other man she had ever known. But she knew that she could not marry him, and believed in her heart that her reasons for refusing him were just reasons. But she remained silent, true to her decision.

When Stephen spoke again it was not to plead with her; he seemed at last to have accepted her refusal for all time. But he asked her reason for absolutely refusing him–not that it mattered much now, since he faced the inevitable, but thought the knowledge might in future guide and strengthen him. He talked rapidly, hinting at beliefs and idolatries, comparing West with East, and East with West, while he stood motionless, one hand upon the fence–earnest, sincere, strong in his request. When he had uttered his last sad word, Helen found herself, as she searched his drawn profile pityingly, no more able to deny him an answer than at the time of their first chance meeting she could have controlled the fate which had brought it about.

"Stephen," she burst out, "I will tell you–though I don't want to tell you–remember! And if in the telling," she hurried on, "I prove rather too candid–please stop me! You will, won't you?"

He nodded listlessly.

"To begin with," she began, quietly, dreading her task, "we as a people are selfish. We are isolated here–are far from the center of things–but only certain things. We are quite our own center in certain other ways. But we are selfish as regards advancement, and being selfish in this way–being what we are and where we are–we live solely for that advancement–for the privilege of doing what we will, and of knowing! It is the first law of the country down here–of my people! We have aims and aspirations and courage all peculiar to ourselves. And when we meet your type, as I met you, we come– (Now, stop me when I get too severe!)–we come to know our own values a little better–to respect ourselves, perhaps–though perhaps, too, I shouldn't say it–a little more. Not that you lack virtues, you Easterners, but they differ from ours–and probably only in kind. And exactly what your type is you yourself have made plain to me during our many little trips together in the saddle. And–and now I fear I must become even more personal," she broke off. "And I am very sorry that I must. Though I know you will forgive me. You will, won't you?" And she looked up at him wistfully. "You thought it might benefit you to know. This is only my opinion. Others may not see it this way. But I am giving it for what it is, and I am giving it only because you asked it and have asked it repeatedly."

He roused himself. "Go on," he said, with evident forced lightness. "I see your viewpoint perfectly."

"Well," she resumed, hurriedly, "you lack ambition–a real ambition. You have ridden horses, played tennis, idled about clubs. You were a coddled and petted child, a pampered and spoiled youth. You attended a dozen schools, and, to use your own language, were 'canned' out of all of them. Which about sums up your activities. You have idled your time away, and you give every promise of continuing. I regret that I must say that, but I regret more deeply that it is true. You have many admirable qualities. You have the greatest of all qualities–power for sincere love. But in the qualities which make one acceptable down here–Wait! I'll change that. In the qualities which would make one acceptable to me you are lacking to a very considerable degree. And it is just there that you fill me with the greatest doubt–doubt so grave, indeed, that I cannot–and I use the verb advisedly–cannot permit myself to like you in the way you want me to like you."

Again he bestirred himself. "What is that, please? What is that quality?"

"I have tried to tell you," she rejoined, patiently. "It is a really worthwhile ambition. You lack the desire to do something, the desire to be something–a desire that ought to have been yours, should have been yours, years ago–the thing part and parcel of our blood down here. It may take shape in any one of a hundred different things–business ventures; personal prospectings; pursuit of art, science; raising cattle–anything, Stephen! But something, something which will develop a real value, both to yourself and to your fellow-man. We have it. We have inherited it. We got it from our grandfathers–our great-grandfathers, in a few cases–men who wanted to know–to learn–to learn by doing. It is a powerful force. It must be a powerful force, it must have been strong within them, for it dragged them out of the comforts of civilization and led them into the desert. But they found what they sought; and in finding what they sought they found themselves also. And what they found–"

"Was something which, having drawn them forward to the frontier, filled them with dislike for those who remained behind?"

"If you wish to put it that way–yes." Her answer was straight and clean-cut.

"But what of those who remained behind?" asked Stephen, alert now. "Surely the quality was there! It must be there yet! Those of the old-timers who remained behind must have stayed simply because of circumstances. Good men often curb the adventurous spirit out of sheer conscientious regard for others who–"

"It is you, Stephen!" interrupted Helen, quietly. "It is you, yourself. All Easterners are not like you, I well know. Yet you and your type are found in all parts of the East."

Stephen stood for a long moment, his eyes fixed on the mystic skyline. Then he turned to her as if about to speak. But there was only the silent message of his longing eyes. Finally he turned away and, as if unconsciously, fell to stroking the horse.

He had nothing to say, and he knew it. The girl was right, and he knew that. She had pointed out to him only what others at different times had mildly tried to make him see. He was a rich young man, or would be after a death or two in his family. But that in itself was no excuse for his inertia. Many had told him that. But he had never taken it seriously. It had remained for the little woman beside him to make him fully realize it. She alone had driven it home so that it hurt. Yet between this girl and the others who had taken him mildly to task there was the difference between day and darkness. For he loved this girl, and if she would not marry him for reasons which he knew he could remedy, then it was up to him to accept her criticism, which was perhaps a challenge, and go forth and do something and be something, and reveal his love to her through that effort. What it would be he did not know. He did know he must get out of the town–get out of the Territory, if needs be–but he must go somewhere in this country of worthy aspiration and live as he knew she would have him live, do something, be something, something that for its very worth to her as well as to all mankind would awaken her ready response. Such a move he realized, as he stood beside her, would be as decent in him as she in her criticism had been eloquently truthful.

The vigor, the relentless certainty, with which she had pointed out his weakness–no one before had had the courage to deal with him like this. And reviewing it all, and then casting grimly forward into his future, he suddenly awoke, as he gently stroked this mettled horse, to a strange likeness between the spirit of horse and mistress. He turned to Helen.

"You are very much alike," he declared–"you and your horse." Then he paused as if in thought. "The spirit of the desert," he went on, absently, "shows itself through all the phases of its life."

Helen brightened "I am glad you think that of us, Stephen," she answered, as if relieved by this unexpected turn. "Pat is truly of the desert. He was born and bred in this land of *amole* and cactus."

"And you?" he asked.

"I also," she replied, gravely. "I too was born and bred in this land of *amole* and cactus." Suddenly she turned her head. "I am afraid they are looking for us."

They returned to the house. Helen's guests were preparing to depart. There was much high humor, and when the last but one was gone, and this one, Stephen, standing on the porch with hat in hand, Helen found that for the moment she had forgotten her distress. At sight of him, however, it all returned to her, and she faced him with earnest solicitude.

"Tell me, Stephen," she burst out, "that you forgive me my unkind words, and that you will try to forget them. But whether you succeed in that or not, Stephen," she hastily added, her voice breaking, "tell me that you will continue to be friendly. We want you, all of us–I want you! I have enjoyed our rides together so much! They have meant much to me, and I hope they have been enjoyable to you. So let us go on, on this accepted basis, and be friends. Tell me you will, Stephen!"

He was silent a long time. Then he told her of his hastily made plans. He was going away from town, of course. He could not remain, under the circumstances. Yet where he was going he didn't know. He would go farther West, probably–go somewhere and try to make good–try to do something worth while, to be something worth while. Saying which, he then thanked her fervently for everything–for her society, for her frank criticism, for having awakened him to an understanding of himself.

Helen stood speechless. She had not anticipated this, that he would go away, that he would leave her. A deep-surging bitterness gripped her, and for a moment she almost relented. But only for a moment. The spell passed, and she looked at him with frank, level eyes.

"I am sorry to hear that, Stephen," she declared, quietly. "We want you with us–all of us. But–but tell me," she concluded, finding the words coming with difficulty–"tell me that you feel no–no antagonism toward me, Stephen, because I can't–can't love you as you want me to love you, and that you understand that–that in deciding as I have I–I only wanted to be true–true to both of us!"

For answer he seized both her hands in his. He gazed straight down into her eyes. "I love you, Helen," he murmured, and then slowly released her fingers.

He left her so quietly that she hardly knew that he was gone. A step on the trail aroused her, and, lifting her eyes, she saw him striding away with shoulders back and head erect, as if awakened to a new manhood. And watching him go, as she felt, for the last time, she could no more control a sob than he at the moment could turn back. For a while she followed him with wistful eyes, then, finding sudden need for consolation, she hurried off the porch and across to the corral. Pat was there to receive her, and she flung her arms around his neck and gave way to sudden tears.

"Pat," she sobbed, "I–perhaps I do love him! Perhaps I have done wrong! I–I–" She interrupted herself. "What shall I do, Pat?" she burst out, bitterly. "Oh, what shall I do?"

Pat could not advise her. But he remained very still, supporting her weight with dumb patience, until she turned away, going slowly back into the house. Then he pressed close into his corner and sounded a shrill, protracted nicker.

That was all.

He saw the door close. He waited, pursuing his old habit, for all the lights to go out. And directly they began to disappear, one by one, first in the lower half of the house, then in the upper half, until all save one were extinguished. This one, as he knew from long experience, was in the room of his mistress. But though he waited and watched till the moon slanted behind the western hills, and the stars to the east dimmed and faded, and the gray of dawn stole across the sky above the mountains–though he waited and watched till his legs ached from long standing, and his eyes smarted from their steady vigil, and the Mexican appeared yawning from the depths of the stable, and from over toward town rose sounds of worldly activity–yet the light in her room burned on. Then the Mexican drove him into the stable. But not even now did he abandon his vigil. He entered his box-stall, with its tiny square window, and fixed his troubled gaze again upon the house. The sky was bright with coming day. From somewhere arose the crow of a rooster. Out on the river trail a team plodded slowly to market.

But the light in the room was still burning.

CHAPTER XII
ADVENTURE

It was late afternoon when Helen came down from her room. She had regained her calm. The Judge had gone about his affairs, her aunt was deep in her siesta, the Mexican woman was bustling about in the kitchen. Refusing this kindly soul's offer of food, she walked listlessly into the library and sank into a huge chair. Spring was well advanced, yet there was an open fire. Elbows upon the arms of her chair, hands clasped under her chin, she turned unseeing eyes upon the flickering flames. Motionless, barely breathing, she was a picture of hopeless grief.

Yet her thoughts were active. One after another the swift-moving events of the night before came to her–a night of delightful happenings and torturing surprises. She recalled that the crowd had been unusually gay, but that Stephen had been unusually quiet and absorbed. She remembered the games, and the story-telling, and the toasting of marshmallows in the grate. But over against these simple pleasures there had been Stephen, entering into the gaiety only because he must, now forcing a smile, now drawing back within himself, until a chorus of laughter would again force him to smile. Yet she had understood, and she had excused him. She had thought him resigned and content to be merely one of the crowd. And then had come that opportunity which evidently he had sought. It had come as a surprise. But with it had come also a sudden desire to be alone with him, and to impress upon him her convictions. So they had gone out into the moonlight, to the corral fence, and to Pat, where she had endeavored to make everything clear. And then their return, and the departure of her guests, and his lingering on the porch, and his decision to go away, to leave her for ever. He hadn't put it in just that way! But that was what he was doing–that was what he had done. He had gone from her for ever.

The thought hurt. It hurt because she knew what part she had taken in it. She knew that she herself had sent him away. And when he had left her she knew, as she knew now, that in her heart she did not want it. For she liked him–liked his society. She liked his care-free manner, his whimsical outlook upon her country, his many natural talents–his playing, and the naïveté of his singing, while he often admitted that his voice hurt him, and so must hurt others. No, she had not wanted him to go away. And somehow it had never occurred to her that he would go for ever. But he was gone, and she could not resign herself. Yet there was no calling him back. She had made a decision, had forced him to understand certain things. So she must accept it. But it hurt. It was slowly dawning upon her that she would never forget him.

Then another thought came to her. Since he was going, and since she had sent him away, it occurred to her that she ought to help him. It seemed to be her duty. Yet she could not determine how. He was going forth to prove himself. He would go where men only could go, and she was but a woman. And she wanted him to prove himself–she knew that–knew it more with every moment that passed. She believed he had it in him. Yet she might help in some way. She wanted to be of some use to him in his undertaking. What could she do?

Suddenly, as she sat there, seemingly powerless, there came a shrill nicker whipping across from the corral–the voice of Pat.

Like a flash she had it! Stephen would go into the cattle country–she believed that. And in the cattle country he would need a horse, a good horse, such a horse as Pat. She would present the horse to Stephen! She would send Pat with him because she herself could not go with him. This she could do. Thus she would help Stephen to find himself, as her ancestors had found themselves. She would help him to become what she wanted him to become–a man–a *man*! Yes, she would give Pat to Stephen. She would send the horse as she had sent the man–forth into the world of deeds–deeds denied her sex.

She rose hurriedly and ascended to her room. At her desk she drew paper and pen toward her.

My dear Stephen [she began her letter],–I am sending Pat to you through Miguel. I wanted to help you in some way. I cannot help you myself directly, but in Pat I feel you will have a valuable aid. Take him–take him with my dearest and best wishes for your success. Pat may actually show you the way–may actually point the way out to you. Who knows? He understands who you are, I know, and I am sure he knows what you have been, and what you still are, to me.

HELEN.

For a moment she sat deep in thought. Then suddenly awaking to the lateness of the hour, she arose and, going to the corral, called to the hostler. Miguel appeared, and she handed him the note, giving him careful instructions the while in regard to the horse. The Mexican smiled and entered the stable in quest of saddle and bridle, the while she turned to Pat in his corner and explained what she was about to do.

"Pat dear," she began, nestling her cheek against his head, "you are going away. You are going with Stephen. Do you remember Stephen?" Emotion began to grip her. "You have served me well, Pat, and faithfully. I hope you will prove as true to your new master. I–I wanted to help him. But I–I couldn't–couldn't–" She could not go on. Gazing up into his eyes she seemed to see him waver–knew that it was because of her blinding tears–and abruptly left him and returned to the house.

In her room she stood weeping at the window overlooking the corral. She saw the Mexican bridle and saddle her pride, saw him carefully tuck away her note, and saw him mount Pat with a great show of importance, as though elated with his commission. Then she saw him ride Pat out of the corral, across into the river trail, and turn toward town. Seeing her horse go from her, perhaps for all time, she turned from the window and flung herself across her bed, where she gave way to her grief. Her Pat was gone! Her Pat–heart of her life– was gone!

Miguel was indeed pleased with his commission. Never before had he been astride this so-wonderful horse. As he rode along, testing the ease of Pat's gait, noting with what readiness he responded to the reins, he fell to wishing that it were not so near dusk, since then he might become the object of envious eyes in town. But he could not control the hour of day, even though he could control the horse's movements. So he cantered along until he reached the town proper, when he slowed Pat into a walk. Lights were being switched on along the avenue, and in their glare he enjoyed to the full whatever admiring glances were turned his way from the sidewalks. But as he neared the hotel where Stephen was stopping he urged Pat into a canter first, then into a gallop, pulling up before the side entrance with a quick reining that brought both the horse and himself to a stop with a magnificent flourish. It was good–as he admitted to himself. Then he slipped to earth. And now his magnificence left him, for he never before had entered this so-beautiful hostelry. Girting in his belt, however, he strode up the steps, faltered on the threshold, and was directed to the clerk. This magnate handed the letter to a bell-boy.

Stephen was seated in his room when he read Helen's note. When he raised his eyes he stared unseeingly at the light across the street, deep in thought.

He knew what this had cost Helen. Riding with her almost every day for months, he could not but understand the depth of her attachment for the horse. Pat for years had been the one big factor in her life. And now she was giving Pat to him, to help him prove himself. It was a great thing to do, so great that he must accept it, and already, at this proof of her interest, he somehow felt assured of success. Also he saw a way open. He would go down into the cattle country, make a connection with some cattle interests, and, with Pat as guide and friend and capable servant, work out his destiny. Exactly what that would be he did not know. But he did know that he was going after it.

He turned to the boy still standing in the doorway. "Tell the man that I'll be down directly," he said. Then he made his way into his mother's suite of rooms.

The frail little woman showed surprise at his decision. But she said nothing. She nodded quiet acquiescence and went on with her instructions to her maid, who was laying clothing away in preparation for the return East in the morning. Evidently she knew her boy. Whereupon Stephen, after explaining further, though no more fully than before, left her, descending to the office.

Miguel was standing awkwardly near the doorway, and with Stephen's appearance touched his hat and led the way outside. Pat was facing three boys, the center of their interest, but when Stephen approached him, and talked to him, he turned and responded with a soft whinny, seeming to understand. Miguel remained at a respectful distance, awaiting orders. Then telling him to wait for a note to be taken to Miss Richards, Stephen re-entered the hotel.

The boys swirled off in play. Miguel stood alone with the horse. There were but few persons on the streets, since it was early evening and people were at supper. Miguel's wandering eyes at length rested upon the swing-doors of a saloon opposite–rested there a long time. Finally, unable longer to resist their spell, he glanced at Pat's bridle, noted that the reins were securely tied, and then yielded to the attention of the saloon. In a moment the swing-doors closed upon him.

They had barely ceased swinging when out of a doorway just down the street stole the figure of a man. He was young, smooth of face, garbed in blue shirt and overalls, with eyes well concealed under a black sombrero low-drawn. He moved out of the shadow cautiously, with many furtive glances about him. Then he swiftly crossed the street, hurried along the sidewalk to Pat, and reached the horse's head and bridle. Untying the reins from the post, he leaped into the saddle. Then he swung Pat around, put light spurs to him, and urged him rapidly across the avenue. Beyond the avenue toward the north lay Stygian darkness. In these black depths he disappeared.

At this moment the clerk in the hotel was aroused by the unusual spectacle of one of his guests–young Wainwright–leaping down the stairs. He looked up with a surprised question. But Stephen ran past him, across the office, without heed. He gained the door, rushed down the steps, and shouted. The boys ceased playing, a passer-by came to a stop, out of the saloon opposite stepped Miguel. Miguel hastened across, drawing his hand over his mouth as he ran. Stephen opened upon him breathlessly.

"He's gone!" he burst out. "I saw it from my window. A young man in blue shirt and overalls. The horse has been stolen!"

Miguel threw up both hands in despair. "*Valgame Dios!*" he cried. "I am lose my job!" He looked about him blankly.

Sick at heart, not knowing what to do, Stephen himself bolted back into the hotel. He entered the telephone booth and rang up the

Judge's office. It was late, but he took a chance. The Judge answered the call. His voice was weary with the strain of a long day.

"Who in thunder wants me at this hour?" he drawled, not unpleasantly. "Can't you let a man–"

Stephen interrupted with an apology. Then he told the Judge of the loss. The Judge's voice changed instantly.

"Fine business!" he snapped. "But I reckon I know who to look for. There's only one man–one gang–in the Territory that would do that in that way. It's a job for the range police." Then his voice softened. "Don't worry, Stephen!" he added. "You just sit tight. I'll take it up with the authorities."

Stephen left the booth and entered the writing-room. Here he added a sad postscript to his note to Helen. Then he went outside, despatched Miguel with the letter, returned to his room and sat down, disconsolate and angry.

To have Pat sent to him with this noble generosity, and then to lose him! Surely fate was more than unkind. The horse, given into his keeping, had been wrested from him at once. Yes, he was all that Helen had intimated that he was–a man incapable of trust, a man such as she could never permit herself–and he recalled her words now with rankling bitterness–to care for in the way he wanted her to care for him. Knowing that Pat was gone from him, and gone in such ignoble fashion, he knew that he never could face the horse's mistress again. This was bitterest of all! For a time he gave way to despair.

Presently he awoke to a sense of stern responsibility. The horse had been delivered. Miguel had safely delivered him. It was all up to him then, Stephen, and to nobody else. He alone was responsible, and it was his duty to get Pat back. Out of his self-doubting this realization came with a sense of comfort. His course now lay clearly before him. He would get the horse back! He *must* get him back! There was nothing else left for him. For if he ever expected to return to Helen, and this was his life's hope, he must return to her with the horse. He could return to her in no other way.

He saw the difficulties. This was a large country, and he knew but very little of its activities. He recalled what the Judge had intimated–that the character of the thieves was such as to offer no encouragement of successful pursuit to any but men schooled to the country and the habits of the thieves. Yet against this and in his favor was the widespread reputation of Pat, and that certainly ought to be of some help in his pursuit. But, difficult or easy–take a month or a year–take five years–he would get Pat and return him to his mistress! The Judge had spoken of range police. Why couldn't he enlist with these men, enlist in any capacity, and accompany them till such time as he should learn the country well enough to venture out alone if necessary in his quest? At any rate, he would have a talk with the Judge–would see him early in the morning. He arose to his feet. The thing was settled in his mind. Also for the first time in his life his view had an object. He would go forth into life, get that which it withheld from him, bring it back and place it before the woman of his choice.

And now, so great is the power, so prompt the reward, of energy rightly applied, he found himself whistling as he began to toss wearing-apparel into a traveling-bag.

CHAPTER XIII
IN THE WASTE PLACES

Pat well knew that this new experience was a strange thing. The trip with the hostler, the unusual hour of day, the appearance of his mistress's friend, the stranger out of the night, the hurried departure from the hotel, all told him that. But whether it was right or wrong, he did not know. His mistress had quite sanctioned his leaving the corral, and so all things developing out of that must have her sanction also–thus worked his instincts. So not once had he rebelled. Nor was he rebelling now. And yet–and this was his emotional conflict–within him was a vague feeling that he should rebel, should kick, buck, toss, and pitch, and throw off this stranger. It grew upon him, this feeling, until, in a section of town unfamiliar to him, he decided to give way to it, to take a chance, anyway, of unseating this man and dashing back into that part of town familiar to him. But he did not. Suddenly a soothing voice restrained, the voice of his rider, which swept away for a time all thought of rebellion.

"So you're Pat!" the man said, and, though his voice was gentle, and perhaps kindly, as Pat judged the human voice, he yet somehow did not like the owner of it. "Well, they hain't lied to me, anyway," went on the voice. "You're one nice piece of horseflesh!"

That was all. But somehow it dispelled all discontent within Pat. Thereafter he thought only of his task, which was that of holding to a devious course through winding alleys and streets well under rein, until he found himself on the river trail and heading south through a section not unfamiliar to him. Then his interest only quickened.

As he went on, it came to him that he rather liked this traveling through the gloom of night. It was a new experience for him, and the trail, familiar to him, yet somehow not familiar, offered much of interest. Ranch-houses, clumps of trees, soft-rustling fields of alfalfa, looming up before or beside him, taxed his powers of recognition as the stars in the heavens, becoming ever more overcast, withdrew, and with them the moon, leaving the earth and its objects finally mere tragic outlines. These objects, rising silently before him, gave him many fitful starts, and seemed to forbid this night-incursion. But he held to the trail, for the most part in perfect contentment, enjoying his unwonted call to duty, but wondering whither it was leading him.

This contentment did not last. It broke as he found himself rounding a bend which he recognized as leading to the river bridge. The change came not through the flicking of his conscience like his former feeling, but through sudden awakening to physical discomfort. For a time he did not know what it was–though he had questioned the new grip on the reins, the rider's seat, his weight. There it was. The man's weight. Miguel had been heavy, of course, but Miguel's seat had been short-lived. This man must weigh fully as much as Miguel, and twice as much as his mistress, and he had been on his back now a long time. There came another something. As Pat grew aware of the weight it seemed to become heavier, so he decided to seek relief of some sort. He dropped back into a walk, grimly taking his comfort into his own control. And, half expecting that the man would force him into a canter again, he continued at a walk. But neither by word nor movement did the man show that he noticed the change. So Pat settled to his task again, once more enjoying quiet satisfaction.

But neither did this last. He soon found another cause for dissatisfaction. He found it because, unconsciously, he was looking for it. He found it this time in the tight grip on his reins, which was setting up a sore chafing in the corners of his mouth. His mistress had never held him so tightly. The result of it, together with his other discomfort, was that he became sullen and antagonistic, and, descending the slight grade to the bridge, he determined to resist. And resist he did. He came to a sudden stop, threw down his head, pitched and bucked frantically. His efforts carried him all over the trail, and once dangerously near the edge and the turbulent waters below. But he found himself unable to throw off the weight.

"Guess maybe–I made–a slight–mistake!" exploded the rider, clamping his knees against Pat. "But go–go to it–old trader!"

Pat accepted the challenge. For this he knew it was. He leaped and twisted; returned to earth with a jolt; pitched and tossed and bucked. And he kept it up, fighting grimly, till he discovered its futility, when he stopped. A moment he stood, breathing heavily, then he set out across the bridge, whisking his tail and wriggling his ears, all in spirited acceptance of reluctant defeat.

He did not attempt further rebellion. Slow-kindling respect stirred within him for this man upon his back–the respect but not love which one entertains toward the mighty, and he gained the end of the bridge and turned south along the trail, partly reconciled. Yet he had not rebelled in vain. The grip on his bit no longer annoyed him, and though the weight still remained heavy, somehow it seemed more endurable now through some cause which he could not determine–probably his increased respect for it. So he trotted along, amiably disposed toward all the world, pleasantly anticipatory of the immediate future, ears and eyes alert and straining toward all things. On his left the river gurgled softly in the desert stillness–a stillness sharply broken. From afar off came a strange call, the long-drawn howl of a coyote. It was not alone. Instantly from a point dead ahead rose another, grooving into the echo of the first in a staccato yelp. Then the first opened up with a choking whine that lifted steadily into an ecstatic mating-call, and Pat saw a black something, blacker even than the night, leap against the far, faint skyline, dangle seemingly a trembling moment, then flash from view across the desert.

Which was but one of the many incidents that served to hold his interest and increase his alertness as he fox-trotted along the road. Nor was one of them without its informing value. For this was his first night journey, and what he saw now would remain with him vividly, helping him to become as successful on night trails as he was now by day.

Something else came to him out of the darkness. It was off to his distant right and well back from the river. It was a tiny gleam of light, shining out of the density of the desert. He watched it with studied interest. It glowed like a cat's eye, and, fascinated, quietly speculative, he kept his eyes upon it until, as he turned a bend in the trail, he saw another light flash into view close beside the first, and equal to it in brilliancy. Suddenly, watching these lights, his interest leaped higher. This was his destination. He instinctively knew it. And presently he was certain of it, for his master, urging him to the right, now sent him along a narrow path that led straight toward the lights.

Within a very few moments Pat found himself before a hulk of an adobe. It was a long, rambling structure, somehow forbidding, and he blinked as he stared with faint apprehension at the lamplight streaming out of two windows. Directly the man dismounted and, making the reins fast to a post, walked toward the house. For a moment Pat saw his tall figure silhouetted in the doorway, to the accompaniment of a quiet chorus of greetings from within, then he saw the door close upon him, and immediately afterward a hand appear at the windows and draw down the shades. And now he felt a great loneliness creep over him, slowly at first, then somehow faster as he heard voices within sink from a cheerful note of greeting to a low rumble of discord.

He began to take heed of objects close around him. He discovered, now that all light was shut off, that he was not alone. To his left stood two horses, with heads drooping, legs slightly spread, reins dangling, quiet and patient in their mute waiting. Promptly with the discovery he took a step in their direction, intent upon establishing friendship. But he found himself checked with a jerk. For an instant he did not understand this. Then he remembered that his reins were tied, and because his mistress never had deemed this necessary he came to feel a kind of irritation, though he made no attempt to force his freedom. Yet, keeping his eyes upon the other horses, he saw that they themselves were free to come and go, that their reins were dangling on the ground. And now he realized that he was under suspicion. He knew what that was from long association with the Mexican hostler, and, smarting under it, he determined to show his new master, and that before many hours had elapsed, he as well as these others was capable of trust.

The door flung open and three men filed out. A fourth remained standing on the threshold, holding up a smoking lamp. Other than the tread of heels no sound accompanied their appearance, no comment, no laughter, no farewells. This made a deep impression upon him, and with further misgivings he watched the men descend the few loose steps and make for the horses, his own master, the tallest of the men, coming slowly toward him. A moment of gathering reins, then all mounted, and one, a squat, powerfully built man, evidently the leader, turned in a southwesterly direction, riding off in the engulfing darkness, heading away from the river. Seeing this, Pat stepped out after him, pressing close upon the heels of his horse, conscious that the third horse, ridden by a little man, was crowding him for second position. But he held stubbornly to his place, and in this place set out along an unmarked trail. He covered mile after mile at a fox-trot, mile after mile in absolute silence, until faint rays of dawn, streaking the sky above a ridge to the east, surprised him into realization of the quick passage of night and his own prolonged duty therein. It was all very strange.

Daylight followed swiftly. From a dull lead color the sky immediately above the ridge, which stretched away interminably north and south, gave way to a pink indescribably rich and delicate. Steadily this pink crept over the heavens, rolling up like the gradual unfolding of a giant canvas, dragging along in its wake hues verging toward golden yellow, until the whole eastern sky, aflame with the light of approaching day, was a conflagration of pinks and yellows in all their manifold mixtures, promising, but not yet realizing, a warmth which would dispel the spring chill left by the long night. Then, with the whole east blazing with molten gold, there came the feeling of actual warmth, and with it the full radiance of day–bringing out in minute detail rock and arroyo and verdant growth, and an expanse of desert unbroken by the least vestige of animal life. At this absence of all that which would suggest the presence of life–adobes, corrals, windmills–Pat awoke again to vague uneasiness and fell to pondering his future under these men, whom he now instinctively knew pursued ways outside the bounds of the civilization of his past.

A voice behind, presumably that of the little man, interrupted the protracted silence. It was high-pitched.

"How's that hoss a-holdin', Jim?"

Pat felt a slight twitch on the reins. Evidently the man had been in deep thought, out of which the voice had startled him. Directly he made answer.

"I got quality here, Glover–I guess. Can't never tell, though. He's a good horse, but he mayn't pan out good for me."

There was further silence.

"Johnson," went on the high-pitched voice again, after a time, "did ye git what Zeke said about the country down there?"

But the leader seemed not to hear. Straight as an arrow, bulking large upon a little gray mare, he moved not the fraction of an inch with the question. Whereupon the little man, after muttering something further about Zeke, relapsed into silence.

Suddenly Pat stumbled and fell to his knees. He quickly regained his feet, however, and resumed the steady forward grind. And grind it now was becoming. His legs burned with a strange distress, his eyes ached from loss of sleep. Throughout his body was a weariness new to him. He was not accustomed to this ceaseless fox-trotting. He could not recall the time when, even on their longest excursion, his mistress had forced him like this. She had always considered him to the extent of granting him many blissful periods of rest. He found himself wanting some such consideration now. He felt that he would like to drop into a walk or to burst into a canter, knowing the relief to be found in any change of gait. But this was denied him. Yet, since the other horses gave no sign of weariness, each appearing possessed of endurance greater than his own, he refrained, through a pride greater even than his distress, from making of his own accord any change in his gait.

Toward noon, as he was brooding over another distress, one caused by gnawing hunger, he felt his master draw down. Also, the others came to a stop. With the men dismounted, he swept eyes over the scene. But he saw nothing that appeared to warrant pause. The place was dead and desolate, barren of all that which had invariably met his gaze when pausing with his mistress. But when one of the men began to build a fire, while the others flung off light saddle-bags from the little gray and the sorrel–an exceptionally rangy horse–he came in a way to understand. Further, with the fire crackling pleasantly and his bridle and saddle removed, he understood fully the cause of this halt. It was time to feed; and, raging with hunger, he forgot all other distress in the thought that now he would have a generous quantity of food, which he believed was due him, since he had more than earned it in his prolonged service through the night. Indeed, so certain was he of reward, he prepared himself for sugar and quartered apples, and, with mouth dripping saliva, stood very still, eyes following every move of his new master.

But he was doomed to bitter disappointment. Instead of sugar and quartered apples, his master tied a rope around his neck and, with a friendly slap, left him to his own devices. Wondering at this, he gazed about him–saw that the other horses were grazing. Disappointed, fretful, stung into action by hunger pangs, he set out in their direction, curious to learn what it was they were feeding upon so eagerly. But, as had happened the night before, he found himself checked with a jerk. He did not like it, for it made him conscious again of his master's suspicions. So he turned a sour gaze upon his unrestricted companions until, forced to it by inner yearnings amounting to acuteness now, he himself lowered his head and fell to grazing.

But he found it all too insufficient. His stomach urgently demanded grain and alfalfa. And he yearned for a little bran-mash. But there were none of these. He saw not even a tiny morsel of flower to appease his inner grumblings, and finally, lifting his head in a kind of disgust, he ceased to graze altogether. As he did so, the men made ready to resume the journey, replacing bridles and saddles and saddle-bags. Pat found himself hopeful again, believing that with the end of this prolonged service, which in view of the distance already traversed must be soon, he would have those things for which his body and soul cried out. And thus he set forth, occupying his former place in the order of advance, moving, as before, at a fox-trot and amid silence from the men. He was still hopeful of better things to come. But it was all a drear experience.

The grind began to tell upon him. As he trotted along, thirst-stricken, miserably nourished, weary from loss of sleep and this ceaseless toil, he sought frankly for cause to rebel, as he had done in the first hour of this strange call to new duty. And he found it. He found it not only in the man's weight, and the infrequent contact of spurs, and the tight grip on the reins, all as on that first occasion, but he found it as well in other things–in the dust thrown up by the little gray ahead, in the sun's rays slanting into his eyes from the west, in the scorching, blistering heat of this same ruthless orb beating down upon his back. Suddenly, cost him what it would, he dropped out of the fox-trot into a walk, prepared to fight for this change of stride to the last breath.

He did not hold to it, however, even though his master, curiously enough, permitted him the change. Pride asserted itself, and after a time, of his own volition, finding the gap between himself and the others much too wide to please him, he broke into a canter and quickly closed the gap, crowding back into his place between the other two horses. That was all of rebellion, though the mood still remained. Bitter, disappointed, nervous, and irritable, he continued forward, wanting things—wanting food and water, wanting sounds of voices, wanting a respite from this unnerving grind. But he made no effort to get them or to show that he wanted them. And he knew why he maintained this attitude of meek acceptance. He was too weak to enforce his demands. He knew that it required energy to buck and pitch, and he knew that he lacked this energy. So he continued along in sullen resignation until, accepting the hint of his instincts, he closed his eyes. This brought relief, and after a time, his movements becoming ever more mechanical, he found himself adrift upon a peaceful sea of semi-coma, oblivious to all trouble—hunger pangs, thirst, weariness. When he returned to full consciousness, somewhat refreshed and fit for farther distances, he found the sun well down the western sky, the cool of evening wrapping him about in delightful zephyrs, and he was still keeping his place between the two horses.

Dusk found him in a small oasis. His master slipped to earth, and with relief Pat gazed about him. He saw a clump of trees, and in their depths, glinting out at him between the trunks, a shimmering pool of water. Also, near these trees, on the edge of the grove, he saw a shack made up of rough logs. But he was interested only in the pool, and, when his master removed his saddle, eagerly and with a soft nicker he stepped toward it. But the man jerked him back. So he waited, realizing that he had been hasty, till his bridle was removed, when again he stepped toward the pool. But again he was jerked back, this time by a firm grip on his forelock. So again he waited while the man placed the disagreeable rope around his neck. With this secure, he found himself led into the grove, where he soon was quenching his raging thirst, and where, after drinking, he felt more kindly not only toward the man, but toward the whole world. When he was conducted back into the open, and the end of the rope made fast to a stake, he lifted his voice in a shrill nicker proclaiming his satisfaction. Then he stood very still, watching the man enter the shack, utterly absorbed in getting that long-delayed reward of sugar and quartered apples.

But again he waited in vain. The man did not reappear; indeed, none of the men reappeared. So after a time, swallowing his disappointment, he turned his eyes upon the other horses. As at noon, they were grazing industriously, and he knew what was in store for him. He regarded them a long moment, trying to bring himself to graze also, but finding that his knowledge of better things would not permit him. Yet there was one pleasant surprise. The little gray, sounding a soft whinny, made her way slowly toward him. This was unexpected friendliness, for the horse had seemed hostile earlier, and he promptly showed his pleasure by licking her neck with lavish attention. And though he found her coat gritty with dust, he continued this generous attention till she lowered her head and resumed her grazing. This reminded him of his own fierce hunger, and he promptly lowered his own head, following her example with a kind of gratitude, and fell to grazing with her, finding in her interest the one ray of light in all the darkness of his distress and continued disappointment. And thus he fed, keeping with her to the limits of his tether, until, soon after the candlelight had whisked out in the shack, she lay down in the yielding sand with a restful sigh. Pat understood this, but he regarded it with uncertainty, knowing that he himself with the coming of night always had protection in a stable. Then, deciding that it was right and fitting, especially as the sorrel also sank into the sand, he himself bent his knees and lay down to rest in the warmth of the desert.

But his lesson in the open was not yet fully learned. Next morning, with the other horses astir, and with the men moving in and out of the shack, he saw his master coming toward him. Reaching him, the man untied the rope from the stake, led him to the pool of water, and permitted him to drink. Then he returned him to the open, and there removed the rope from him entirely. But despite this he found that he was not free from suspicion. For now the man tied a short rope around his fore ankles, and strode back into the shack, leaving him, as before, to his own devices.

Half expecting the man to return with sugar and apples, Pat watched him take himself off with mild anticipation. But as the man did not return he bethought him after a time of his sterner hunger, and took prompt step in the direction of a tuft of grass. Instantly he felt a sharp twitch at his ankles and fell headlong. For a moment he lay dazed, utterly at a loss to understand, thrashing about frantically in futile effort to regain his feet. Then he became calm again, and brought craftiness instead of brute force to bear upon the trouble. He regained his feet. Then he studied the cause of the disaster, and finally stepped out again, cautiously now, having learned his lesson. So he did not stumble. But he did feel the check around his ankles again. Steadying himself, he saw clearly the cause of his previous discomfiture, but he did not accept it as defeat. Casting his eyes toward the other horses, he awoke to the fact that they, as well as himself, were hobbled. Watching them, studying them, he finally saw one rear, strike out with his front legs, and draw his hind legs up to meet the advance. So that was it! He now knew what he himself must do. Feeling out his hobbles carefully, gathering quick courage the while, he himself at length reared, struck out with fore legs, followed up with hind legs, and found himself directly over the tuft of grass. This was pleasant, and he promptly began to nibble it, finding it no less toothsome–perhaps more toothsome–for the effort. And when he had finished this he gazed about for others, and, seeing others, moved upon each in turn as he had moved upon the first, rearing and striking, following it with hind legs, rearing and striking again, following again with hind legs, all successfully. And so he learned his second great lesson in the open.

Thus he began his life in the desert. Fraught as it was with much discomfort, both spiritual and physical, he yet found much of interest in it all, and he was destined to find in it, as time went on, much more of even greater interest. And in the days which followed, and the weeks and months following these, because he showed that he was willing and anxious to learn, to attune himself to the life, he aroused in all who came in contact with him, men as well as horses, an esteem and affection which made life smoother and more pleasant for him than it might otherwise have been.

CHAPTER XIV
A PICTURE

A hundred miles west from the shack, stretching away from it in an almost unbroken expanse, was a desert within the desert. *Amole* and sagebrush and cactus vied with each other to relieve the dead, flat, monotonous brown. Without movement anywhere, save for the heat-waves ascending, this expanse presented an unutterably drear and lonesome aspect. It terminated, or partly terminated–swerving off into the south beyond–in a long sand-dune running northeast and southwest. This mighty roll lay brooding, as did the world-old expanse fringing it, in the silence of late morning. Overhead a turquoise sky, low, spotless, likewise brooding, dipped down gracefully to the horizon around–a horizon like an immense girdle, a girdle which, as one journeyed along, seemed to accompany him, rapidly if he moved rapidly, slowly if he moved slowly–an immense circle of which he was the center. The sun was glaring, and revealed here and there out of the drifts a bleached skeleton, mutely proclaiming the sun as overlord, while over all, around and about and within this throbbing furnace, there seemed to lurk a voice, a voice of but a softly lisped word–solitude.

Suddenly, like a mere dot against the skyline, there appeared over the giant dune to the north a single horseman. A moment he seemed to pause on the crest, then began the long descent, slowly, with almost imperceptible movement. He was not more than under way when another dot appeared against the skyline, a second horseman, close behind the first, who, like the first, after seeming to pause a moment on the crest, dipped into the long slope with almost imperceptible movement. A third dot appeared, two dots close beside each other, and these, like the others, dipping into the descent with almost imperceptible movement, for all the world like flies reluctantly entering a giant saucer. And then appeared another, the fifth, and then no more. The last also seemed to pause a brief moment on the crest, and also dipped with almost imperceptible movement into the long descent.

They struck the floor of the furnace. Details began to emerge. One was a fat man, another was a gaunt man, a third was a little man–all smooth of face. Then there was a man with a scrubby beard. And there was another smooth-faced man, riding a little apart from the others, a little more alert, perhaps, his garments not their garments, his horse a little rounder of outline, a little more graceful of movement. They might have been in conversation, these riders out of the solitude. But all were heavily armed. And all rode slowly, leisurely, taking their own good time, as if this in itself was duty, with orders uncertain, or with no orders at all. They rode on across the desert within the desert, presenting three-quarter profile, then, with an hour passing, full profile, then, with another hour passing, quarter profile, and now, with yet another hour passing, five agreeable backs–broad, most of them, all topped with sombreros, and all motionless save for the movement of their mounts. On and on they rode into the south, underneath a blistering sun at full zenith. They became mere dots again upon the pulsating horizon, mere specks, and disappeared in the shimmering haze.

Solitude, the voice of solitude, the death-stillness, throbbing silence, reigned once more. Not an animal, not an insect, not a tree, struck the eye. The arid and level floor was again clean of movement. The sun glared, revealing here and there out of the drifts a bleached skeleton, in this speechless thing mutely proclaiming its own sway. Beneath the sun the horizon, an immense girdle, swept round in unbroken line, pulsating. The turquoise sky hung low, spotless and shimmering, brooding, dipping smoothly down to the horizon and to the long sand-dune running to northeast and southwest. Skirting this dune, reaching to it out of the east, then swerving off to the south beyond, lay the almost unbroken expanse, the desert within the desert, its dead, flat, monotonous brown relieved here and there with alternating sagebrush and cactus and *amole*, stretching back a distance of a hundred miles to the shack.

CHAPTER XV
CHANGE OF MASTERS

The interior of the shack was comparatively bare. On the floor, which was of adobe, and therefore hard and smooth as cement, were five three-legged stools and a table, all crude and evidently shaped out of saplings from the grove. There was but a single window, high up, tiny and square, containing neither glass nor frame, which looked out upon the south. Built against the walls were some shelves, upon which lay a scant supply of tinware, and in the opposite wall was a tier of bunks, just now littered with soiled blankets. Evidently this place had sheltered these men frequently, for each moved about it with easy familiarity, and obviously it was a retreat, a rendezvous, a hiding-place against the range police.

A game of cards was about to be started. The three men were seated round the table, and before two of them–the younger man, Jim, and the heavy-set man, the leader, Johnson–was an even distribution of chips. The third man, Glover, was smoking a short-stemmed pipe, evidently having been cut out of the play.

"Jim," said Johnson, showing his perfect teeth with an unpleasant grin, "we'll hop right to this! I think my little proposition here is fair and square. Thirty dollars in money against that black horse out there. I told you where you could get a good horse, and you got one sure enough! And he's yours! But I've taken a kind of shine to him myself, and why ain't this a good way to push it over? My little gray and thirty dollars in money. What's the matter with it?"

The other did not appear greatly pleased, nevertheless. Thoughtfully he riffled the cards a long moment. Then he looked up into Johnson's black eyes steadily.

"Poker?" he asked, quietly.

"Draw poker," replied the leader, giving his black mustache a satisfied twist. He jerked his head in the direction of the chips. "Win all, take all," he added.

Jim lowered his eyes again. He was not more than a boy, this outlaw, and he had formed a strong attachment for the black horse. And because he had come to understand Pat and to appreciate him, he hated to think of the horse's serving under this bloodless man opposite. Pat's life under this man would be a life of misery. It was so with all of Johnson's horses. Either they died early, or else, as in the case of the little gray, their spirits sank under his cruelty to an ebb so low that nothing short of another horse, and one obviously capable of rendering successful protection, roused them to an interest in their own welfare. This was why the little gray, he recalled, had approached the black the first night after reaching the shack. Evidently she had recognized in him an able protector, should he care to protect her, against the brutality of her master. And so to play a game of cards, or anything else, with a view to losing possession—

"I don't hear you saying!" cut in the cold voice of the other upon his thoughts. "Ain't the stakes right?"

Jim looked up. "I guess so," he said. "I'm tryin' to figure— percentages and the like."

Again he relapsed into thought. He feared this man as he feared a snake. For Johnson had a grip on him in many ways, and in ways unpleasant to recall. So he knew that to refuse meant a volley of invectives that would end in his losing the horse anyway, losing him by force, and a later treatment of the animal, through sheer spite, the brutality of which he did not like to contemplate. So he did not reply; he did not dare to say yes or no. Either way, the horse was gone. For Johnson was clever with the cards, fiendishly clever, and when playing recognized no law save crookedness.

"Jim," burst out Johnson, controlling himself evidently with effort, "I want to ask you something. I want you to tell me something. I want you to tell me who it was grubstaked you that winter you needed grubstaking mighty bad. I want you to tell me who it was got you out of that scrape over in Lincoln County two years ago. I want you to tell me who it was took care of you last winter—under mighty trying circumstances, too—and put you in the way of easy money this spring! But you needn't tell me," he suddenly concluded, picking up the cards savagely. "I know who it was without your telling me, and you know who it was without my telling you. And now what's the returns? When I give you a chance to come back a little—in a dead-square, open game of cards–you crawl into your shell and act like I'd asked you to step on the gallows."

Jim permitted himself a quiet smile. "I don't think I'm playing the hog, exactly," he rejoined, evenly. "I guess maybe I'm thinking of the horse as much as anything. And not so much of him, either, maybe, as of you, the way you handle horses if they don't dance a two-step when you want a two-step. In about a week, Johnson," he continued, mildly, "you'd have that horse jabbed full of holes with them Mexican rowels of yours! He wouldn't stand for that kind of affection, or I'm no judge of horseflesh. He ain't used to it; he ain't that kind of a horse–your kind! You ought to see that yourself. You don't want no spirited horse like him, because either you'd kill him or he'd kill you. *I* can see it, if you can't!"

"We'll now cut for deal," interposed Johnson, grimly.

"Take myself," went on the other, half smiling "why I like the idea of keeping him. I used to kill cats and rob nests and stone dogs when I was a kid; but later I learned different. I didn't kill cats and rob nests after that; dogs I got to petting whenever I'd meet one. I got acquainted with animals that way. Made the acquaintance from both angles–seeing how they acted under torture, then learning how they acted under kindness. I know animals, Johnson," he added, quietly. "And an animal to me is an animal and something more. A horse, for instance. I see more in a horse than just an easy way of getting around. But that ain't you. You're like a man I once knowed that kept a dog just because the dog was a good hunter. If I couldn't see more in a dog than just what he's fit for, I'd quit the sport."

"Now we'll cut for deal."

Jim had been rocking back and forth easily on two legs of his stool. He now dropped forward squarely on the floor and nodded assent.

"Cut for deal," he said, quietly. "You!"

The game began. Glover, who evidently found interest in discussions, but none whatever in a game of cards, tilted back against the wall and began to talk, now that the argument was over.

"Zeke tells me," he began in a nasal voice, tamping the tobacco into the bowl of his pipe reflectively, "as how they's a bunch o' Injun renegades movin' south'ards off the reservation on a hell-toot. I meant to speak of it afore, but forgot, as usual. Jim's talk here o' animals lovin' each other that away reminds me." He lifted gray eyes to Johnson. "Didn't Zeke say nothin' to you about that, neither?" he asked, evidently mindful of some other grave oversight on the part of "Zeke."

Johnson did not reply until after three or four rounds of the cards. "Zeke told you a lot of things that hour you sat with him alone," he rejoined, with broad sarcasm. "Zeke must like you!"

"Mebbe," agreed Glover, accepting the remark with all seriousness. "He says as how Fort Wingate is out, and I remarks that sich a move about terminates the performance. He agrees with me–says fust squint them renegades gits at regular troops they'll hunt gopher-holes as places o' ginerous salvation."

The others remained silent. The game was going decidedly against Jim. It had gone against him from the first–as he had known it would. Yet he continued to play, watchful of his opponent, keen to note any irregularities. Yet he had discovered nothing that might be interpreted as cheating. Still he was losing, and still, despite all beliefs to the contrary, he entertained hope, hope that he might win. If he did win, he told himself, Johnson was enough of a white man to accept the defeat and leave the horse where he was. Yet his chips were steadily dwindling; the cards persistently refused to come his way; only once thus far had he held a winning hand. But he played on, becoming ever more discouraged, until, suddenly awaking to an unexpectedly good hand, he opened the pot. The raises followed back and forth swiftly, but he lost again. And now Johnson, as he mechanically drew the chips toward him, broke the silence.

"Zeke got you all worked up, didn't he?" he declared, turning his eyes upon Glover. "As for renegades," he went on, beginning to deal the cards again, "I've knowed 'em–hull droves of 'em–to stampede on the whistle of a rattler." Evidently he was returning to good humor.

Glover took his pipe from his mouth. "Renegades gits stirred up every jest so often," he observed. "I s'pose it's because of the way they feel about things. Being run offen the reservations thataway ain't nowise pleasant, to begin with, and then havin' to hang around the aidges for what grub their folks sees fit for to sneak out to 'em ought to make it jest that much more monotonous–kind of. Reckon I'd break out myself–like a man that eats pancakes a lot–under sich circumstances. Zeke says this band–the latest gang to git sore–is a-headin' dead south. Talks like we might run agin trouble down there. More'n one brand, too–the police and the reg'lars all bein' out thataway. They're all out–Zeke says."

The others were absorbed in play, and so made no retort. Whereat Glover, with a reflective light in his eyes, continued:

"I've seen something myself," he went on, evidently mindful of Johnson's observation. "I've seen better men than Injuns stampede on less than rattlesnakes–and cover a heap more ground in a lot less shorter time. What I'm talkin' about is skunks," he explained, to nobody in particular–"hydrophoby skunks–their bite. Why," he continued, warming to his subject and seemingly ignorant of its myths, "I once seen a man ride into San Mercial with his face that white it wouldn't 'a' showed a chalk mark! And he was holdin' up his thumb like it was pizen–which it was! And he was cuttin' for old Doc Struthers that fast his cayuse was sparkin' out of his ears. Bit by a hydrophoby skunk–yes, sirree. Got to the Doc's just in time, too! But he allus was lucky–the Doc! Money jest rolled into that party all the time. But some folks don't jest quite make it–horses gives out, or something. And if they ain't got the sand to shoot the finger off–"

A sudden shadow across the window checked him. He quietly reached for his gun. Also, Johnson lifted quick eyes to the window. And now Jim turned his head. Directly Glover rose to his feet; Johnson got up off his stool; Jim flung to the door. A moment they stood tense. Then Jim moved cautiously to the window. He gazed outside. As he did so his features relaxed. Presently he returned to the table.

"That horse," he explained, eyes twinkling.

The others returned to their places. All were visibly relieved. But Glover did not go on with his yarn. Lighting his pipe again, he fell to smoking in thoughtful silence.

Jim picked up his cards. He saw four kings. But he felt no elation. Before him was a mere dribble of chips, and he knew that he could not hold out much longer. Johnson was coldly surveying his own cards, and after a studied moment opened the pot. Jim thrust forward half his small stack, followed by Johnson with a raise, whereupon Jim placed all he had upon the board. That closed the game. The other spread out his cards generously, and Jim, glancing listlessly at four aces, rose from the table. Turning to the window, he saw Pat still lingering near the shack. He gazed at him a long moment in silence.

"He's yours," he said, finally, facing Johnson. "Reckon I'll go outside for a little air."

Outside, he made straight for Pat, removed the hobbles, led him into the grove. As the horse quenched his thirst, Jim sat down with his back against a tree and removed his hat.

"Sorry, old-timer," he began, quietly, "but it can't be helped. We–" He interrupted himself; shoved Pat away a step. "That's better," he went on, smiling. Then, as Pat looked puzzled, "On my foot–yes," he explained. "All of your own, too, of course!" he added. "But one of mine, too!" He was silent. "As I was remarking," he continued, after a moment, "we've got to beat him some other way. You're a likely horse."

He lowered his eyes thoughtfully. He did know of a way to beat Johnson. That way was to mount Pat, ride hard for the open, and race it out against the little gray mounted by Johnson. But already he could see the vindictive and cursing Johnson in pursuit, discharging guns before him. So the idea was hopeless, for he knew that Johnson even now was alert for some such move. But even if it were feasible, he realized that he never could rid himself of the man. Others had tried, as he well recalled–tried to break away from him for all time, with a result in no way to Johnson's credit. Two had never been seen again, which pointed grimly to the fact that Johnson lived up to his favorite maxim, which was that dead men tell no tales. Another was the case of that poor luckless devil who, through some mysterious workings of the law, having broken with Johnson, had been arrested and convicted of a crime long forgotten. But Jim knew, as others closely associated with Johnson knew, that it was Johnson who indirectly had sent the unfortunate one to the penitentiary. So it required courage, a kind of unreasoning desperation, to quit the man and the life he led.

Suddenly Jim took a new hold upon himself. What, he began to ask himself, was getting into him? Why was he suddenly thinking of quitting Johnson? What would he do if he did quit him? To his kind all decent channels were closed for any but the exceptional man. But that wasn't it! Why was he arguing with himself along these lines? What was getting into him? He felt as if some good and powerful influence was come into his life! He had felt like this in Denver when a Salvation Army lassie had approached him. But this wasn't Denver! Nor was there a woman! What was it, anyway? He could not decide.

He arose and laid his hand upon Pat's forelock.

"It's a regular case," he said, leading the horse out of the grove, "for something to turn up. It generally does, anyway," he concluded. "Don't it, Old Gravity?"

CHAPTER XVI
PAT TURNS THIEF

A week passed before Pat knew of his change in masters. But that was not strange. Busily engaged in keeping himself alive on scant herbage, he took but little interest in anything else. Besides, his young friend continued to make much of him, talking in soothing tones and gently stroking his sides, and the little gray, holding herself faithfully near, also maintained quiet evidence of friendliness. So he had no reason to suspect change. But one morning, with camp broken, and saddle-bags flung out, and the window sealed over, and the door shut and barred, and the other horses bridled and saddled, there came to him in the person of the large man himself–a person he had instinctively disliked–the first sign of the change in his fortune.

The man approached, bridle on arm, to remove his hobbles. He remained motionless under this, and prepared also to accept the bridle quietly. But in bridling him the man was rough to an extent he had never before known–forcing an oddly shaped bit against his tongue, and twisting and turning his sensitive ears as if these delicate organs were so much refractory leather or metal. Then came the saddle, and with it further torture. The forward belt was made snug, which he was accustomed to and expected; but when the rear girdle was cinched so tight that he found difficulty in breathing, he became nervous and wanted to protest. It was all very unusual, this rough handling, and he did not understand it. The effect of the tight cinch was peculiar, too. With the knot tied firmly, he felt girded as for some great undertaking, his whole nervous system seemed to center in his stomach, and all his wonted freedom and buoyancy seemed compressed and smothered. With all this, and the man in the saddle and spurring viciously, he realized grimly the change in masters.

They set out at a fox-trot, continuing their southwesterly direction. It was an unmarked course from the beginning, leading them steadily down into the Mogollon range, and, as before, Johnson was occupying the lead, with Jim next behind, and Glover bringing up the rear. And, as on the first leg of the journey, all rode in silence.

So Pat was in the lead, and while he found his new master half as heavy again as the other, he also found compensation for the increased weight in the position which he occupied. Not that he was proud to be in the lead; nothing from the beginning of this adventure had caused a thrill of either joy or pride. But he did find in his new place freedom from dust cast up by the heels of his companions, and he trotted along in contentment, to all outward appearances. But it was only an appearance of content. Within were mixed emotions. While he felt pleasure at being active again, while he was resigned in a way to his hunger pangs, and he was glad that his friends, the little gray and the young man, were still with him, yet against all this was a sense of revolt at the unnecessary tightness of the cinch, the hard hand on the reins, and the frequent touch of spur and heel and stirrup against his sides. Finally the feeling which began at that initial torture in bridling swelled with the consequent annoyances into approaching revolt. He became ugly and morose.

This soon revealed itself. He was crossing a wide arroyo. Without counting costs, grimly blind to the result, he burst out of the fox-trot into a canter. He held to this a thrilling moment, and then, finding himself keyed to greater exertions, abandoned the canter and broke into a sharp run. It was all done quickly, the changes of stride lapping almost within his own length, and his heart leaped and pounded with delight, for the change somehow relieved him.

But it was a mistake. Quickly as it was done, he found himself almost as quickly jerked up, swung viciously around, and his sides raked with ruthless spurs. He gasped a moment under the smarting fire of the spurs, then, as in the old days, reared in a towering rage. And this was a mistake. Too late he found the man's weight overbalancing him. He struggled to recover himself, plunged over backward, and down, striking the earth heavily. Hurriedly he regained his feet, but not so the man, not till the others sprang to his assistance. Then he realized what he had done, realized it fully as he caught the venomous gleam in the man's eyes and heard the storm of abuse volleying from his lips. Then, looking at the man, and listening to his raging outburst, he conjured up out of the dim past memories of the Mexican hostler and of that single encounter in the white corral. And now his fear for the man left him.

"I'll kill him! I'll shoot the horse!" roared Johnson, his face yellow underneath the tan. He reached toward his side-arms.

But he did not shoot. With his face white and drawn Jim strode to Pat's head, while Glover, quick to understand, played the solicitous attendant, assisting the limping Johnson into the saddle. And that closed the incident. Presently all were riding along again, with Johnson, wincing under internal distress, holding his reins more loosely than before.

But it was not without its good. As on that other occasion in the corral, Pat had learned something. He had measured a man, and he knew, and knew that the man knew, that he had come off victor. But it gave him no secret gratification. He continued to trot along, holding steadily to the gait, subtly aware of the slackened rein and of the wrenched and loosened girdle, until, with the coming of noon, the blessed relief from the weight of the man, the ill-fitting saddle, and the over-tight girth, came also an agreeable surprise. He was turned out to graze without hobble or tether, and for this consideration he felt faint glimmerings of respect for his new master. Making free at first with the other horses, he set off to enjoy to the full his new-found liberty.

But as he pursued ever farther the elusive vegetation in the joy of freedom, he presently awoke to his great distance from camp, and, indeed, from the other horses. Conscious of a sudden gripping loneliness and a certain apprehension, he began to retrace his way. As he did so, out of the silence came a nasty whirring sound, and suddenly he felt a rope settle over his head. Surprise, then anger, displaced his loneliness and apprehension; he jerked back to escape the rope. But it held fast. He braced his legs and began to pull steadily. But the harder he pulled the worse the rope choked him. Finally he ceased all effort and turned his eyes along the rope. At the far end stood the little mare, legs braced in the sand, and astride her, stolid and grim, and with eyes narrowed, the figure of the large man. At sight of him Pat began to pull again, more through ugliness now than desire to escape, until he found that he was dragging the little gray out of her stiffened hold. Then he slackened off. Also, as she wheeled back toward camp, he set out amiably after her. In camp he found his young friend scattering and deadening the coals of the camp-fire, and the little man making up the saddle-bags. This told him that the journey was to be resumed, and he stood quiet and peaceful as he was being bridled and saddled, and afterward he trotted along under the guidance of his master without show of anger or rebellion. Indeed, though the sun was hot, and the unmarked trail tedious, and the weight on his back heavier than ever, he felt less fretful and more contented than at any time since leaving the little ranch beside the river–possibly because of the thrill of his double encounter.

Ahead and on either hand the desert soon began to break and lift. As they went on the dunes grew to be hills and heights, growing, looming, closing in upon them. Now and again a clump of trees or a shoulder of rock or a stretch of foliage stepped out in relief against the brown of the landscape, revealing more than once ideal grazing-land. Also, as they penetrated deeper into this broken country, the sky overhead showed change. From a spotless blue it revealed tiny splotches of gray-white cloud scudding before upper currents. With the passing hours these clouds became heavy, sullen, and threatening, until the sun, dipping into the west, sinking in a kind of hazy moisture, left the heavens completely overcast, cold and bleak and forbidding–a dense mass of cloud-banks down to the tip of ridge and range. And now came dusk, short and chill, and with it the slow ascent of a long grade, leading them up to a ridge, low and ragged, trailing away interminably to north and south in the gloom. Complete darkness found them deep among high hills.

The men drew rein beside a little stream. They watered the horses, and then, throwing off saddle-bags and gathering brush, they built a tiny fire. Glover appeared nervous and worried, and when the meal was ended turned to mount and be off again. But Johnson called him back. Johnson was seated on the ground, close beside Jim, and Glover sat down with them. Thus they waited, silent, reflective, watching, while about them pressed the close night, seeming by its touch to impart to them something of its solemnity. Off at one side the horses, bridled and saddled, waited also–watching and waiting, motionless, and over them all brooded a stillness that was mighty and portentous. Thus they waited for two hours, wrapped in profound silence, and then Johnson, after scanning the sky, rose and made for the horses. The others quickly followed him. Their trail led into a narrow defile. Up this winding way they rode, with Johnson in the lead, up and ever up, until they burst through a clump of brush at the top. There they drew rein and again waited, silent, reflective, watching. Presently Glover, with eyes turned eastward, uttered a grunt which meant relief.

The clouds in the eastern sky were breaking. Through the heavy banks came a faint glimmering of moonlight. At first but a hair-line, it widened out, reaching up and across the sky, developing steadily into the semblance of a frozen flash of heat lightning, until all the eastern heavens showed a shimmering expanse, broken here and there by black clouds sullenly holding their own, which flooded the underscudding desert in beautiful mottled gray-green coloring. Wider and wider the light spread, up and away on either hand, moving stealthily across the sky, until the sheen of it broke over the ridge itself, and then swept beyond to the west, laying bare a broad expanse of mesa dotted with gray-green specks that told of the presence of hundreds of cattle. And now the sullen clouds took to weaving, swaying under the pressure of upper-air currents, the specks below beginning to lift and fall with the motion of the clouds like bits of wreckage undulate on the sea. The air-drifts descended, came closer, fanning the cheeks of the men, rustling through the leaves which crowned the ridge, and breaking the heavy silence. The air-currents flicked the desert with their freight of swift-moving shadows, causing strange movement among the bits of wreckage– the cattle. It was a glorious march, lighting up the western expanse beneath and revealing a flat country, unbroken by dune or cleft as far as the eye could penetrate. So the light moved on, crowding before it sullen shadows which presently disappeared.

Johnson broke the stillness. "We'd better move along down," he said, and shook Pat's reins.

The horses began the long descent. As compared with the upward climb they made slow progress. Forced to feel their way, they moved always in halts and starts, over saplings, around bulging rocks, along narrow ledges, and at length gained the mesa, where the men drew rein. Johnson, sweeping his eyes coolly over the field of his campaign, began to give orders.

"Jim," he snapped, "cut in over there–that arroyo–and crowd 'em around to the south. Don't go too deep." Then, as Jim caught up his reins, "Glover, swing off this side–close in. We'll keep close in down to the line. Hop along!"

Pat remained standing. He turned his eyes after the little gray and her rider. He saw the pair swing up over a rise of ground at a gallop, dip from view into a hollow, and appear again on the level beyond. Across this they rode, speeding to the opposite slopes, then slackening as they ascended, making quietly among the nervous cattle, horses and riders moving with the easy certainty that told of much experience. Then he saw the head and shoulders of the young man above the surging herd, crowding a part of it slowly in his direction, to the right, to the left, forward and around, always making steadily toward him. It was interesting, and he continued to watch the cool steadiness of the man and the easy control of the horse, until he caught sight of the other, riding the opposite flank, but also crowding steadily toward him. He fell to watching this man, who, not so tall as Jim among the herd, but as quietly active, was also pressing to right and left and forward and around among the cattle, relentlessly cutting them out. Soon there was a general forward movement, the young man riding on the far side, the little man closing up the rear, and this brought the whole herd, some bellowing loudly, others in sullen silence, still others contentedly munching, directly opposite. Then he felt the prick of spurs, and, throwing himself eagerly at the task, he galloped around behind the advancing cattle, falling into the position now abandoned by the little man, who cantered around and forward upon the left flank. It was exciting, and for a moment he thrilled. Then came the only interruption.

A big steer, breaking suddenly out of the herd, tore madly to the rear. Pat, nearest the escaping beef, was spurred in pursuit. It was unexpected, the spurring, and it was savage, and, jolted out of soothing reflection, he flattened his ears and balked. The man spurred him again and again and again, finally raking his sides mercilessly. Whereupon Pat balked in earnest, bucking and pitching viciously. At this the man swung his quirt, cutting Pat repeatedly over head and ears. Yet Pat continued to plunge, holding grimly to his lesson, which was to teach this man the futility of this treatment. He did not throw the man off, but neither did he go ahead. Finally the man ceased his brutality, and evidently coming to understand, headed Pat after the moving herd without spur or quirt. Then Pat, though still rankling under the cruelty, sprang eagerly forward, desirous of showing his willingness to serve when rightly used.

That was all. The night passed quietly, the men, alert to their tasks, each separated from the other, riding stolidly into golden dawn. But not till late, with the sun half-way to its zenith, and then only because of safe distance from possible detection, did they draw rein. Saddle-bags were thrown off, though bridle and saddle were left on in case of emergency, and the horses were turned out on short tethers. The men risked a fire, since they were in the shadow of a ridge, and when the coffee-pot was steaming seated themselves on the ground, in a close circle. For the first time since midnight one spoke. It was Johnson.

"We'll hold west of Lordsburg," he declared, sweeping his eyes gloatingly over the herd. "Francisco Espor and his gang over the line'll weep when they see that bunch–for joy!"

Jim leaned back upon one elbow. "What was that rumpus last night," he inquired, "right after we started?" Then he showed his thoughts. "I mean, the horse."

Johnson swung his head around. For a moment he appeared not to understand. Then suddenly his eyes lost their good-humored twinkle and grew hard.

"Lost one," he answered, abruptly. "The horse stalled." He narrowed his eyes as he stared vindictively at Pat. "I must take a day off, after we get over the line," he snapped, "and break that animal to saddle, bridle, spur, quirt, and rope. He 'ain't never been broke, that horse, and he's naturally mean!"

Jim sat up. "Not with me," he declared, quietly, "when we got acquainted. You ain't taking him right, that's all."

Johnson eyed him surlily. "You're a wonderful piece!" he snapped; and then, by glint of eye and jerk of head showed that he dismissed the subject.

But Jim seemed to feel otherwise. "Maybe I am," he retorted, turning absent eyes in the direction of the horse. "But I ain't all. I happen to know of another wonderful piece. I'm only a one-territory piece."

Johnson grinned. "Go on," he urged, politely.

"There's no 'go on' to it," rejoined Jim, revealing equal politeness. "I'm only thinking of a piece I happen to know that runs about a man that's wanted more or less in seven states and two territories. Running double, he's hard to get."

Johnson reached over coolly and struck him nastily across the mouth. Then as coolly he sat back, while Jim slowly rose to his feet. His eyes were blazing.

"Thanks," he said, tensely. "I've heard a lot about your killings," he went on, breathless with anger. "I guess maybe that's the way—"

"Hush!" broke in Glover, excitedly, his eyes upon the ridge to the east.

The others turned. Moving slowly along the crest, disappearing, reappearing, disappearing again, was the figure of a man. They gazed a long moment, when the figure dropped from view again. They continued to gaze, silent, rigid, watchful, peering narrowly against the morning sunlight. Presently the figure reappeared, lower against the gray background, moving slowly as before, evidently crouching. Lower it came, quarter down the slope, half-way, then again disappeared. Johnson broke the tense silence.

"Sheepherder!" he snapped, and turned savage eyes back upon Jim.

But Glover leaped to his feet. "If that's a sheepherder," he cried, making for the horses at a run, "then I'm a sheep!"

CHAPTER XVII
A RUNNING FIGHT

A rifle-shot forced instant action. Jim whirled away from the camp-fire and saddle-bags and sprang toward the horses, while Johnson, leaping up with the agile twist of an athlete, gained his feet running. Jim headed grimly for Pat, but Johnson reached him a breath in advance. Snatching up the reins and mounting, he dug Pat viciously with his huge rowels. At that Pat balked. The man swore and cursed and spurred again; but the horse remained obdurate. Seeing this, Johnson stopped spurring. Thereupon Pat flung forward, dragging his tether clear of its stake, and crowded close beside the gray. Jim was mounted on the gray, bending low in the saddle, racing in frantic pursuit of Glover. Mounted on the sorrel, Glover was well in the lead, speeding straight into the west, riding at right angles to the ridge, galloping hard for the open desert. The echo of the shot reverberated again faintly, and around them closed a tense silence.

Others were making for the open. Out of the underbrush, riding easily, burst a handful of rangers. Stephen was one of them. As they swept into the clear country, well-armed, well-mounted, the look on their strong, bronzed faces told of their purpose, which was to get the thieves alive, if possible. Down the long slope they galloped, hats low against the sunlight, elbows winging slightly, heads and backs slanting to the winds, speeding like a group of centaurs. Other than Stephen, there were four of these range police. Men of insight, of experience, keen in the ways of the lawless, knowing best of all the type ahead, they rode without strain, without urging, knowing that this was a long race, a matter of endurance, a test, not for themselves so much as for the horses, those of the pursued as well as their own. Loosely scattered, they rode, eyes not upon the thieves, but upon the horses carrying the thieves, as if hopeful for another break like that shown at the start by the magnificent black.

Thus rode the rangers. Not so Stephen. Stephen knew no such laws. All he knew was that after long weeks of futile riding, here at last was Helen's Pat galloping madly away from him. Lashing and spurring his own bay mare, resolute and determined, he gradually began to pull away from the others.

Ahead, Johnson began slowly to gather in his trailing tether-rope. Almost without visible effort he wound it around his saddle-horn. Whereupon Jim, evidently aroused to like danger of tripping, set to work at the loop around the little gray's neck. The knot was tight, and his position cramped, but he persisted, and, with it loose, tossed the rope away. Glover already was free from his trailing rope, having taken the time at the outset hurriedly to cast it off. And he was still in the lead, the sorrel carrying him without seeming effort, and moving steadily away from the others, each long stride gaining half as much ground again as the swinging gait of Pat or the quick and nervous reaching of the little gray. But all were moving at top speed, racing desperately across the desert, leaping sand-dunes, dipping into hollows, mounting eagerly over larger dunes, on and on like the wind, sending up with each fling of hoof swirling clouds of dust and gravel. It was a grim effort.

Such a time comes to but few men. And such a crisis tests the mettle of men and shows the differences. Gripped in a primal emotion, fear for life, weak men show strength, and strong men weakness. Harmless men murder, murderous men weep, blasphemous men pray, praying men curse. Yet under such a stress strong men often reveal greater strength, rising to physical and spiritual heights of reserve that mock a following fate, even as praying men often pray harder and more fervently than ever they prayed in times of calm. Individual in peace, mankind is individual in war. It is the way of man.

And thus it was with these three hurtling forward in the shadow of doom. Glover, ever weak, ever apprehensive, yet always considerate of others, now revealed unexpected strength and appeared considerate only of himself. Crouching in his saddle, apparently mindful of but a single thing–escape–he lashed his horse brutally, swinging his quirt rhythmically, now and again darting cold eyes backward. Johnson, given by nature to bravado and bluster, was even more defiant in this supreme moment. He rode with a plug of tobacco in hand, biting off huge pieces frequently, more frequently squirting brown juices between lips white as the telltale ring around his mouth–a ring as expressive as the hollows beneath his glittering eyes. And Jim, ever worried, ever conscious of himself, sat in his saddle easily, now that he was about to reap the harvest of his ill-sown seeds, riding with eyes on the horse alongside–Pat–studying with coolly critical gaze the animal's smoothness of gait, wonderful carriage of head, unusual and beautiful lifting of forelegs. Thus, in this valley of the shadow, each was his true self and something more, or less, as the chaotic spirit within viewed the immediate future or scanned the distant past.

Another shot from the posse–a screaming bullet high overhead–a command to stop! But they did not stop. Instead, Johnson, rising in his stirrups, unholstered a huge revolver and fired point-blank at the rangers. It was the wrong thing to do, and instantly Jim drew away from the leader. This left a clear gap between, and exposed the speeding Glover ahead to fire from the rear. And suddenly it came, a volley of rifle-shots, and Glover, stiffening suddenly, was seen to clutch at his saddle-horn. Also, he turned his head and shoulders as if to cry out. But he uttered not a sound. Evidently the jostling of his sorrel forbade. He turned his head to the front again, and, slumping low in his saddle, began frantic use of spur and quirt. But the sorrel had lost his stride, and before he could regain it Jim and Johnson had dashed alongside. Jim swung close and looked at Glover. Glover returned the gaze, and again appeared about to speak. But now the sorrel flung forward into his stride, and the movement seemed to decide Glover against all utterance.

But Jim understood. He held close to Glover, but turned his eyes after Johnson. Instantly he scowled and his mouth drew grimly down. For Johnson was swinging off at a tangent, riding out of the set direction, rapidly pulling away from them. For one sullen moment Jim regarded him; then turned his head to the rear. One of the rangers, a young man mounted on a graceful bay–with the rangers, yet apparently not one of them–was riding well forward out of the group. Understanding Johnson's move now, comprehending his utter selfishness in thus swinging away from them, Jim gazed pityingly at Glover. But Glover did not notice him. He himself was following the swift-riding Johnson with blazing eyes, and suddenly he exploded in vindictive anger.

"Put a hole in him!" he cried, hoarsely. "Shoot him! Shoot him, Jim! I–I can't!"

But neither could Jim. It was not his nature. Yet there was one thing he could do. And this he did. He took fresh hold on the reins, and, grim and deliberate and vengeful, swung about after Johnson. Further, in swinging his horse about he purposely crowded the sorrel over also. This brought both in direct pursuit of Johnson, and soon they overtook him. But not because of their greater speed.

Suffering from an unwonted raking of spurs, Pat had taken to sudden rebellion–balking at first, then beginning to buck, flinging about in all directions except the way desired by the fugitive on his back. Riding close and noting this, Jim felt glad beyond all decency. He even chuckled with satisfaction, conscious almost of a desire to dismount and hug the black. Then his feeling changed. He regretted his glee, became fearful for the man, and called sharply to the horse. And now Pat came to a stand. This for a moment only. Then of his own accord he sprang forward again, speeding as eagerly now as but a moment before he had rebelled, and soon he was galloping alongside the gray. Eminently pleased with the whole performance, Jim again chuckled in delight and burst forward at top speed.

Nor was this rebellion lost on Stephen. Riding well forward of the others, when he saw Pat offering resistance he whipped and spurred his mount in the hope that Pat would hold out. But Pat did not hold out, though Stephen knew that he would have, had he but understood. Also, there was his handicap–handicap of the others also. Neither he nor they dared to fire lest they should shoot the black. Occasionally the thieves spread apart, thus giving a chance for a shot with safe regard for Pat. But these openings were infrequent. All they could do was ride in the hope that the thieves might be seized with panic at last and give themselves up.

But no such thought came to the fugitives. Johnson, after his galling experience with Pat, looked more grimly determined than ever to get away. Presently he struck back again. He drew a revolver, rose in his stirrups, and fired twice to the rear. It was not without result. Up from the rangers swept a chorus of yells, and Jim, turning his head, saw the foremost pursuer, the young man who was evidently not a ranger, circle headlong over his tumbling horse. He turned to the front again, and, understanding what would follow, whipped and spurred furiously. Suddenly the answer came. The desert awoke in a fusillade of shots, and Jim saw Glover, who once more was in the lead, drift out of his saddle, slip down much as a child descends from its high-chair, and fall to earth in a crumpled heap. He swerved and dashed alongside. For an instant he drew rein and studied the still face. Then he lifted his eyes, gazing off absently toward the distant skyline, the mellow haze in the hills, the shimmering of heat-waves above the dunes, the glistening reflections of light off myriads of tiny sand cubes. Glover–poor Glover–had paid the price, and had paid it in silence.

He wheeled his horse and sped after Johnson. He overtook him swinging up over a slight elevation. Dead ahead, not more than two miles distant, he saw a long grove of trees. It gave him hope. Here was a chance for effective resistance. Here both he and Johnson could dismount, drive the horses into shelter, seek shelter themselves, and open fire upon the posse. His spirits kindled. He would shoot to kill, as he knew Johnson would shoot to kill, and then, with the rangers helplessly disabled, he would mount Pat, mount the black this time, and if Johnson became ugly he would shoot him. Then he would ride to the east, ride out of this life, and with the horse take up a decent existence somewhere, abandoning crime forever. He would–

More shots from the rear interrupted him. Evidently the rangers, mounting over the rise themselves, had also caught sight of the grove. Evidently, too, they were taking no chances against such a stand as he was contemplating. At any rate, the firing became rapid and continuous, and it was deadly, for suddenly he saw Johnson wilt in the saddle, drop his revolver, drop the reins, and clutch at his left arm. Also he heard a cry–heard it sharp and clear above the pounding of the gray's hoofs and the creak and crunch of his own saddle-leather.

"I'm hit! I'm hit, boy! They–they've got me!" Pat himself heard the outcry and felt the loosened rein. It puzzled him. He did not know whether to keep going or to slacken down. But he kept on going–going hard. Yet he would have welcomed a halt. He was weak and faint. He could not remember the time, save that memorable day on the mesa, when he had run so hard and so continuously. Yet ahead lay trees, and instinctively he accepted them as his destination. In that grove perhaps was water, an opportunity for rest, and abundance of food. So he continued forward, grimly conscious of his burning ankles, his pounding and fluttering heart and heaving and clamoring lungs–plunging forward under the weak urging of his heavy master, responding now through force of habit–feeling that because he was in motion he must continue in motion. It was a numb, mechanical effort, involuntary and apart from him, as much apart from his control as was the beating of his heart.

Another volley came from the rear, and with it another violent change in his master. The man cried out and loosened his feet in the stirrups. Yet Pat continued to gallop until he felt the weight slowly leaving him, felt it go altogether, felt it dangling from one stirrup. Then he came to a stop. As he did so the little gray dashed past–his friend. And now great loneliness gripped him. He started forward. But the weight in his stirrup checked him. He came to a stop again. Then he wanted to nicker in protest, but he found that he could not. He was too weak to utter sound. So he stood there, his eyes upon the little gray and her rider, watching them hurtling toward the grove. Then the thudding of hoofs came to his ears from the rear, and, slowly turning, he saw a group of horsemen riding wearily–one hatless; another with flaying quirt; a third with smoking carbine; a fourth, a large man, smooth and red of face, riding heavily–all galloping toward him.

But they did not hold his interest. His heart and soul lay with the little gray mare, and, turning to the front again, he saw mare and rider swinging out of sight around the end of the grove. Confidently he watched for their appearance beyond. Presently he saw them sweep into view again–moving at a gallop, swinging across a wide plain that held them clear to his straining eyes–saw them grow faint and fainter, small and ever smaller–become a hazy speck on the horizon–finally disappear from view in the engulfing dunes and vales of the surrounding desert. And now, weakened as he was, he sounded a forlorn, protracted nicker of protest.

The rangers pulled up, breathless. They dismounted stiffly, released the weight from Pat's stirrup, and carried it off a little ways. He watched them a moment, noting their ease of movement and business-like air, and then turned his gaze to the horses. All were strange to him, and he looked them over frankly, resting his eyes finally upon a chunky white. Instinctively he knew that this horse was mean, and he hated mean horses as he hated mean men. Observing that this one showed his teeth freely at him, the while holding his small ears almost constantly flat, he measured him for difficulties in the future, if the association were to continue. Then he turned his eyes back to the men.

As he did so, out of the silence rode a single horseman. He was mounted upon the sorrel, and Pat wondered at this. But as the man drew near and Pat saw a blood-smeared, ghastly face, he wondered still more. For there was something familiar about this lone rider, and he took a step toward him. Presently he saw him gain the outer edge of the circle, and then a strange thing happened. He saw the young man begin to weave in his saddle, saw two of the others suddenly leap for him–saw them reach him just in time to save him from tumbling limply to the ground. Then he noted another queer thing. He saw the young man's left arm dangle oddly from the shoulder; saw the young man himself grasp it, wincing with excruciating pain, and saw him turn wide eyes suddenly toward him. Then he heard the man speak.

"Look–look him over!" he cried, and his voice was a curious mixture of distress and restrained excitement. "I–I don't want him–him to go back–to go back–hurt–hurt in–in–"

And now Pat saw the strangest thing of all. He saw the young man slowly close his eyes and sink back into the arms of the others as one dead. He saw the others exchange troubled glances and lay the insensible form down tenderly on the sand. It was all very unusual, something new in his life; and, not knowing what else to do, yet somehow feeling that he should do something, be it never so little, he lowered his head and sounded a trembling nicker into the silence.

CHAPTER XVIII
AN ENEMY

There was water in the grove, and the men made camp at the edge of the trees. "The Doc," which was what the rangers early had affectionately nicknamed Stephen, was suffering a compound fracture of the left arm, together with numerous bruises and scratches about the head and face. He had had a nasty fall. His horse had stumbled and almost instantly died as the result of the big cattle-rustler's shots. The men set and splinted Stephen's arm as best they could, and they bandaged his head with rare skill; but it was deemed advisable for him to remain quiet for a time.

So Stephen lay listlessly smiling at the bantering of the men, too sick at heart really to take interest in any living thing. His arm pained him, and his head ached, while throughout his body he was sore and stiff and well-nigh incapable of moving. But not once following the first complete collapse did he let go of himself, although when the men set his arm it seemed that he must. Somehow he was contented that everything was as it was. True, he was hurt. But also he had found Pat, had recovered the horse for Helen, and the horse now was within sound of his voice, did he but care to lift it. His physical hurts would get well, his spiritual hurts never without the recovery of the horse. And now he had the horse.

One morning it became apparent that their food-supplies would soon need replenishing. So it was decided to break camp for the nearest town, a Mexican settlement some eighty miles to the southwest. Stephen had been walking about somewhat cheerfully for three or four days, and his condition was such that he could ride forward slowly without danger to his arm. So they broke camp, utilizing the sorrel as a pack-horse–there now were two extra saddles and bridles–and set out, Stephen, of course, mounted upon Pat.

Once more Pat found himself following an unmarked and desolate trail. Moving always at a walk now instead of the conventional fox-trot, he found his service, save for this and one other thing, identical with that under his previous masters. The single other difference was that instead of irritating silence, these men unwittingly soothed him with their talk and swift exchange of jokes. Thus the hours passed, until noon came, when, with his bridle and saddle removed, and pungent odors of savory cooking tickling his nostrils, he received the privilege of grazing over the whole desert unhobbled and untethered. But this, liberal as it seemed, brought him nothing of the nourishment his soul craved. After an hour or two of lazy wandering, while the men passed the time at cards, he was sent forward again along the ever-mysterious trail. And thus he moved, through the long hot afternoon, the cool and lingering twilight, on to a night camp where once more he was turned loose with the other horses to glean as best he might life-giving sustenance from the scant herbage. But it was drearily monotonous.

Throughout it all, however, there was one who kept his interest alive. It was the white horse. In the camp holding himself aloof, as if superciliously refraining from close contact, on the trail this horse took to revealing his antagonism. He would stand a short way from him while they grazed, lay back his ears and whisk his tail, and, whenever the chance came, he would snap viciously at the other horses. Pat understood the meaning of all this, and held himself ready to resist attack, yet he simply looked at the horse with a kind of amused speculation. Nor at any time did he feel grave apprehension. That he did not take the horse seriously lay in the fact that after drawing near in this fashion and bristling nastily the white horse would quickly draw away again, steadily and craftily, and then fall to worrying one of the other horses, usually one of smaller size that quite obviously feared him.

There came the time when the white did not confine his threatenings to the grazing-periods. He became aggressive on the march. Though less free to give battle here, which was possibly his reason, he would frequently jockey close, and either flash his head around with teeth snapping, or else, as if to make Pat feel inferiority, would plunge forward to a point immediately in front, and in this position fling back choking dust or gravel. At such times the round-faced man, the white's master, would drag him away mightily, or, if he was not quick enough, then the sorrel, drowsing along behind on a lead-rope, would unconsciously offer resistance. But it was all very disagreeable, and Pat, while finding that it broke up the monotony of the journey, yet at length found himself also becoming irritated.

He finally gave way to it. It was his nature to brood over annoyances and sometimes to heap grains of injustice into mountains of woes. He fell to thinking of his general lot, his misfortunes, the lack of proper food, the occasional lack of water, until he became sullen and peevish. The change showed in sudden starts at unusual sounds which brought sharp protests from his young master, and then he began to refuse to eat. This was grave, and he knew it. But he could not or would not help it; he never knew quite which it was. But he did not eat. Instead of moving about with the other horses, nose to ground, mouthing the bunch-grass, he would mope by himself well away from the other horses, standing with head hanging and ears inert, all in motionless silence. As the water-holes became farther apart, and the grazing worse yet, he did this more and more, until the white horse, evidently seeing his lack of spirit, became a source of downright aggravation, frequently taking lightning nips at him. At such times Pat would lift his head and hold himself erect and vigilant during the grazing-period, but he brooded, none the less, and as persistently refused to eat.

This was not lost upon Stephen or the rangers, neither his refusing to eat nor the white's antagonism. They spent hours discussing both. Having found in Pat none of the regular symptoms of disease, yet aware that something grave was the matter, the rangers fell to discussing Pat's condition with much earnestness, frequently interrupting their arguments on the one subject to declare that the white horse, provided Pat held out and healed up against his complaint, would get a fight such as was never before witnessed in the desert. That they were evenly matched both as to build and strength was recognized; that Pat was possessed of a reserve that told of finer courage all agreed. Yet in this last lurked opportunities for argument; and argue they did, sometimes long into the night, the little man known as the Professor and the rangy individual with the scrubby beard showing the greatest vehemence. Yet despite all their arguments, to which Stephen invariably listened in smiling silence, none as yet had offered good reason for the villainous attitude of the white toward the peaceful Pat.

"*I* know!" suddenly declared the man with the scrubby beard one evening, after the tin dishes had been cleared away. "It's jealousy!"

He narrowed his eyes out through the darkness in the direction of the horses. "Who ever 'u'd believe old Tom out there 'u'd show jealousy? I see it, though, the first day. You recollect we made a heap of the black, kind of petting him up some, and Tom, bein', as he sure is, an intelligent hoss, I reckon he figured it out that he'd played the game and been faithful all along, and then to see himself set back that way by a complete stranger, it jest nachelly made him sore. Same as it would you or me, mebbe, if we was informed polite and all that from headquarters that they was a new man comin' to jine us that was the pure quill whichever way you looked at him. Old Tom is bein' et up with jealousy, I'm regretful to say."

"Animiles feels things a heap more'n humans does," put in the little man known as the Professor. "But they're more reserved in showin' 'em out. Yit when they do show 'em out, they're a lot less polite about it than humans."

"Nachelly," snapped the lean man, glaring savagely across the fire at the other. "But that ain't tellin' us what ails the black," he went on, dropping the subject of the white and taking up with the symptoms of the black, evidently through perverseness. "He's solemn and dumpish," he declared, thoughtfully, "like he might have distemper. But he 'ain't got distemper. And his teeth ain't sharp, yet he don't eat at all. And I can't see anything the matter with his insides."

"Did you look?" inquired the Professor, innocently, but with a quick wink at Stephen.

"Yes, I–" began the lean man, only to check himself with an angry snort. Then he shifted the topic again, reverting to the case of old Tom. "That white hoss'll about push that matter to a finish," he declared. "See if what I say don't pan out! Tom he'll just about obey that law o' nature which animals has knowed from long before the ark, but which us humans is just gettin' a hold on. He'll remove the cause–old Tom will–or get himself removed. He ain't nobody's fool– nor never was!" And he rested his eyes significantly upon the Professor.

The Professor was busy, however. He had pulled a deck of cards from his hip pocket, and now was riffling them with pointed interest. Directly he began to deal them around, carefully overlooking the lean man as he did so. But the latter, dropping over upon one elbow, permitted the game to proceed without offering objection to the oversight, a peculiar one, since he was in the full glare of the fire.

That argument was closed.

But next morning Pat received unexpected attention. His young master approached him, looped a rope around his neck, and gave the end to the large man, who mounted the white. Then the lean man bridled and saddled the sorrel for the young man, who evidently was unable conveniently to do these things with his one hand. After this he loaded Pat with the extra saddles and bridles, and thus they set out. It was a not unfavorable change, and Pat, while harboring mixed emotions, since he now was trailing along behind the white, yet found himself in a lighter mood. Feeling little jealousy of the white, however, he soon forgot the changed relations, finding in his own position a new viewpoint upon the cavalcade which was interesting. For now he could survey the whole squad, five horses of varied size and action, and this, as he studied the individual gait of each, was not without its pleasure. Also, being, as he was, free from the weight of a man, he felt an airy lightness that was positively refreshing. And finally, since he was out of reach of the nagging white, this blessing alone made him grateful. So he followed along, working yet not working, with a feeling of complete composure such as had not been his for many a day.

Still his composure did not last. The novelty wore off toward noon, and he found himself morose and introspective again. Sounding the depths of his grievances, he at length took to thinking of the white corral beside the river. Not in many a day had he thought of the ranch. But he was recalling it now, not through affection, not because it was home to him, but because, brooding over his many discomforts in the open, he was suddenly remembering that his life had not always been this–that he knew actual comfort, knew what it was to have his wants gratified. And recalling these facts, he naturally recalled that which had made them possible–the little ranch in the valley. So he let his thoughts linger there. Faint and elusive at first, those other days became finally quite vivid, days of expectancy and gratification, days of sugar and quartered apples, days of affection and love-talk from his pretty little mistress. And how he missed them all! How he missed them–even the Mexican hostler and the brown saddler and the old matronly horse–his mother by adoption! But they were gone from him now, gone for all time out of his life. Yet though he believed them gone, he continued to brood on them, to live each day over again in his thoughts, till the men ahead dismounted suddenly. Then he was glad to turn his attention to other matters, things close around him. One of these was the coming of the lean man with a pair of familiar objects in his hands–this after the noonday meal.

"Well, my bucky," he began, turning critical eyes over Pat, "I been studyin' your case a heap, and I've come to think I'm old Doctor Sow himself. Your young man here is knocked out of all possible good," he went on, as Stephen smilingly approached, "and so it occurred to me, sir, as how you ain't sick no more'n I be. What ails you is you're an aristocrat–something that's been knocked around unusual–what with them rustlers and with us that's worse than rustlers–and got yourself all mussed up and unfit! All you need is a cleanin'–that's what ails you! You're just nice furniture–a piece o' Sheraton, mebbe–that's all over sweepings, and I'm the he-maid that's going to dust you off. Hold still, now."

So Pat, after taking a step toward Stephen, who now was stroking him tenderly, held very still, not only under the soothing caress, but under the operation–for such was the cleaning–since he was gritty beyond belief. Also, after the operation he felt immeasurably better, and better still when Stephen led him to a tiny stream and he had relieved his thirst. But that was not all of joy. Turned loose with the other horses, he fell to grazing eagerly, actually finding it good, and once lifting a long and shrill nicker in gratitude for this change in his condition. Nor did his delight stop here. With camp broken, and his young master, instead of returning him to the lead-rope, bridling and saddling him awkwardly with one hand, he set out along the trail at a gait so brisk that it brought a startled exclamation from the young man, who promptly pulled him down. But though he was forced to keep a slow gait, yet frequently during the afternoon, conscious of his fresh coat and the sense of buoyancy it gave him, he flung up his head and nickered loud and joyfully. Also, with night once more descending, and the stars twinkling in the blue-black heavens, and the sheen of a rising moon flooding the desert, he moved about among the other horses with a vigor that was almost insolence, seizing tufts of grass wherever he saw them, heedless of others' rights.

Around the fire sat or sprawled the men. Two of them were industriously mending, one a shirt, the other a bridle. The Professor and the man with the scrubby beard were complacently smoking, while Stephen, glad to stretch out after the day's ride with an arm that constantly distressed him, was reclining upon a blanket, staring into the flames and conjuring up in their leaping tongues numerous soothing pictures. As he sat there the man with the beard suddenly addressed him.

"Doc," he drawled, removing his pipe from between whiskers that glinted in the light of the fire, "now that you've got him, what are you thinking of doing with that horse?"

"I'll take him back," replied Stephen, pleasantly.

The other was silent. "Shore!" he rejoined, after a moment. "But take him back where?"

"Where he belongs."

There was further silence. "Excuse me!" finally exclaimed the other. "I was thinking as mebbe you'd take him whence he came."

Stephen sat erect and looked at the other. He was smoking again complacently.

"Whence come you?" asked Stephen, after a time.

The other slowly removed his pipe. Then he told him. Then Stephen spoke. And then the man rose stiffly, crossed solemnly to him and shook hands with him cordially.

"I knowed you was white the fust day I see you," he declared. Then he waved a vague hand over the others. "They've all–all of 'em– traveled that way. I was raised–"

A sudden shrill scream out in the darkness interrupted him. It was a horse. The cry stirred the entire camp. The Professor arose, sauntered out, whistling, whirled, and called back sharply. The others ran toward him; the large man struck a match. The white horse was limping on three legs. They bent over and examined the fourth. The match went out. All straightened up. As they did so Pat sounded a shrill nicker.

"Busted!" exclaimed the large man, quietly. "Well, I'm a goat! That black horse has kicked old Tom clear over the divide. I–I'm clean done! Quick as lightning, too! No preambles; no circumlocutions; no nothing. Just put it to him. Good Lord!" Then he regretfully drew a revolver. "I reckon you boys better stand back."

A shot broke the quiet, and the desert shivered and was still again. The white horse sank to the ground. Stephen walked to Pat, struck a match, and looked him over critically. Pat was torn and bleeding in two places along the neck, but otherwise he needed no attention. Stephen patted him thoughtfully, gratefully, fighting the horror of what might have been had this splendid horse weakened in the crisis. No wonder the little girl in the valley worshiped him.

But he said nothing. After a time he returned to the fire and sat down among a very sober group of men. Presently the man with the scrubby beard broke the quiet. His voice sounded hollow and distressed.

"I knowed it," he declared. "Though I thought old Tom 'u'd done better." He began to roll a cigarette. "Pore old Tom! He's killed; he's dead–dead and gone." With the cigarette made, he snatched a brand from the fire and lighted it. He fell to smoking in thoughtful silence, in his eyes a look of unutterable sadness.

The Professor bestirred himself. "Tell me," he asked, lifting his gaze to the heavens reflectively–"tell me, does any of you believe that horses–any animiles–has souls?"

The lean man glanced at him. His eyes now had the look of one anxious to express his views, but cautiously refused to be baited. Finally he made answer.

"If you're askin' my opinion," he said, "I'll tell you that I know they have." He was silent. "I know that animals has the same thing we've got," he continued–"that thing we call the soul–but they've got it in

141

smaller proportions, so to speak. It's easy as falling off a bucking bronc. Take old Tom out there. Take that Lady horse that got killed two years ago by rustlers–take any horse, any dumb animal–and I'll show you in fifteen different ways that they've got souls."

"How?"

The lean man glared. "Now 'how'!" he snapped. "You give me a mortal pang. Why don't you never use your eyes once like other and more decent folks? Get the habit. You'll see there ain't any difference between animals and humans, only speech, and they've got that!"

The large man smiled. "Let's have it, Bob," he invited. "Where'll we look for it first?"

The lean man showed an impatience born of contempt. "Well," he began, tossing away his cigarette, "in desires, first, then in their power to appreciate, and, finally, in their sense of the worth of things. They have that, and don't you think they hain't. But they've got the others, too. Animals like to eat and drink and play, don't they? You know that! And they understand when you're good to 'em and when you're cussed mean. You know that. And they know death when they see it, take it from me, because they're as sensitive to loss of motion, or breathing, or animal heat, as us humans–more so. They feel pain, for instance, more'n we do, because, lackin' one of the five–or six, if you like–senses, their other senses is keyed up higher'n our'n."

The Professor looked belligerent. "Get particular!" he demanded.

"I won't get particular," snapped the other. "S'pose you wrastle it out for yourself–same as us humans." Evidently he was still bitter against this man. "That Lady horse o' mine," he went on, his eyes twinkling, addressing himself to the others, "she had it all sized about right. She used to say to me, when I'd come close to her in the morning: 'Well, old sock,' she'd say, throwin' her old ears forward, 'how are you this mornin'?–You know,' she'd declare, 'I kind o' like you because you understand me.' Then she'd about wipe her nose on me and go on. 'Wonder why it is that so many of you don't! It's easy enough, our language,' she'd p'int out, 'but most o' you two-legged critters don't seem to get us. It's right funny! You appear to get 'most everything else–houses, and land, and playin'-cards, and sich. But you don't never seem to get us–that is, most o' you! Why, 'tain't nothin' but sign language, neither–same as Injuns talkin' to whites. But I reckon you're idiots, most o' you, and blind, you hairless animals, wearin' stuff stole offen sheep, and your ugly white faces mostly smooth. You got the idee we don't know nothin'–pity us, I s'pose, because we can't understand you. Lawzee! We understand you, all right. It's you 'at don't understand us. And that's the hull trouble. You think we're just a lump o' common dirt, with a little tincture o' movement added, just enough so as we can run and drag your loads around for you. Wisht you could 'a' heard me and old Tom last night, after you'd all turned in, talkin' on the subject o' keepin' well and strong and serene o' mind. Sign language? Some. But what of it, old whiskers? Don't every deef-and-dumb party get along with few sounds and plenty of signs? You humans give me mortal distress!'

"And so on," concluded this lover of animals. "Thus Lady horse used to talk to me every mornin', tryin' to make me see things some little clearer. And that's all animals–if you happen to know the 'try me' on their little old middle chamber work." He fell silent.

The others said nothing. Each sat smoking reflectively, gazing into the dying flames, until one arose and prepared to turn in. Stephen was the last except the Professor and the man with the scrubby beard. And finally the Professor gained his feet and, with a glance at the last figure remaining at the fire, took off his boots and rolled up in his blanket. For a long moment he stared curiously at the other bowed in thought.

"Ain't you goin' to turn in?" he finally inquired. "You ain't et up by nothin', be you?"

The lean man slowly lifted his head. "I was thinkin'," he said, half to himself, "of a–a kind of horse's prayer I once see in a harness-shop in Albuquerque."

The other twisted himself under his blanket. "How did it go?" he asked, encouragingly. "Let's all have it!"

The lean man arose. "'To thee, my master,' it started off," he began, moving slowly toward his blanket. Suddenly he paused. "I–I don't just seem to remember it all," he said, and sat down and pulled off one of his boots. He held it in his hands absently.

The Professor urged him on. "Let her come," he said, his face now hidden in the folds of his covering. "Shoot it–let's hear."

"'To thee, my master, I offer my prayer,'" presently continued the other, turning reflective eyes toward the flickering coals. "'Feed me, water me, care for me, and, when the–the day's work is done, provide me with shelter and a clean, dry bed, and, when you can, a stall wide enough for me to lie down in in comfort. Always be kind to me. Talk to me–your voice often means as much to me as the reins. Pet me sometimes, that I may serve you the more gladly and know that my services are appreciated, and that I may learn to love you. Do not jerk the reins, and do not whip me when going up-hill. And when I don't understand you, what you want, do not strike or beat or kick me, but give me a chance to understand you. And if I continue to fail to understand, see if something is not wrong with my harness or feet.'"

The Professor's blanket stirred. "Go on!" he yelled. "Sounds all right. Go ahead! Is that all?"

"I disremember the rest," replied the other. "Let's see!" He was silent. "No," he finally blurted out, "I can't get it. It says something about overloading, and a-hitching where water don't drop on him, and–Oh yes! 'I can't tell you when I'm thirsty,' it goes on, 'so give me cool, clean water often. Never put a frosty bit in my mouth; first warm it by holdin' it a moment in your hands. And, remember, I try to carry you and your burdens without a murmur, and I wait patiently for you long hours of the day and night. Without power to choose my shoes or path, I sometimes stumble and fall, but I stand always in readiness at any moment to lose my life in your service. And this is important, and, finally, O my master! when my useful strength is gone do not turn me out to starve, or sell me to some cruel owner to be slowly tortured and starved to death; but do thou, my master, take my life in the kindest way, and your God will reward you here and hereafter. You will not consider me irreverent, I know, if I ask all this in the name of Him Who was born in a stable.'"

The Professor's blanket stirred again. "Go on," he demanded in muffled tones. "Is that all?"

The lean man slipped off his second boot. "No," he replied, quietly, "that ain't all."

"Well, go ahead. It's good. That horse must 'a' been a city horse; but go on!"

"Only one more word, anyway," was the rejoinder. He was still holding his boot.

"What is it?"

"Why"–the voice was solemn–"it's 'Amen.'"

"Aw, shucks!" came from the depths of the blanket.

The lean man turned his head. "Say, you!" he rasped, belligerently.

"What?"

For answer the boot sailed across the camp.

The Professor popped his head out of the blanket, drew it back suddenly, popped it out again, all strongly suggestive of a turtle.

There was a hoarse laugh, then silence, but none of those men forgot the Prayer of the Horse.

CHAPTER XIX
ANOTHER CHANGE OF MASTERS

The next morning Pat had a change from the tedium of the desert. With the others he struck into a narrow canyon that led out to a beaten trail upon a rolling mesa. The trail wound diagonally across the mesa from the south and lost itself in snake-like twistings among hills to the north. Guided to the right into this trail, Pat found himself, a little before noon, in a tiny Mexican settlement. It was a squat hamlet, nestling comfortably among the hills, made up of a few adobes, a lone well, and a general store. The store was at the far end, and toward this his young master directed him.

As they rode on Pat noticed a queer commotion. Here and there a door closed violently, only to open again cautiously as they drew opposite, revealing sometimes two, sometimes three, sometimes five pairs of black eyes, all ranged timidly one pair over another in the opening. Dogs skulked before their approach, snarling in strange savagery, while whole flocks of chickens, ruffling in dusty hollows, took frantically to wing at their coming, fleeing before them in unwonted disorder. And finally, as they moved past the well, a half-grown boy, only partly dressed, hurtled out of the side door of one house, raced across a yard to the front door of another house, and slammed the door shut behind him in a panic.

It was all very strange, and it made a deep impression upon him. Also it evidently impressed the men, for as they drew rein in front of the store, with its dust-dry shelves and haunting silence, all asked quick questions of the proprietor, a little wizened, gimlet-eyed Mexican who was leaning in the doorway. After glancing over their accoutrements with a nod of understanding, he answered, explaining the reason for the agitation.

It was all the result of a raid. Three days before a band of marauders had swept down from the north, ransacked pigstys and chicken-coops and corrals, and galloped off madly to the south. Yes, they had plundered the store also. Indian renegades–yes. He could not say from what reservation. Yes, they were armed, and in warpaint, and riding good horses–all of them. No, he could not say–about thirty in the band, perhaps. He–What? Yes, he had alfalfa and, if they wished, other things–beans and rice and canned goods. No, the renegades had not wholly cleaned out the store. Yes, he had matches. No, they had not– What? *Vino?* To be sure he had *Vino!* He would get–how many bottles?–right away! It was in the cellar, where he kept it cool, and reasonably safe from all marauders–including himself. With this slight witticism he disappeared into the store.

The men dismounted. They sat down upon the porch, and one of them, the large man, removed his hat, produced a blue bandana, and fell to mopping his red face. The day was warm, and the settlement, lying low under surrounding peaks, received none of the outside breezes. Also, it was inert now, wrapped in the quiet of a frightened people. There was no movement anywhere save that of ruffling hens in the dust of the trail, and the nearer switching of horses' tails. Once this stillness was broken. Among the houses somewhere rose feminine lamentations, wailing sobs, the outburst cutting the quiet with a sharpness that caused the men to turn grave eyes in its direction. And now the keeper of the store reappeared, bearing three bottles of wine in his arms, and numerous supplies, which the men accepted and paid for. Then all led their horses back to the well, which was in a little clearing, and there prepared to make camp, throwing off saddle-bags and accoutrements and building a fire while they planned a real meal.

Pat was enjoying all this. The settlement had a faintly familiar look, and he half expected to see a swarthy Mexican, whip in hand, approach him with abusive tongue. Also, after weeks of far horizons and unending sweeps of desert, he found in this nearness of detail pleasurable relief. It was good to see something upright again without straining across miles of desolation, even as it was good to see adobes once more, with windows and doors, and smoke curling up out of chimneys. He felt a deep sense of security, of coziness, which he had been fast losing on the broad reaches, together with his sight for short distances. For his eyes had become affected since leaving the white corral beside the river, although with this he was aware of a peculiar gain. His sense of hearing now was most acute, and he could hear the least faint sounds–sounds which, before his taking to the open, he could not have heard. So he was enjoying it all, feeling real comfort, a kind of fitness, as if he belonged here and would better remain here for ever. Then, with a generous supply of alfalfa tossed to him, as to the other horses, he became convinced that he should remain in this little settlement for all time.

Along in the afternoon the storekeeper, accompanied by a native woman, who was tear-stained and weeping, crossed the settlement. At the moment the men, lounging about on blankets, were discussing ways and means for Stephen. He need not continue with them now, they informed him, unless he wanted to. Arrangements could be made here to get him to a railroad in some kind of vehicle, leading Pat behind. But it was up to him. They weren't hurrying him away, by any means, yet it sure was up to him to get proper treatment for his arm, which showed slow signs of recovery.

Stephen was considering this when the two Mexicans approached. The proprietor of the store started to explain, when the little woman draped in a black mantilla interrupted him with further sobbing and a pointing finger–pointing back across the settlement.

"*Caballeros*," she began, "you coom please wit' me, I–I haf show you soomt'ing." Then again she burst into weeping.

Startled, Stephen arose, and the others gained their feet. They set out across the settlement. They struck between some adobe houses, crossed some back yards, dodged under clothes-lines, and found themselves in a tiny graveyard. The woman brought them to a stop before a fresh mound of earth. Here she knelt in another outburst of tears, while the gimlet-eyed storekeeper explained.

It was a little boy twelve years old. The marauders had stolen his pig. He had bitterly denounced them, and one–evidently the leader–had shot him. It was too bad! But it was not all. In one of the houses, the large house they had passed in coming here, lay an old man, seventy-eight years of age, dying from a rifle-shot. Yes, the renegade Indians had shot him also. What had he done? He had defended his chickens against theft. It was too bad! It was all too bad! Could not there something be done? To live in peace, to live in strict accord with all known laws, such was the aim and such had been the conduct of these people. And then to have a band of cutthroats, murderers, thieves, descend upon their peace and quiet in this fashion! It was all too bad!

The rangers turned away from the scene. All save the woman set out across the settlement, returning to the camp in silence. Seated once more, they fell to discussing this situation. And discussing the tragedy, they reverted to Stephen and his own troubles, light in comparison. They themselves, they acknowledged, had their work all cut out for them. It was what they got their money for. But there was hardly any use, they pointed out, in Stephen's accompanying them on this mission. Yet he could go if he wanted to. What did he say?

And Stephen, gazing off thoughtfully toward the tiny mound of fresh earth, and seeing the little woman prostrated with grief upon the grave, knew that Helen, herself bitter with loss, and no doubt needing Pat as much almost as this woman needed her own lost one, would have him do what he wanted to do. And what he wanted to do, felt as if he must do, was to accompany these men, go with them, disabled though he was, and help as best he could to bring down retribution upon the renegades. And he made known his wishes to the others, finally, expressing them with a note of determination.

As they bridled and saddled, leaving all equipment not actually required, the proprietor of the store, his small eyes eager, stood close and frequently repeated his opinion that murder in even more gruesome form had been committed to the north. Then they set out, following the direction taken by the Indians, riding briskly, keyed up to energy through hope of encounter, although Stephen suffered not a little from the jolting of his arm. Dropping down from the hills, they swung out upon the mesa, and thence made into the south along a winding trail. Ordinarily they would have lingered to accept the strained hospitality of the settlement. But this was duty, duty large and grave, and, conscious of it all, they pressed forward in silence. The renegades' tracks stood out clearly, and the rangers noted that some of the horses were shod, others only half shod, while the greater number were without shoes at all. This told of the marauders' nondescript collection of mounts, and also acquainted them with the fact that many of the animals had been stolen. On through the afternoon they rode, making but little gain, since the tracks became no fresher. When darkness fell, though still in the open without protection of any kind save that offered by a slight rise of ground, they dismounted and prepared to make camp.

Throughout the afternoon Pat had felt something of the grim nature of this business. This not only because of the severe crowding which he had endured–though that had told him much–but because of the unwonted silence upon the men. So he had held himself keenly to the stride, rather liking its vigor after long days of walking, finding himself especially fit to meet it after his recent change of food. And although the sun had been swelteringly hot, yet the desert had been swept with counteracting breezes, and, with night finally descending, he had felt more than ever his fine mettle, and now, even though his master was painfully dismounting, he felt fit to run his legs off at the least suggestion.

This fitness remained with him. When his young master turned him loose at the end of a generous tether, he stepped eagerly away from the firelight and out into the light of a rising moon, not to graze, for he felt no desire to graze, having eaten his fill and more at noon, but to give vent to his high spirits in unusual rolling in the sands. This he quickly proceeded to do, kicking and thrashing about, and holding to it long after the men about the fire had ceased to come and go in preparing their meal, long after they had seated themselves in the cheerful glow, smoking and talking as was their habit.

The Professor noticed it. He looked at the man with the beard pointedly. "That Pat hoss he's workin' up another job o' cleanin' for you," he observed. "Seemed in an awful hurry, too," he added, then dropped his eyes innocently.

The other was punching new holes in his belt with an unwieldy jack-knife. He suddenly gave off twisting the point of the knife against the leather and lifted it menacingly in the direction of his tormentor.

"Look-a-here, Professor," he retorted, "I ain't feelin' any too pert right now, and I'll take a hop out o' you if you don't shet up!"

The Professor looked grieved. "What's the matter of you?" he inquired.

"Never you mind!" The knife went back to the leather again. "Let that horse roll if he wants to! It ain't any skin off your hands!"

150

Which was the key-note of all assembled save the Professor. All except him appeared tense and nervous and in no way inclined to joke. For a time after the lean man's rebuke they engaged in casual talk, then one after another they drew off their boots and rolled up in their blankets. All but Stephen. His arm was throbbing with unusual pain. It was still in splints, and still bandaged in a sling around his neck, and since it always hurt him to change positions, he remained seated beside the fire, wrapped in sober thought. Outside, in the green-white light of the moon, he heard the horses one by one sink to rest. Around him the desert, gripped in death-stillness, pressed close, while overhead the star-sprinkled dome of heaven, unclouded, arched in all its wonted glittering majesty. A long time he sat there, keenly alive to these things, yet thinking strange thoughts, thoughts of his loneliness, and what might have been, and where he might have been, had he never met the girl. These were new thoughts, and he presently arose to rid himself of them and turned in, and soon was in a doze.

Some time later, he did not know how much later, he was aroused by a sound as of distant thunder. But as he lifted his head the sound disappeared. Yet when he dropped his head back again he heard it. He pressed his left ear close to earth. The sound grew louder and seemed to come nearer. Again he lifted his head. As before, he could hear nothing save the snoring of the large man and the dream-twitching of the Professor. He gazed about him. The camp was still. He peered outside in the moonlight. The horses were all down–at rest. At length he dropped back once more, closed his eyes sleepily, and soon dozed a second time.

But again he was aroused. He whipped up his head. The sound was thundering in his ears. He heard trampling hoofs–many hoofs–immediately outside. He leaped to his feet. He saw horsemen–Indians–the renegades–crowding past, riding frantically to the north. He called sharply to the others, who were already waking and leaping to their feet. He turned to the horses. They were all there, standing now, alert and tense. Wheeling, he stared after the Indians. They were speeding away like the wind, close huddled, fleeing in a panic. He watched them, dazed, saw them ascend a rise, become a vacillating speck in the moonlight, and drop from view in a hollow beyond the rise. He turned to the men. All stood in mute helplessness, only half comprehending. He opened his mouth to speak, but as he did so there came a sudden interruption.

It was a bugle-call, rollicking across the desert, crashing into the death-like hush which had settled upon the camp. He turned his eyes toward the sound–to the south. Over a giant sand-dune, riding grouped, with one or two in the lead, swept a company of cavalrymen. Down the slope they galloped, moonlight playing freely upon them, bringing out every detail–the glint of arms, the movement of hat-brims, the lift and fall of elbows–pounding straight for the camp. Another blast of the bugle, crisp and metallic, and they swerved; they drew near, nearer still, came close on the right, and swept past in a whirlwind of sounds, thundering hoofs, cursing men, slamming carbines, creaking saddles, snorting horses. So they swept on into the north, pushing, crowding, jostling, throwing back flying gravel, odors of sweat, swirling dust-clouds. They mounted rapidly over the rise, and became, as the pursued, vacillating specks, and then disappeared in the hollow beyond.

Stephen recovered himself. He swept his eyes again over the horses. He saw a change among them. Three were calm, but not the other two. Both of them were weaving faintly, and, even as he sprang to them, one sank slowly to the ground. Wondering, dazed, gripped in apprehension, he bent over it. The horse was a stranger, and it was gasping its last breath. Dismayed, he turned to the other. This horse also was a strange horse, and it was white with foam and panting, also run to death. Astonished, cold with apprehension, he looked for Pat. But neither Pat nor the sorrel was to be seen. Then the truth overwhelmed him. The renegades, seeing fresh horses here, had made a swift change. Pat was gone!

For one tense moment he stood spellbound. Then he sprang into action. He dressed as best he could, called to the others to bridle and saddle a horse, and leaped into the saddle. His whole body rebelled at the movement. But he set his jaw grimly, and, clutching at his bandaged arm, yet keeping his grip on the reins, he spurred frantically after the cavalry. As he dashed away he shouted back his purpose.

But the men, standing with wide eyes turned after him, heard only the end:

"I'll get him in spite of hell!"

CHAPTER XX
FIDELITY

Meantime Pat was running at top speed across the desert. Yet he was trying to understand this strange call to duty. Roused from fitful slumber by trampling hoofs, he had felt an excited hand jerking him to his feet, and after that a slender rope looped round his lower jaw. Then he had been urged, with a wriggling form on his bare back, frantic heels drumming his sides, and a strange voice impelling him onward past a surging crowd of horsemen, still only half awake, out into the open. When he was well in the fore, he had found himself crowded to his utmost–over sand-dune, into arroyo, across the level– around him thundering hoofs, panting horses, silent men, all speeding forward in the glorious moonlight. It was a strange awakening, yet he had not entertained thoughts of rebellion, despite the fact that he had not liked the flaying rope, the soft digging heels, the absence of bridle and saddle. It was strange; it was not right. None of it had checked up with any item of his experience. Yet, oddly enough, he had not rebelled.

Nor was he harboring thoughts of rebellion now. Racing onward, smarting with each swing of the lash, he found himself somehow interested solely in holding his own with the other horses. Suddenly, alert to their movements, he saw a cleft open in their surging ranks, made by the fall of an exhausted horse. Yet the others did not stop. They galloped on, unheeding, though he himself was jerked up. Then followed a swift exchange of words, and then the unhorsed man mounted behind Pat's new master. Carrying a double load now, Pat nevertheless dashed ahead at his former speed, stumbling with his first steps, but soon regaining his stride and overtaking the others. And though it cost him straining effort, he felt rewarded for his pains when one of the men uttered a grunt which he interpreted as approval. But it was all very strange.

A canyon loomed up on his left. He had hardly seen the black opening when he was swung toward it. He plunged forward with the other horses, and was the first to enter the canyon's yawning mouth. Between its high walls, however, he found himself troubled by black shadows. Many of them reached across his path like projections of rock, and more than once he faltered in his stride. But after passing through two or three in safety he came at length to understand them and so returned to his wonted self-possession.

But he was laboring heavily now. His heart was jumping and pounding, his breath coming in gasps, but he held to the trail, moving ever deeper into the hills, until he burst into a basin out of which to the right led a narrow canyon. Then he slowed down and, turning into the canyon, which wound and twisted due north and south in the bright moonlight, he continued at a slower pace. But his heart no longer was in the task. The weight on his back seemed heavier; there was a painful swelling of his ankles. He knew the reason for this pain. It had come from unwonted contact with hard surfaces and frequent stepping on loose stones in this strange haste with a strange people in the hills. Yet he kept on, growing steadily more weary, yet with pride ever to the fore, until a faint light began to streak the overhead sky, stealing cautiously down the ragged walls of the canyon. Then he found himself pulled into a walk.

He was facing a narrow defile that wound up among the overhanging crags. Glad of the privilege of resting, for a walk was a rest with him now, he set forward into the uninviting pass. Up and up he clambered, crowding narrowly past boulders, rounding on slender ledges, up and ever up. As he ascended he saw gray-white vales below, felt the stimulus of a rarer air, and at last found his heart fluttering unpleasantly in the higher altitude. Yet he held grimly to his task, and, when broad daylight was streaming full upon him, he found himself on a wide shelf of rock, a ledge falling sheer on one side to unseen depths, towering on the other to awe-inspiring heights. Here he came to a halt. And then, so tired was he, so faint with exhaustion, so racked of body and spirit, that he sank upon the cool rock even before the men could clear themselves from him, and lay there on his side, his eyes closed, his lungs greedily sucking air.

The glare of full daylight aroused him. Regaining his feet, he stared about him. He saw many strange-looking men, and near them many dirty and bedraggled horses. He turned his eyes outward from the ledge. He saw around him bristling peaks, and below them, far below, a trailing canyon, winding in and out among hills toward the rising sun, and terminating in a giant V, beyond which, a connecting thread between its sloping sides, lay an expanse of rolling mesa. It was far from him, however–very, very far–and he grew dizzy at the view, finding himself more and more unnerved by the height. At length he turned away and swept his eyes again over the horses, where he was glad to find the rangy sorrel. Then he turned back to the men, some of whom were standing, others squatting, but all in moody silence.

As he looked he grew aware that a pair of dark eyes were fixed upon him. He stared back, noting the man's long hair and painted features and the familiar glow of admiration in his eyes. Believing him to be his new master, he continued to regard him soberly until the man, with a grunt and a grimace, rose and approached him. Pat stood very still under a rigid examination. The man rubbed his ankles, turned up his hoofs, looked at his teeth; and at the conclusion of all this Pat felt that he had met with approval. Also, he realized that he rather approved of the man. Then came a volley of sounds he did not understand, and he found himself touched with grave apprehension. But not for long. The man led him across the ledge to a tiny stream trickling down the rocks, walking with a quiet dignity he long since had learned to connect with kindliness. This and the fact that he led him to water determined his attitude.

Toward noon, as he was brooding over hunger pangs, he was startled by excited gutturals among the men. Gazing, he saw one of the men standing on the edge of the shelf, pointing out through the long canyon. With the others, Pat turned his eyes that way. Between the distant V dotting the mesa beyond rode a body of horsemen. They were not more than specks to his eyes, proceeding slowly, so slowly, in fact, that while he could see they were moving he yet could not see them move as they crawled across the span between the canyon's mouth. Interested, gripped in the contagion of the excitement round him, he kept his eyes upon the distant specks until the sun had changed to another angle. But even after this lapse of time, so distant were the horsemen, so wide the canyon's mouth, they had traveled only half-way across the span. Yet he continued to watch, wondering at the nervousness around him, conscious of steadily increasing heat upon him, until the last of the slow-moving specks, absorbed one by one by the canyon's wall, disappeared from view. Then he turned his eyes elsewhere.

The men also turned away, but continued their excited talk. But even they after a time relapsed into silence. What it was all about Pat did not know. He knew it was something very serious, and suddenly fear came to him. He saw some of the men lie down as if to sleep, and he feared that they intended to remain here for ever, in this place absolutely destitute of herbage. But after a time, made sluggish by the attitude of the men, he himself attempted to drowse. But the heat pulsating up off the rocks discouraged him, and he soon abandoned the attempt, standing motionless in the hot sun.

A change came over him. He took to brooding over his many discomforts–hunger pangs, loss of sleep, bothersome flies, the pain of his swollen ankles. As the day advanced his ankles swelled more, and grew worse, the flies became more troublesome, and his inner gnawings more pronounced. So the time went on and he brooded through the still watches of the afternoon, through the soft stirrings of evening, on into night again. With the coming of night light breezes rose from the spaces below to spur his fevered body into something of its wonted vigor. And the night brought also preparations among the men to journey on. This he welcomed, even more than the cooling zephyrs.

There was some delay. His master entered upon a dispute with the horseless man. The voices became excited and rose to vehement heights. But presently they subsided when Pat himself, anxious to be active, sounded a note of protest. Yet the argument proved to his benefit. Instead of mounting him behind his master, the odd man swung up behind another man on the sorrel. Then he was permitted to move forward, and as he approached the narrow defile he sounded another nicker, now of gratification.

The pass dropped almost sheer in places. As he descended, more than once he was compelled to slide on stiffened legs. In this at first he felt ecstatic danger thrills. But only at first. Soon he wearied of it, and he was glad when he struck the bottom, where, after being guided out of shadow and into broad moonlight, he found himself moving to the west in a deep canyon. With the other horses he burst into a canter, and continued at a canter hour after hour, following the winding and twisting canyon until daylight, with its shadows creeping away before him, revealed to his tired eyes a stretch of mesa ahead, dotted with inviting clumps of bunch-grass. Then of his own volition he came to a stop and fell to grazing. Soon all the horses were standing with mouths to earth, feeding eagerly.

The men, sitting for a time in quiet conversation, finally dismounted, laughing now and then, and casting amused glances toward the black horse.

Soon they mounted again to take the trail. Instead of riding with the other on the sorrel, the odd man swung up on Pat's back behind his master. But as Pat no longer suffered from hunger, he complacently accepted the return of the double load. Then all moved forward. Pat jogged out of the canyon, turning to the right on the desert, and moved rapidly north in the shadow of the hills. He held to his stride, and toward noon, rounding a giant ridge projecting into the desert from the hills, he saw ahead on his right, perhaps two miles distant across a basin, the mouth of another canyon. Evidently his master saw it also, and obviously it contained danger, for he jerked Pat down to a walk. Almost instantly he knew that the danger was real, for the man, sounding a sharp command to the others, brought him to a full stop. Then followed an excited discussion, and, when it ended, Pat, gripped in vague uneasiness, found himself urged forward at top speed. Yet in a dim way he knew what was wanted of him. He flung himself into a long stride and dashed across the wide basin, across the mouth of the canyon, into the shadow of the hills again. Breathless, he slackened his pace with thirty excited horses around him, mad swirling clouds of dust all about, and before him the oppressive stillness of the desert. They were safely past the danger zone.

He pressed on at a slow canter. Ahead the mesa revealed numerous sand-dunes, large and small, rising into the monotonous skyline. Plunging among them, he mounted some easily, others he skirted as easily, and once, to avoid an unusually large one, he dropped down into the bed of an arroyo, traveled along its dry course, and then clambered up on the desert. But it was wearying work, and, becoming ever more aware of his double load, he began to chafe with dissatisfaction. Yet he held to his gait, hopeful of better things–

he was always hopeful of better things now–until he reached another dune, larger than any as yet encountered, when once more he broke out of his stride to circle its bottom. As he did so, of his own volition he checked himself. Dead ahead he saw horses scattered about, and beyond the horses, rising limply in the noon haze, a thin column of smoke. Also, he felt both his riders stiffen. Then on the midday hush rose the crack of firearms from the direction of the camp.

His master lifted a shrill voice. He felt a mighty pull at his head. He swung around like a flash. Then came the flaying of a rope and frantic urging of heels. He plunged among the surging horses, dancing and whirling excitedly, and out into the open beyond. He set his teeth grimly, and raced headlong to the south, galloping furiously, tearing blindly over the desert. He headed straight for the distant basin, straight for the mouth of the canyon, hurtling forward, struggling mightily under his double load. He did not know it, but he was speeding into a tragic crisis.

The others overtook him. They were carrying but single loads. But they did not pass him. He saw to that. He burst forward into even greater speed, clung to it grimly, forged into a position well in the lead. And he held this place–around him frenzied horses, frantic riders; behind him, to the distant rear, shot after shot echoing over the desert; before him the baking sands, shimmering heat-waves, sullen and silent. He raced on, swinging up over dunes, dropping into hollows, speeding across flats, mounting over dunes again, on and on toward the basin and the mouth of the canyon–and protection.

But again disaster.

Suddenly, out of the canyon poured the cheerful notes of a bugle. On the vibrant wings of the echoes, streaming into the basin from the canyon, swept a body of flying horsemen. Instantly he checked himself. Then his master sounded a shrill outcry, swung his head around violently, and lashed him forward again. He hurtled headlong, dashing toward the distant ridge, the peninsula jutting out into the desert. Grimly he flung out along this new course. But he kept his eyes to the left. He saw the horsemen there also swerve, saw them spread out like a fan, and felt his interest kindle joyously. For this was a race! It was a race for that ridge! And he must win! He must do this thing, for instinctively he knew that beyond it lay safety. There he could flee to some haven, while cut off from it, cut off by these steady-riding men on his left, he must submit to wretched defeat. So he strained himself harder and burst into fresh speed, finding himself surprised that he could. In the thrill of it he forgot his double load, forgot the close-pressing horses, forgot irritating dust. On he galloped, racing forward with machine-like evenness–on his left the paralleling horsemen, to his rear yelling and shooting, on his right his own men and horses, and for them he felt he must do big things.

Suddenly the shooting in his rear ceased. Evidently these men had received some warning from the riders on his left. Then he awoke to another truth. The horsemen on his left were gaining. It troubled him, and he cast measuring eyes to the front. He saw that he was pursuing a shorter line to the ridge; he believed he still could reach it first. So again he strained on, whipping his legs into movement till they seemed about to snap. But the effort hurt him and he discovered that he was becoming woefully tired. Also, the double weight worried him. It had not become lighter with the miles, nor had he grown stronger. Yet he galloped on with thundering hoofs, the tranquil desert before him, the thud of carbines against leather to the left, behind him ominous silence. But he kept his eyes steadily to the left, and presently he awoke to something else there, something that roused him suddenly and in some way whipped his conscience. For now he saw a white figure amid the khaki, racing along with them–a part of them and yet no part of them–a familiar figure wearing a familiar bandage. This for a brief moment only. Then he took to measuring distances again; saw that the cavalrymen were holding to the course steadily, racing furiously as he himself was racing for the ridge. Would he win?

A shrill outcry from his master, and he found himself checked with a jerk. It was unexpected, sudden, and he reared. The movement shook off the second man. Dropping back upon all-fours, Pat awoke to the relief the loss of this load gave him. Grimly determining to hold to this relief, he dashed ahead, following the guidance of his master in yet another direction, hurtled away before the second man could mount again.

He found that he was speeding in a direction almost opposite from the ridge. He did not understand this. But his regret was not long lived. Casting his eyes to his left in vague expectancy of seeing the familiar spot of white again, he saw only his own men and horses, and beyond them the smiling desert. Puzzled, he gazed to the right. Here he saw the cavalrymen, and though puzzled more, he yet kept on with all his power. As he ran he suddenly awoke to the presence of a new body of horsemen on his distant left, a smaller band than the cavalrymen, men without uniforms, most of them hatless, all yelling. He remembered this yell, and now he understood. He was speeding toward the mouth of the canyon; had been turned completely around. And thus it was, he knew, that the horsemen once on his left were now on his right, and the madly yelling group at his rear was now on his left. He awoke to another realization. This was a race again, a race with three new entrants now–all three making toward the canyon. Would he win?

He fell to studying the flanking groups. On his right, riding easily, bent to the winds, their heavy horses swinging rhythmically, their accoutrements rattling, galloped the cavalry–steady, sure of themselves, well in hand. On his left, riding furiously, without formation, dashed the smaller group of riders–their horses wrangling among themselves, one or two frequently bucking, all flinging forward in excited disorder. This disorder, this evident nervousness, he feared. He knew somehow that the first real trouble would come from this source. He knew men to that extent. And suddenly his fears were realized. With the three converging lines of direction drawing closer, and the mouth of the canyon but a short distance away, out of this group on his left came a nasty rifle-fire, followed by a mighty chorus of yells. There was a result at once. Close beside him a horse stumbled; the man astride the horse was thrown headlong; from the cavalrymen on his right came a single shrill, piercing outcry–a cry to desist! But he did not understand this. Nor did he heed it. Galloping forward, eyes upon the ever-nearing canyon, he at length became grimly conscious of approaching defeat–of the firm and ruthless closing in upon him from either side of the two bands. And now, and not till now, realizing as he did that the thing was beyond him, that he could not reach the canyon first–

now, and not till now, though soul and body were wrecked by exhaustion, Pat abated his speed.

Instantly pandemonium broke loose. He heard the firing on his left increasing. He felt his master make ready to return it. He saw others around him, twisting vengefully into position, open with repeating rifles. Then the cavalrymen, evidently forced into it by the others, swung to the fray with their carbines, which began to boom on his right. The whole basin echoed and re-echoed sharp reports. Across his eyes burst intermittent flames. His ears rang with shots and yells. The shooting became heavier. Bullets sang close about him–seemed centered–as if the enemy would cut down his master at once and disrupt the others through his loss. The bullets sang closer still. And now immediately about him men and horses dropped, upsetting other riders, tumbling over sound horses–all in a seething chaos. He became dazed. His eyes were blinded with the flashes, and his ears ached with the crash and tumult. He grew faint. A dizziness seized him. But on he labored, his head aching, his eyes growing dimmer, his limbs numb and rebellious, his heart thumping in sullen rebellion, his ears bursting with the uproar.

Another change swept over him. Mist leaped before his eyes. The roaring in his ears subsided. His legs flew off–he had no legs! The mist became a film. Yet he could see–see faintly. He saw a mad jumble of flying men and horses–a riotous mixture of color, arms, and firearms whirling and interlaced, a grim, struggling mass in death-grips. It swept close–crashed over him, struck him full. He felt the impact–then another. The ground rose and struck him. And now there fell upon him a great and wonderful peace–and a blank–then a voice, a familiar voice, and he drifted into unconsciousness.

He was wakened by a fiery liquid in his throat. He slowly opened his eyes. He saw men and horses, many of them, standing or reclining in small groups. He saw them between the legs of a group immediately around him–men gazing down at him pitifully. As he lay thus dazed he heard the familiar voice again. It was sounding his name. He struggled to his feet. Steadying himself against his dizziness, he looked curiously at the young man standing before him. And suddenly he recognized him. This was his young master with the white around his arm and neck–the young man who had ridden him into the Mexican settlement, and who had been so good to him there, giving him generous quantities of alfalfa. He–But the voice was sounding again.

"You poor dumb brute!" said Stephen, quietly; and Pat liked the petting he received. "You've just come through hell! But–but if they get you again–anywhere, friend of mine–they'll wade through hell themselves to do it." He was silent. "Pat, old boy," he concluded, finally, "you're going back home! I–I'm through!"

A strange thing took place in Pat. Hearing this voice now, and seeing the owner of it, though he had seen him and heard his voice many times just before this last heartbreaking task under a strange master, he suddenly found himself thinking of the little ranch beside the river, and of his loving mistress, and also the cold and cruel Mexican hostler. And, thinking of them, he found himself thinking also of another, one who had accompanied him and his mistress on many delightful trips in the valley and up on the mesa in the shadow of the mountains. And now, thinking of this person, he somehow recognized this young man before him fully, and wondered why this had not come to him before. For this was the same young man– curiously pale, curiously drawn and haggard–but yet the same man. Understanding, understanding everything, he nickered softly and pressed close, mindful of yet another thing–something that had helped to make his life on the little ranch so pleasant and unforgettable. What he was mindful of, and what he now sought, was sugar and quartered apples.

CHAPTER XXI
LIFE AND DEATH

The third group in the affray consisted of cowboys. Weary and bedraggled, yet joyous at the suppression of the uprising, they set out for home about noon. Stephen, mounted upon Pat, accompanied them. They headed into the northwest, riding slowly, talking over the affair, while Stephen explained in part his interest in the black horse. Night found them near a water-hole, and here they went into camp, Stephen weak and distressed, his whole body aching, his arm and shoulder throbbing in agonizing pain. The men proved attentive and considerate; but he lay down exhausted and courted sleep, hardly hearing what they said. Sleep came to him only fitfully, and he was glad when break of day brought a change. They rode on through the second day, usually in sober silence, on into another dusk and another night of torture. A third day and a third dusk followed, but there was no camp this time. Continuing forward, just before dawn, with the moon brilliant in the heavens, they reached a cluster of buildings. One of them was a dwelling with a fence around it as a protection against cattle and horses, and to the rear of this all dismounted. Stephen led Pat into a spacious stable, and, with the assistance of the others, unsaddled and unbridled him, watered and fed him generously, then left him for the night.

Instantly Pat began to inquire into his condition and surroundings. He was stiff and sore and a little nervous from the events of the past few days, and he found the stable, spacious though it was, depressing after his protracted life in the open. Yet there were many offsetting comforts. He had received a generous supply of grain and all the water he could drink. Then there was another comfort, though he awoke to this only after sinking to rest. His stall was thickly bedded with straw, which was comfort indeed, and though he had become accustomed to the pricking of the desert sand, he nestled into the straw with a sigh of satisfaction. To his right and left other horses stirred restlessly, and from outside came an occasional nicker, presumably from some unroofed inclosure. All these sounds kept him awake for a time, and it was approaching day before he felt himself sinking off into easy slumber.

He was awakened by the coming of a stranger into his stall. It was broad daylight, and he hastily gained his feet, mystified for an instant that he should be sleeping in broad day, and not a little troubled by his strange surroundings. The new-comer was a fat youth with a round and smiling face, who, as he raked down the bedding, talked in a pleasing drawl.

"Pat," he began, shoving him over gently, "you're shore some cayuse. Wouldn't mind ownin' a piece o' you myself. But I was goin' for to say there's trouble come onto you. That mighty likable pardner o' yours is gone in complete–sick to death. We've telephoned for the doc, but he's off somewheres, and we've got to wait till he gits back. But it's shore too bad–all of it. Steve he's got a nasty arm and shoulder, and he's all gone generally. Mighty distressin' I call it."

With this he slapped Pat heartily and left him.

When he had gone Pat felt a depression creeping over him. It became heavier as the hours passed. He knew that his young friend was somewhere about, and could not understand why he failed to come to him himself, instead of sending this stranger. Then, with the hours lengthening into a day, and the days dragging into a week, with only the smiling stranger coming to him regularly, and petting and stroking and talking to him, he came to feel that something of grave and serious nature was going on outside. So he longed to get out of the stable, out into sunlight and away from this restraint, and to see for himself what it was that was holding his master from him.

Then late one afternoon he heard a step approaching. It was his master's step, yet it was very different. It was slow and dragging, and while the voice was the same, yet there was a note of hollowness as he spoke that did not belong there, a note as if it required great effort to speak at all. But in spite of this he recognized his young master, and sounded a welcoming nicker, anxious to be off. For somehow he believed that now he would be taken out into the sunlight. Nor was he disappointed. After a moment's petting the young man led him outdoors, and there began to bridle and saddle him, slowly, with many pauses for breath, all as if it hurt him, as indeed it must, since he still wore the white bandages. Then there appeared a group of interested young men, suddenly, as though they had just discovered the proposed departure.

"See here, Steve," one of them exploded, "this ain't treating us a bit nice. You're a mighty sick man. I ain't saying that to worry you, neither; but I can't see the idee of your hopping out of bed to do this thing. You stick around till the doc comes again, anyway. Now, don't be a fool, Steve."

Stephen continued slowly with his saddling. "It's decent of you fellows," he said, quietly. "And I don't want you to think me ungrateful. It's just a feeling I've got. I want to get this horse back where he belongs."

Another of the group took up the attempt at persuasion. "But you're sick, man!" he exclaimed, beginning to stroke Pat absently. "You won't never make the depot! You owe it to everybody you've ever knowed to get right back into bed and stay there!"

But Stephen only shook his head. Yet he knew that what the boys said was true. He was sick, and he knew it. He realized that he ought to be in bed. And he wanted to be in bed. But already he had suffered too much, lying inert, not because of his arm and the fever upon him, though these were almost unbearable, but because of the haunting fear, come to him ever more insistently with each passing day, that since Pat had escaped from him twice thus far, he was destined to escape from him a third time. Sometimes this fear took shape in visions of a blazing fire in the stable, in which Pat was burned to a crisp; again it took form in some malady peculiar to horses which would prove equally disastrous. At last, unable to withstand these pictures longer, he had crept out of bed, dressed as best he could, and stolen out of the house, bent upon getting Pat to the railroad, and there shipping him east to Helen at whatever cost to himself. So here he was, about to ride off.

"You're–you're mighty decent," he repeated, hollowly, by way of farewell. "But I've got to go. And don't worry about my making the station," he added, reassuringly. "I have the directions, and I'll get there in time to make that ten-thirty eastbound to-night." He clambered painfully up into the saddle.

A third member of the group, the round-faced and smiling cowpuncher, opened up with his pleasing drawl. "Why'n't you stay over till mornin', then?" he demanded. "The ranch wagon goes up early, and you could ride the seat just like a well man."

But Stephen remained obdurate, and, repeating his thanks and farewells, he urged Pat forward at a walk because he himself could not stand the racking of a more rapid gait. The men sent after him expressions of regret mingled with friendly denunciations, but he rode steadily on, closing his ears grimly against their pleas, and soon he was moving slowly across the Arizona desert. His direction was northwest, and his destination, though new to him, a little town on the Santa Fé.

As he rode forward through the quiet of the afternoon he found his thoughts a curious conflict. At times he would think of the girl, and of his love for her, and of the long, still hours spent in the ranch-house brooding, especially the nights, when, gazing out at the stars, he had wondered whether she knew, or, knowing, whether, after all, she really cared. They had been lonely nights, fever-tossed and restless, nights sometimes curiously made up of pictures–pictures of a runaway horse and of a girl mounted upon the horse, and of long walks and rides and talks with her afterward, and of the last night in her company, outside a corral and underneath a smiling moon, the girl in white, her eyes burning with a strange glow, himself telling his love for her, and hearing in return only that she did not and could not return that love.

These were his thoughts at times as he rode forward through the desert solitude. Then he would awaken to his physical torture, and in this he would completely forget his spiritual distress, would ask why he had flung himself into this mocking silence and plunged into all this misery and pain. He knew why–knew it was because of the girl. But would it have been better to accept her dismissal and, returning to the East, let her pass out of his memory? In his heart he knew that he could not.

There followed the thought of his responsibility for Pat, and of what was left for him to do. He recalled the theft, and his weeks of futile riding to recover the horse, and the thrill accompanying risk of life when he finally recovered him. And after that the second theft, and another and more dreadful ride when he raced through the night after the cavalry–the torture of it, the agony of his arm, the shooting, and the grappling hand to hand, and Pat sinking with exhaustion, and the thrill again, his own, at having the horse once more in his possession. It was *worth* it–all of it–and he was *glad*–glad to have had an object for once in his life. And he still had that object, for was he not riding the horse on a journey which would end in placing Pat in the hands of the adorable girl who owned him?

Thus he rode through the afternoon and on into an early dusk. Suddenly awaking to the Stygian darkness around him, he gave over thinking of the past and future and turned uneasy thoughts upon the present. Above him was a black, impenetrable dome, seemingly within touch of his hand; around and about him pressed a dense wall that gave no hint of his whereabouts. Yet he believed that he was pursuing the right direction; and, forgetting that Pat, no more than himself, knew the route, he gave the horse loose rein. Thus for an hour, two hours, three, he rode slowly forward, when like a flash it came to him that he was hopelessly lost. He reined in the horse sharply.

For a time he sat trying to place himself. Failing in this, he raised his eyes, hoping for a break in the skies. But there was no glimmer of light, and after a while, not knowing what else to do, he sent Pat forward again. But his uneasiness would not down, and presently he drew rein again, dismounted, and fell to listening. There was not a breath of air. He took a step forward, his uneasiness becoming fear, and again stood motionless, listening, gripped by the oppressive stillness of the desert. It crept upon him, this death-quiet, seemed to close about him suffocatingly. Suddenly he started. Out of the dense blackness had come a voice, weak and plaintive. He turned tense with excitement and listened keenly.

"Hello, there! This–over this way!"

He could see nothing; but he moved in the direction of the voice. After a few strides he was stopped by a consciousness of something before him, and there was a constrained groan.

"Careful, man–I'm hurt. Unhorsed this morning. Been crawling all day for shade. Strike a match, will you? God! but it's a night!"

Stephen struck a light. As it flared up he saw prone in the sand a young man, his face drawn with pain, his eyes dark and hunted. The match went out. He struck another. The man was pitifully bruised and broken. A leg of his trousers had been torn away, and the limb lay exposed, strangely twisted. His track, made in crawling through the sand, stood out clearly, trailing away beyond the circling glow of light. A moment of flickering, and the second match went out.

"Which way were you headed, friend?" Stephen asked, pityingly. His heart went out to the stricken stranger. He wanted to ask another question, too, but he hesitated. But finally he asked it. "Who are you, old man?"

For a moment the fellow did not reply. The silence was oppressive. Stephen regretted his question. Then suddenly the man answered him, weakly, bitterly, as one utterly remorseful.

"I'm Jim," he blurted out. "Horse-thief, cattle-rustler."

Stephen bit his lip. More than ever he regretted that he had asked. Well, something had to be done, and done quickly. Could he but feel sure of his direction, he might place this unfortunate upon Pat and walk with him to the railroad town, where proper medical and surgical attendance could be obtained. But this he was unable to do, since he fully realized he was astray.

"Brother," he suddenly explained, "I was headed, myself, toward the railroad. A little before dark I lost my way. Do you happen to know–"

"Sit down," interrupted the other, faintly. "I've been–been lost–a week."

Stephen sat down thoughtfully. All hope of serving the man for the present was gone. He must wait till daybreak at least. Then somebody or something might appear to show him the way out. He thought of the ranch wagon, and of Buddy's offer, and it occurred to him that unless he was too far off the regular course he might attract Buddy. It was a chance, anyway.

"I've been 'most dead, too, for a week," suddenly began the other. "I 'ain't eat regularly, for one thing–'most a month of that, I reckon. Been times, too, when I couldn't–couldn't find water. I didn't know the country over here. Had to change–change horses a couple times, too. Because–" He checked himself. "I made a mistake–the last horse. He give me all–all that was comin'–"

A nicker from Pat interrupted him. Stephen felt him cringe. Directly he felt something else. It was a cold hand groping to find his own. The whole thing was queer, uncanny, and he was glad when the man went on.

"Did–did you hear that?" breathed the fellow, a note of suppressed terror in his voice. "Did you hear it, friend? Tell me!" His voice was shrill now.

Stephen reassured him, explaining that it was his horse. But a long time the man held fast, fingers gripping his hand, as if he did not believe, and was listening to make sure. At length he relaxed, and Stephen, still seated close beside him, heard him sink back into the sand.

"I was getting away from–from–Oh, well, it don't–don't make any difference." The fellow was silent. "I needed a–a horse," he continued, finally. "My own–the third since–since–my own had played out. I was near a ranch, and–and it was night, and I–I seen a corral with a horse standing in it–a gray. It was moonlight. I–I got the gate open, and I–I roped him, and–" He interrupted himself, was upon one elbow again. "It was a stallion–a cross-bred, maybe–and–and say, friend, he rode me to death! I got on him before I knowed what he was. Bareback. He shot out of that corral like he was crazy. But I–I managed to hold–hold to him and–if he'd only bucked me off! But he didn't. He just raced for it–tore across the country like a cyclone. He rode me to death, a hundred miles, I bet, without a stop. And I held on–couldn't let go–was afraid to let go." He was silent. "Are you–you dead sure, friend, that was your horse?"

Stephen again reassured him, realizing the fear upon the man and now understanding it. But he said nothing.

"And then somewhere off here he throwed me," went on the man. "But he–he was a raving maniac. He turned on me before I could get up, and bit and kicked and trampled me till I didn't know nothing– was asleep, or something. When I came to–woke up–he was still hanging around. He's around here yet! I heard him all day– yesterday! He's off there to the east somewheres. He's–he's looking for me. I kept still whenever I'd see him or hear him, and then when he'd move off out of sight, or quit–quit his nickering, I'd crawl along some more. I'm–I'm done, stranger," he concluded, weakly, dropping over upon his back. "I'm done, and I know it. And it was that horse that–that–" He was silent.

Stephen did not speak. He could not speak after this fearsome tale. Its pictures haunted him. He could see this poor fellow racing across the desert, clinging for life to that which meant death. His own condition had been brought about through a horse, a horse and wild rides at a time when he should have been, as this unfortunate undoubtedly should have been, in bed under medical care. For a moment he thought he would tell him a tale of misery equal to his own, in the hope that he might turn him from thoughts of his own misfortunes. But before he could speak the other broke in upon his thoughts with a shrill outcry. He had raised himself upon one elbow again, and now was pointing toward the eastern sky.

"Look!" he cried. "Look off there!"

Stephen turned his eyes in the direction of the pointing finger. He saw a faint light breaking through the black dome of the sky. As he watched it, it trickled out steadily, like slow-spreading water, filtering slowly through dense banks of clouds, folding them back like the shutter of a giant camera, until the whole eastern sky was a field of gray clouds with frosty edges, between which, coming majestically forward through the green-white billow, appeared finally a moon, big and round and brilliant, casting over the earth a flood of wonderland light, streaming down upon the dunes and flats in mystic sheen, bringing out the desert in soft outline. Near by, the light brought out the form of Pat, standing a short distance off with drooping head, motionless in all the splendor of his perfect outline. Stephen turned back to the man. He found him staring hard at the horse. He did not understand this until the fellow burst out excitedly, his eyes still fixed on Pat.

"Whose horse is that?" he demanded. "Tell me. Do you own that black horse?"

Stephen slowly shook his head. He thought the question but another expression of the stranger's nervous apprehension due to his experience. Yet he explained.

"He belongs back in New Mexico," he said, quietly–"the Rio Grande Valley. He was stolen last spring. Been ridden pretty hard since, I guess. I happen to know where he belongs, though, and I was taking him to a shipping-point when I lost my way. That's the horse you heard nicker a while ago," he added, soothingly.

The man sank flat again.

"I stole him," he blurted out. "I–I hope you'll get him back where he belongs. His–his name is Pat. He's–he's the best horse I ever rode." He relapsed, into silence, motionless, as one dead.

Stephen himself remained motionless. He looked at the man curiously. He believed that he ought to feel bitter toward him, since he saw in him the cause of all his own misery. But somehow he found that he could feel nothing but pity. In this man with eyes closed and gasping lips Stephen saw only a brother-mortal in distress, as he himself was in distress, and he forgave him for anything he had done.

He looked at Pat, understanding the temptation, and then turned his eyes pityingly toward the man–the stranger, dozing, murmuring strangely in his sleep. Seeing him at rest, and realizing the long hours before daybreak, Stephen finally dropped over upon one elbow, and prepared to pass the night as best he could. He was suffering torture from his arm and shoulder, and burning with the fever shown in his hot skin and parched lips.

The night passed restlessly. He saw the first rays of dawn break over the range and creep farther and farther down the valley, throwing a pale pink over the landscape and sending gaunt shadows slinking off into the light. A whinny from Pat aroused him. He arose painfully, gazed at the man at his feet, and then turned his eyes toward the distant horizon. A second whinny disturbed him and he shifted his gaze. Far above two great buzzards, circling round and round, faded into the morning haze. From a neighboring sand-dune a jack-rabbit appeared, paused a quivering moment, then scurried from view. The morning light grew brighter. A third whinny, and

Pat now slowly started toward him. But again he fastened his eyes upon the distant horizon, hoping for a sight of the ranch wagon. But no wagon appeared. At length he turned to the horse. Pat stood soberly regarding the man, his ears forward, head drooping, tail motionless, as if recognizing in this mute object an erstwhile master. And suddenly lifting his head, he sounded a soft nicker, tremulously. Then again he fell to regarding the still form with strange interest.

The form was still, still for all eternity. For the man was dead.

Stephen sat down. He was shaking with fever and weakness. He placed a handkerchief over the face in repose, almost relieved that peace had come to this troubled soul. Then he thought of possible action. He realized that he was utterly lost. He had Pat, and for this he was thankful, since he knew that he could at least mount the horse and leave him to find a way out. But the horse alone must do it. He himself was bewildered, for the desert in broad day, as much as in the long night, revealed nothing. On every hand it lay barren, destitute of movement, wrapped in silence, seeming to mock his predicament. Yet he could not bring himself to mount at once. He sat motionless, suffering acutely, knowing that the least exertion would increase his pain—a machine run down—not caring to move.

Suddenly, off to the east appeared a horse—a gray. It cantered majestically to the top of a dune, and stood there—head erect, nostrils quivering, ears alert, cresting the hillock like a statue. Stephen shivered. For instinctively he knew this to be the gray stallion, the cross-bred, that had trampled the form beside him. His first impulse was to mount Pat and spur him in a race for life; his second impulse was to crouch in hiding in the hope of escaping the keen scrutiny of that merciless demon. He chose the race. Springing to his feet, he leaped for Pat, and he grasped the saddle-horn. In his haste he slipped, lost his stirrup, and fell back headlong. The shock made him faint, and for a time he was unconscious. Shrill neighing aroused him, and, hastily gaining his feet, he saw Pat running lightly, well-contained, to meet the swiftly advancing gray stallion. Then events moved with a terrible unreality.

The gray screamed defiantly and leaped toward Pat faster and faster. Pat braced his legs to meet the assault. But no assault came. With rare craft the gray suddenly checked himself, coming to a full stop two lengths away. Here, with ears flat and lashing tail, he glared at Pat, who, equally tense, returned defiance. Thus they stood in the desert, quiet, measuring each other, while Stephen, crouched, watching them, remembering the lifeless form beside him, prayed that Pat would prove equal to the mighty stallion. He had no gun. Pat alone could save him. If Pat were conquered nothing remained but death for both. For with Pat dead–and surely this masterful foe would stop at nothing short of death–Stephen realized that he himself, in his present condition, would never see civilization again. He could not walk the distance even if he knew the way, nor could he hope to mount the victorious stallion, should Pat be defeated, because only one man had done that, and that man lay dead beside him. The thought of being alone in the desert with the dead struck chill to his heart. He recalled his first ride with Helen, and her tales of men and horses in the early days, and what it meant to a man to have his horse stolen from him. It was all clear to him now, and he clenched his sound hand till the nails cut the flesh. Unless Pat fought a successful fight he was doomed to die of thirst, even if the stallion did not attack him. As he looked at Pat, his only hope in this dread situation, he prayed harder and more fervently than before that his champion would win.

Pat thrilled with the sense of coming battle, but he did not fear this horse. He remembered that once he had struck down a rival, and before that he had twice given successful battle to men–to a finish with the Mexican hostler, another time when he had brought his enemy to respect and consider him. Therefore he had no reason to fear this horse, even though he saw in the gray's splendid figure an enemy to be carefully considered. But not for an instant did Pat relax. For this was a crafty foe, as shown by his sudden halt, which Pat knew was the prelude to a swift attack. So he watched with keen alertness the flattened ears, the lashing tail–his own muscles held rigid, waiting.

The gray began a cautious approach. He put forward his legs one after another slowly, the while he held his eyes turned away, as if he were wholly absorbed in the vastness of the desert reaches. This was but a mere feint, as Pat understood it, and yet he waited, curious to know the outcome, still holding himself rigidly on guard. Closer came the gray, closer still, until he was almost beside him. Pat heard the whistle of his breath and saw the wild light in his eyes, and for an instant feared him. Yet there was no attack. The gray calmly gained a point immediately alongside and stopped, head to Pat's rump, separated from him by not more than half his length. Yet he did not attack; but Pat did not relax. And again they stood, end to end now and side by side, until Pat, coming finally to think, against his better judgment, that this was, after all, only a friendly advance, became less watchful. Then the blow fell. With a shrill scream that chilled Pat's heart the gray leaped sideways with a peculiar broadside lunge intended to hurl him off his feet. It was a form of attack new to Pat, and therefore never known to his ancestors, and before he could brace himself to meet it he found himself rolling over and over frantically in the sand.

He sprang up, screaming with rage, while the gray was trampling him with fiendish hoofs. He steadied himself, resisted the onslaught, took the offensive himself. He lunged with bared teeth, sank them into yielding flesh, and wheeled away quickly. But not fast enough. The gray slashed his rump. He turned back, tore the gray's shoulder, wheeled sharply, attacked with lightning heels, and darted away again. But again the gray sprang upon him, ripped his rump a second time, and sprang off like a fiend. Raging, vindictive, Pat hurtled after him, and snapped again and again, drawing hot blood pungent of taste and smell, and then he leaped aside. But not far enough. The gray dashed into him, enveloped him in a whirlwind of clashing teeth and flashing heels, and wheeled away in a wide circle, screaming to the heavens, leaving Pat, with a dozen stinging wounds, dazed and exhausted.

But Pat was quick to recover himself. Also, he took council. Never had he fought like this. His battle with the white horse had been brief–brief because of sudden releasing of weeks of venom stored within him by the white's continuous nagging, brief because of the white's inability to spring from each attack in season to protect himself. But no such sluggishness hampered this enemy, and he grimly realized that this was a struggle to the death. But he felt no fear. He respected the other's craft and wit and strength. Yet he

175

knew that he himself had strength, while he realized that strength alone would not conquer. Craft and wit must serve with strength. Having strength, he himself must adopt the other qualities, must adapt himself to the occasion, exercise wit and craft, wait for openings, feint and withdraw, feint and attack, until, wearying this enemy, and puzzling him, there would come the chance to strike a death-blow. He knew what the death-blow was–knew it from his encounter with the white. He must inflict it first, lest the gray anticipate him, for the gray undoubtedly knew, also, from his experience and from his ancestors, what the death-blow was.

After a moment of gasping breath and gradually clearing eyes he felt self-control and assurance return. Since his enemy appeared to be waiting, he himself continued to wait. He waited three minutes, five minutes, ten, until the nervous tension would permit him to wait no longer. Remembering his plans, and emulating the first approach of the gray, he started slowly toward him, putting forward one foot after another quietly, his eyes upon the distant horizon. He even outdid the gray in his craft. As he drew near, he suddenly took on the manner of one seeking friendliness, nickering once softly, as if he had had enough of this and would ask reconciliation. But his ruse failed. The gray was wise with the wisdom of the world-free. Plunging suddenly upon him, he snapped for his ears, but missed. His teeth flashed at Pat's neck, lodged, and ripped the flesh. He whirled, lashed out with his heels, missed, and sped away. Pat wheeled again and again, almost overthrown, and staggered away.

Again he took council with himself. He was not beaten, he knew that. But neither was the enemy beaten. He knew that also. And he knew he must bide his time. Twice he had closed with the enemy, and twice he had come away the worse. Nothing was to be gained by this method. He must bide his time, wait for an encounter, dodge it if the moment proved unpropitious, but refrain from close attack. He must wait for his chance.

As he stood there, alert to every least thing, he suddenly awoke to tease breathing close behind him. For one flaming moment he was puzzled. Then he remembered that he had been watching the gray out of the corner of his eye. He had seemed to be off guard, and the other had stolen cautiously around behind him, evidently to take advantage of this chance. He swallowed hard. The enemy was stealing upon him. He wanted to wheel, believed he ought to wheel if he would save himself, but he did not. Instead, he brought craft into play. He listened patiently, intensely alert, and bided his time. The breathing came closer, closer still, and stopped. He heard the enemy swallow. He conquered his longing to turn, and remained still as death. The gray drew no closer. He seemed to be waiting, also biding his time. And now it became a test, a matter of nervous endurance, each waiting for the other. Around them pressed the desert solitude. There was no sound anywhere. The sun beat down upon the earth remorselessly. And still Pat waited, but not for long. There was a soft tread behind him, and he knew that he had won in the contest of endurance. With the footfalls he heard spasmodic breathing. And yet he waited. But he was ready to strike–to deal the death-blow. Closer came the restrained breathing, was close behind him. Then he struck with all his strength.

And his lightning heels found their mark. He heard the crack of bone and a long, terrible scream. He wheeled and saw the gray limping away. Gripped in sudden overwhelming fury, sounding a cry no less shrill than that of the gray, he leaped upon the enemy, bore him to earth, and, knowing no mercy, he trampled and slashed the furiously resisting foe into a bleeding mass. Then he dashed off, believing that it was all over. He turned toward Stephen and flung up his head to sound a cry of joy. But he did not sound it, for, taken off his guard, he suddenly found himself bowled over by the frenzied impact of the gray.

And Stephen, tense with suspense, felt hope sink within him. For the gray stallion, even with fore leg broken, was smothering the prostrate Pat in a raging attack. He saw Pat struggle time and again to gain his feet. At last, only after desperate effort, he saw him rise. He saw him spring upon the crippled gray and tear his back and neck and withers until his face and chest were covered with blood. And then–and at sight of this he went limp in joy and relief–he saw Pat wheel against the gray and lash out mightily, and he saw the gray drop upon breast and upper fore legs–hopelessly out of the struggle. For Pat had broken the second fore leg, and this fiend of the desert was down for all time.

And now Pat did a strange thing. As if it suddenly came to him that he had done a forbidden thing–for, after all, he was a product of advanced civilization–he flung up his head a second time and sounded a babyish whimper. Then he trotted straight to Stephen, there to nestle, as one seeking sympathy, under his master's enfolding arms. And Stephen, understanding, caressed and hugged and talked to him in a fervor of gratitude, until, awaking to the distress of the stallion, he staggered to his feet, intent upon a search for a revolver in the clothing of the still form. He found one, unexpectedly, in concealing folds, and with it shot the gray. Then he dragged himself to Pat, clambered dizzily into the saddle, gave the horse loose rein.

Pat set out at a walk. He was bleeding in many places, and he was sore and burning in many others. But he did not permit these things to divert him from his task. He went on steadily, going he knew not whither, until he felt his master become inert in the saddle. This troubled him, and, without knowing precisely why he did it, he freshened his gait and continued at a fox-trot well into the morning, until his alert eyes suddenly caught sight of a thin column of dust flung up by galloping horses and swiftly revolving wheels. Then he came to a halt, and, still not understanding his motives, he pointed his head toward the distant vehicle and sounded a shrill nicker.

The effort brought disaster. He felt his young master slip out of the saddle, saw him totter and sink in a heap on the sand. And now he understood fully. Throwing up his head again, he awoke the desert with an outcry that racked his whole body. But he did not stop. Again and again he flung his call across the silence, hurling it in mighty staccato in the direction of the ranch wagon until he saw the man suddenly draw rein, remain still for a time, then start up the horses again, this time in his direction. And now, and not till now, he ceased his nickering, and, in the great weariness and fatigue upon him, let his head droop, with eyes closed, until his nose almost touched the ground.

And although he did not know it, in the past four hours this dumb animal had in every way lived up to the faith and trust reposed in him by the little woman in the distant valley.

CHAPTER XXII
QUIESCENCE

After long jogging behind the ranch wagon Pat found himself back in a stable. He found himself attended once more by the round-faced and smiling young man who had looked after him before. This friend put salve upon his wounds, and after that, for days and days, provided him with food and water, sometimes talking to him hopefully, sometimes talking with quiet distress in his voice, sometimes attending to his wants without talking at all. It was all a dread monotony. The days became shorter; the nights became longer; a chill crept into the stable. All day long he stamped away the hours in restless discontent, longing for a change of some sort, longing for a sight of his young master, wanting to get out into the open, there to race his legs off in thrilling action.

Once this wish was granted. The weather was quite cold, and his round-faced friend came to him that morning showing every sign of haste. Hurriedly he bridled and saddled Pat, rushed him out of the stable, flung up across his back, and put spur to him with such vigor that he was forced into a gait the like of which he had not taken since his breathless speeding to the accompaniment of shots. Out across the desert he raced, breasting a cold wind, on and on till he found himself in a small railroad town. Here he was pulled up before a little cottage, and saw his friend mount the front steps and pull a tiny knob in the frame of the door. A moment of waiting and he saw a portly man appear, heard sharp conversation, saw his friend run down the steps. Then again he felt the prick of spurs, and found himself once more cantering across the desert. But not toward home. Late in the afternoon, wearied and suffering hunger pangs, he found himself in another small town and before another tiny cottage, with his friend pulling at a knob as before, and entering into crisp conversation with the person who answered, a lean man this time, who nodded his head and withdrew. After this he once more breasted the cold winds, worse now because of the night, and continued to breast them until he found himself back in the stable.

Thus he had his wish. But it was really more than he had wanted, and thereafter he was content to remain in peace and rest in the stable. But he was not always confined to the stable now. His friend began to permit him privileges, and one of these was the spending of long hours outdoors in a private corral. Here, basking in the sunlight, which was not free from winter chill, he would spend whole days dreaming and wondering–wondering for the most part about his master, the master he liked, and finding himself ever more distressed because of his continued absence. Sometimes, in the corral, he would see men walk slowly in and out of the ranch-house, or come to a halt outside his fence and stand for long minutes gazing at him, a look in their eyes, he thought, though he was not quite sure, of pity mingled with sorrow. But though these men came to him frequently, yet they rarely ever spoke to him; even as his round-faced friend, though still regularly attentive, rarely ever spoke to him now. It was all mysterious. He knew that something of a very grave nature was in the air, but what it was and why his real master never came to him as did the other men, he did not know, though sometimes he would be obsessed with troubled thoughts that all was not well with the young man.

Then one day, with spring descending upon the desert, he saw something that quickened his interest in life. He saw a door open in the house, saw a very thin young man appear on the threshold, saw him slowly descend the steps and walk toward him. It was his master. Yet was it? He pressed close to the fence, gazed at the man long and earnestly. Then he knew. It was indeed the same young man. He was much thinner now than when last he had come to him, and he seemed to lack his old-time energy, but nevertheless it was he. In a moment he knew it for certain, for the man held out a long, thin, white hand and called his name.

This was the beginning of the end. Thereafter two and three times a day the young man came to him, sometimes in the corral, sometimes in the stable, but always with each successive visit, it seemed to Pat, revealing increasing buoyancy and strength. And finally there came a day, bright and warm, when his master came to him, as it proved, to remain with him. The young man was dressed for riding, and he was surrounded by all the men Pat had ever seen about the place, and not a few whose faces were new to him. They led him out of the stable into the open, a dozen hands bridled and saddled him, then all crowded close in joyful conversation.

"Well, sir," began the round-faced young man, slapping Pat resoundingly upon the rump, "you're off again! And believe me I'm one that's right sorry to see you go. I don't care nothin' about this pardner o' yours–he don't count nohow, anyway. He's been sick 'most to death, shore, but he's all right now as far as *that* goes. His arm is all healed up, and he's fit in every other way–*some* ways–yet he's takin' himself off from as nice people as ever dragged saddles through a bunk-house at midnight. But that ain't it. He's takin' old black hoss away with him, and it don't jest set. I shore do hate to see you go."

Which seemed to express the opinions of the others. And somehow, even when his master was in the saddle and everything pointing to a final departure, Pat found himself hating to go. But duty was duty, and after his master had gathered up the reins and all had cordially shaken hands he broke into a canter, and, followed by a chorus of mighty yells, headed into the interminable desert, within him the feeling of one upon the threshold of new life, or of old and delightful life returned. Before he realized either the lapse of time or the distance traveled, he found himself cantering into the little railroad town he had visited so hurriedly in the winter. And there followed another experience new to Pat–a journey by train back to his home.

CHAPTER XXIII
THE REUNION

Stephen awoke quite late in the morning after his arrival in Pat's home town. Standing before a window in his room at the hotel, he saw a young woman cantering across the railroad tracks in the direction of the mesa. It was Helen, and, at sight of her, for a brief and awful moment he wavered in his decision. Then he remembered his suffering, and the determination made while convalescing, and, hastening his toilet, he hurried through breakfast and made his way to the livery-stable where Pat had spent the night. Pat nickered joyful greeting, as if understanding what was to come. Bridling and saddling him, Stephen mounted and rode into the street at a canter. He turned into the avenue, crossed the railroad tracks, and mounted the long, slow rise to the mesa at a walk. He moved slowly because he wanted time to think, to pull himself together, to the end that he might hold himself firmly to his decision in this last talk. And yet–and this was the conflict he suffered–he could hardly restrain himself, hold himself back, from urging Pat to his utmost.

He reached the first flat in the long rise. Absorbed in troubled reflections, he was barely conscious of the nods from two men he passed whom he knew–Hodgins, kindly old soul, book in hand; Maguire, truest of Celts, a twenty-inch slide-rule under his arm. Nodding in friendly recognition, both men gazed at the horse, seeming to understand, and glad to know that he was back. Mounting the second rise, he saw another whom he knew. A quarter of a mile to his left, on the tiny porch of a lone adobe, sat Skeet under a hat, feet elevated to the porch railing, head turned in a listening attitude, as though heeding a call, or many calls, from the direction of a brick-and-stone structure to the southwest. Everywhere familiar objects, scenes, stray people, caught his eye as he rode slowly out upon the mesa, trying to get his thoughts away from the immediate future, from Helen, his successful return of the horse, and that other thing, his determination to leave this spacious land for ever.

Suddenly he saw her. She was standing beside her brown saddler, her hand upon the bridle, gazing thoughtfully toward the mountains, now in their morning splendor. He rode Pat to a point perhaps twenty feet behind her, and then quietly let go of the reins and dropped to earth. For a moment he stood, his heart a well of bitterness; then, taking Pat's rein, he stepped toward her, quietly and slowly, intent upon making her surprise complete, because of her great love for the horse. She continued motionless, her hand upon the bridle, facing the mountains, and he came close before she turned.

He stopped. She stood perfectly still, eyes upon him, upon the horse, a slow pallor creeping into her face. Presently, as one in a spell, she let fall the reins, slowly, mechanically, and stepped toward him, a step ever quickening, her face drawn, in her eyes a strange, unchanging glow, until, when almost upon him, she held out both arms in trembling welcome and uttered a pitiful outcry.

"Stephen! Pat!" she sobbed. "Why–why didn't you–" She checked herself, came close, reached one arm around Pat, the other around Stephen, and went on. "I am–am glad you–you have come back– back to me." Her white face quivered. "Both of you. I–I have suffered."

And Stephen, swept away by the tide of his great love, and forgetting his determination, forgetting everything, bent his head and kissed her. She did not shrink, and he kissed her again. Then he began to talk, to tell her of her wonderful horse. Slowly at first, hesitating, then, as the spirit of the drama gripped him, rapidly, sometimes incoherently, he told of his adventures with the horse, and of Pat's unwavering loyalty throughout, and of that last dread situation when both their lives depended upon Pat's winning in a death-grapple with a wild horse. And then, as the gates of speech were opened, he showed her his own part, telling her that as Pat had been true to her trust, so he himself had tried to be true to her faith and trust, and was still trying and hoping, against his convictions, that she understood, that she would consider his love for her and would take him, because he loved her wholly and he needed her love to live. His tense words broke at last, and then he saw her looking up at him through tear-dimmed eyes and smiling, and in the smile he saw the opening of a life new and wonderful.

After a little she turned to Pat. She fell to stroking him in thoughtful silence. Then she turned back.

"I had heard much of what you have been through," she began, slowly, her voice soft and vibrant with deep sympathy, in her eyes that same steady glow. "The rangers reported to headquarters, and headquarters reported to Daddy. They told of the running fight, Stephen, and how–how you were hurt. And they told of the renegades, and their descent upon your camp, and of Pat's disappearance. And they told of the way you mounted another horse, hurt and sick though you were, and rode off in pursuit. But from there they knew nothing more. But they had spoken of the cavalry, and I wrote to Fort Wingate, inquiring, and they told me what they knew–that you had joined them and ridden with them through that dreadful fight, though they had tried to keep you out of it on account of your condition, and that afterward you had gone off with some cowboys–they didn't know to what ranch. So I looked up every brand in that section, Stephen," she went on, her voice beginning to break. "And I wrote to every place that might by any possible chance know something. But nobody knew. And–and–there I–I was stopped. You had been swallowed up in that desert, and I–I knew you must be ill–and I realized that I–I had sent you into it all." She sobbed and leaned her head against him. "I couldn't do anything, Stephen. I was helpless. All I have been able to do at any time, Stephen, was to–to sit at a window and wait–wait to hear from you–wait for your return–and hope, hope day in and day out that– that you were safe. I–I have–have suffered, Stephen," she concluded, sobbing wretchedly now. "I have suffered–suffered so much!"

He drew her close in his arms, united at last in complete understanding. The brown saddler, left free, wandered away indifferently; but Pat remained beside them, and presently they felt the tender touch of his beautiful head, as if in comprehension and blessing. Their hands went out to him, and Pat nickered softly at the love in their caress. Then Stephen gently raised Helen's sweet, tear-stained face to his, and in her eyes he read the certainty of the great happiness of years to come, while Pat, raising his head proudly to the desert, stood above them as if in solemn protection.

THE END

ZANE GREY'S NOVELS

May be had wherever books are sold. Ask for Grosset & Dunlap's list

THE LIGHT OF WESTERN STARS

Colored frontispiece by W. Herbert Dunton.

Most of the action of this story takes place near the turbulent Mexican border of the present day. A New York society girl buys a ranch which becomes the center of frontier warfare. Her loyal cowboys defend her property from bandits, and her superintendent rescues her when she is captured by them. A surprising climax brings the story to a delightful close.

DESERT GOLD

Illustrated by Douglas Duer.

Another fascinating story of the Mexican border. Two men, lost in the desert, discover gold when, overcome by weakness, they can go no farther. The rest of the story describes the recent uprising along the border, and ends with the finding of the gold which the two prospectors had willed to the girl who is the story's heroine.

RIDERS OF THE PURPLE SAGE

Illustrated by Douglas Duer.

A picturesque romance of Utah of some forty years ago when Mormon authority ruled. In the persecution of Jane Withersteen, a rich ranch owner, we are permitted to see the methods employed by the invisible hand of the Mormon Church to break her will.

THE LAST OF THE PLAINSMEN

Illustrated with photograph reproductions.

This is the record of a trip which the author took with Buffalo Jones, known as the preserver of the American bison, across the Arizona desert and of a hunt in "that wonderful country of yellow crags, deep canons and giant pines." It is a fascinating story.

THE HERITAGE OF THE DESERT

Jacket in color. Frontispiece.

This big human drama is played in the Painted Desert. A lovely girl, who has been reared among Mormons, learns to love a young New Englander. The Mormon religion, however, demands that the girl shall become the second wife of one of the Mormons–

Well, that's the problem of this sensational, big selling story.

BETTY ZANE

Illustrated by Louis F. Grant.

This story tells of the bravery and heroism of Betty, the beautiful young sister of old Colonel Zane, one of the bravest pioneers. Life along the frontier, attacks by Indians, Betty's heroic defense of the beleaguered garrison at Wheeling, the burning of the Fort, and Betty's final race for life make up this never-to-be-forgotten story.

Grosset & Dunlap, Publishers, New York

NOVELS OF FRONTIER LIFE BY
WILLIAM MacLEOD RAINE

HANDSOMELY BOUND IN CLOTH. ILLUSTRATED.

May be had wherever books are sold. Ask for Grosset and Dunlap's list

MAVERICKS.

A tale of the western frontier, where the "rustler," whose depredations are so keenly resented by the early settlers of the range, abounds. One of the sweetest love stories ever told.

A TEXAS RANGER.

How a member of the most dauntless border police force carried law into the mesquite, saved the life of an innocent man after a series of thrilling adventures, followed a fugitive to Wyoming, and then passed through deadly peril to ultimate happiness.

WYOMING.

In this vivid story of the outdoor West the author has captured the breezy charm of "cattleland," and brings out the turbid life of the frontier with all its engaging dash and vigor.

RIDGWAY OF MONTANA.

The scene is laid in the mining centers of Montana, where politics and mining industries are the religion of the country. The political contest, the love scene, and the fine character drawing give this story great strength and charm.

BUCKY O'CONNOR,

Every chapter teems with wholesome, stirring adventures, replete with the dashing spirit of the border, told with dramatic dash and absorbing fascination of style and plot.

CROOKED TRAILS AND STRAIGHT.

A story of Arizona; of swift-riding men and daring outlaws; of a bitter feud between cattle-men and sheep-herders. The heroine is a most unusual woman and her love story reaches a culmination that is fittingly characteristic of the great free West.

BRAND BLOTTERS.

A story of the Cattle Range. This story brings out the turbid life of the frontier, with all its engaging dash and vigor, with a charming love interest running through its 320 pages.

Grosset & Dunlap, Publishers, New York

JACK LONDON'S NOVELS

May be had wherever books are sold. Ask for Grosset & Dunlap's list.

JOHN BARLEYCORN. Illustrated by H. T. Dunn.

This remarkable book is a record of the author's own amazing experiences. This big, brawny world rover, who has been acquainted with alcohol from boyhood, comes out boldly against John Barleycorn. It is a string of exciting adventures, yet it forcefully conveys an unforgetable idea and makes a typical Jack London book.

THE VALLEY OF THE MOON. Frontispiece by George Harper.

The story opens in the city slums where Billy Roberts, teamster and ex-prize fighter, and Saxon Brown, laundry worker, meet and love and marry. They tramp from one end of California to the other, and in the Valley of the Moon find the farm paradise that is to be their salvation.

BURNING DAYLIGHT. Four illustrations.

The story of an adventurer who went to Alaska and laid the foundations of his fortune before the gold hunters arrived. Bringing his fortunes to the States he is cheated out of it by a crowd of money kings, and recovers it only at the muzzle of his gun. He then starts out as a merciless exploiter on his own account. Finally he takes to drinking and becomes a picture of degeneration. About this time he falls in love with his stenographer and wins her heart but not her hand and then–but read the story!

A SON OF THE SUN. Illustrated by A. O. Fischer and C. W. Ashley.

David Grief was once a light-haired, blue-eyed youth who came from England to the South Seas in search of adventure. Tanned like a native and as lithe as a tiger, he became a real son of the sun. The life appealed to him and he remained and became very wealthy.

THE CALL OF THE WILD. Illustrations by Philip R. Goodwin and Charles Livingston Bull. Decorations by Charles E. Hooper.

A book of dog adventures as exciting as any man's exploits could be. Here is excitement to stir the blood and here is picturesque color to transport the reader to primitive scenes.

THE SEA WOLF. Illustrated by W. J. Aylward.

Told by a man whom Fate suddenly swings from his fastidious life into the power of the brutal captain of a sealing schooner. A novel of adventure warmed by a beautiful love episode that every reader will hail with delight.

WHITE FANG. Illustrated by Charles Livingston Bull.

"White Fang" is part dog, part wolf and all brute, living in the frozen north; he gradually comes under the spell of man's companionship, and surrenders all at the last in a fight with a bull dog. Thereafter he is man's loving slave.

Grosset & Dunlap, Publishers, New York

STORIES OF RARE CHARM BY
GENE STRATTON-PORTER

May be had wherever books are sold. Ask for Grosset and Dunlap's list

LADDIE.

Illustrated by Herman Pfeifer.

This is a bright, cheery tale with the scenes laid in Indiana. The story is told by Little Sister, the youngest member of a large family, but it is concerned not so much with childish doings as with the love affairs of older members of the family. Chief among them is that of

Laddie, the older brother whom Little Sister adores, and the Princess, an English girl who has come to live in the neighborhood and about whose family there hangs a mystery. There is a wedding midway in the book and a double wedding at the close.

THE HARVESTER.

Illustrated by W. L. Jacobs.

"The Harvester," David Langston, is a man of the woods and fields, who draws his living from the prodigal hand of Mother Nature herself. If the book had nothing in it but the splendid figure of this man it would be notable. But when the Girl comes to his "Medicine Woods," and the Harvester's whole being realizes that this is the highest point of life which has come to him–there begins a romance of the rarest idyllic quality.

FRECKLES.

Decorations by E. Stetson Crawford.

Freckles is a nameless waif when the tale opens, but the way in which he takes hold of life; the nature friendships he forms in the great Limberlost Swamp; the manner in which everyone who meets him succumbs to the charm of his engaging personality; and his love-story with "The Angel" are full of real sentiment.

A GIRL OF THE LIMBERLOST.

Illustrated by Wladyslaw T. Brenda.

The story of a girl of the Michigan woods; a buoyant, lovable type of the self-reliant American. Her philosophy is one of love and kindness towards all things; her hope is never dimmed. And by the sheer beauty of her soul, and the purity of her vision, she wins from barren and unpromising surroundings those rewards of high courage.

AT THE FOOT OF THE RAINBOW.

Illustrations in colors by Oliver Kemp.

The scene of this charming love story is laid in Central Indiana. The story is one of devoted friendship, and tender self-sacrificing love. The novel is brimful of the most beautiful word painting of nature, and its pathos and tender sentiment will endear it to all.

Grosset & Dunlap, Publishers, New York

JOHN FOX, JR'S.

STORIES OF THE KENTUCKY MOUNTAINS

May be had wherever books are sold. Ask for Grosset and Dunlap's list

THE TRAIL OF THE LONESOME PINE.

Illustrated by F. C. Yohn.

The "lonesome pine" from which the story takes its name was a tall tree that stood in solitary splendor on a mountain top. The fame of the pine lured a young engineer through Kentucky to catch the trail, and when he finally climbed to its shelter he found not only the pine but the foot-prints of a girl. And the girl proved to be lovely, piquant, and the trail of these girlish foot-prints led the young engineer a madder chase than "the trail of the lonesome pine."

THE LITTLE SHEPHERD OF KINGDOM COME

Illustrated by F. C. Yohn.

This is a story of Kentucky, in a settlement known as "Kingdom Come." It is a life rude, semi-barbarous; but natural and honest, from which often springs the flower of civilization.

"Chad," the "little shepherd," did not know who he was nor whence he came–he had just wandered from door to door since early childhood, seeking shelter with kindly mountaineers who gladly fathered and mothered this waif about whom there was such a mystery–a charming waif, by the way, who could play the banjo better than anyone else in the mountains.

A KNIGHT OF THE CUMBERLAND.

Illustrated by F. C. Yohn.

The scenes are laid along the waters of the Cumberland, the lair of moonshiner and feudsman. The knight is a moonshiner's son, and the heroine a beautiful girl perversely christened "The Blight." Two impetuous young Southerners fall under the spell of "The Blight's" charms and she learns what a large part jealousy and pistols have in the love making of the mountaineers.

Included in this volume is "Hell fer-Sartain" and other stories, some of Mr. Fox's most entertaining Cumberland valley narratives.

Ask for complete free list of G. & D. Popular Copyrighted Fiction

Grosset & Dunlap, Publishers, New York

B. M. Bower's Novels

THRILLING WESTERN ROMANCES

Large 12 mos. Handsomely bound in cloth. Illustrated

CHIP, OF THE FLYING U

A breezy wholesome tale, wherein the love affairs of Chip and Della Whitman are charmingly and humorously told. Chip's jealousy of Dr. Cecil Grantham, who turns out to be a big blue eyed young woman is very amusing. A clever, realistic story of the American Cowpuncher.

THE HAPPY FAMILY

A lively and amusing story, dealing with the adventures of eighteen jovial, big hearted Montana cowboys. Foremost amongst them, we find Ananias Green, known as Andy, whose imaginative powers cause many lively and exciting adventures.

HER PRAIRIE KNIGHT

A realistic story of the plains, describing a gay party of Easterners who exchange a cottage at Newport for the rough homeliness of a Montana ranch-house. The merry-hearted cowboys, the fascinating Beatrice, and the effusive Sir Redmond, become living, breathing personalities.

THE RANGE DWELLERS

Here are everyday, genuine cowboys, just as they really exist. Spirited action, a range feud between two families, and a Romeo and Juliet courtship make this a bright, jolly, entertaining story, without a dull page.

THE LURE OF DIM TRAILS

A vivid portrayal of the experience of an Eastern author, among the cowboys of the West, in search of "local color" for a new novel. "Bud" Thurston learns many a lesson while following "the lure of the dim trails" but the hardest, and probably the most welcome, is that of love.

THE LONESOME TRAIL

"Weary" Davidson leaves the ranch for Portland, where conventional city life palls on him. A little branch of sage brush, pungent with the atmosphere of the prairie, and the recollection of a pair of large brown eyes soon compel his return. A wholesome love story.

THE LONG SHADOW

A vigorous Western story, sparkling with the free, outdoor, life of a mountain ranch. Its scenes shift rapidly and its actors play the game of life fearlessly and like men. It is a fine love story from start to finish.

Lightning Source UK Ltd.
Milton Keynes UK
UKHW012057071019
351184UK00001B/68/P